SHE
GETS
THE
GIRL

ALSO BY RACHAEL LIPPINCOTT

The Lucky List

ALSO COWRITTEN BY RACHAEL LIPPINCOTT

Five Feet Apart
All This Time

SHE GETS THE GIRL

Rachael Lippincott and Alyson Derrick

SIMON & SCHUSTER BFYR

NEW YORK LONDON TORONTO SYDNEY NEW DELHI

SIMON & SCHUSTER BFYR

An imprint of Simon & Schuster Children's Publishing Division

1230 Avenue of the Americas, New York, New York 10020

Text © 2022 by Rachael Lippincott and Alyson Derrick

Jacket illustration © 2022 by Poppy Magda

Jacket design by Lizzy Bromley © 2022 by Simon & Schuster, Inc.

SIMON & SCHUSTER BOOKS FOR YOUNG READERS

and related marks are trademarks of Simon & Schuster, Inc.

For information about special discounts for bulk purchases, please contact
Simon & Schuster Special Sales at 1-866-506-1949 or business@simonandschuster.com.

The Simon & Schuster Speakers Bureau can bring authors to your live event.
For more information or to book an event, contact the Simon & Schuster Speakers Bureau at
1-866-248-3049 or visit our website at www.simonspeakers.com.

Interior design by Hilary Zarycky

The text for this book was set in Bell.

Manufactured in the United States of America /First Edition

2 4 6 8 10 9 7 5 3 1

Library of Congress Cataloging-in-Publication Data

Names: Lippincott, Rachael, author. | Derrick, Alyson, author.

Title: She gets the girl / Rachael Lippincott and Alyson Derrick.

Description: First edition. | New York : Simon & Schuster Books for Young Readers, 2022. |
Audience: Ages 14 and Up. | Summary: Alex Blackwood is really good at getting the girl she wants,
but coming from a broken home with an alcoholic mother she finds commitment difficult, even when
she thinks she is in love; impossibly awkward Molly Parker has a crush on the cool Cora Myers, but
she does not know how to even start a conversation, much less make a connection; now they are all at
college in Pittsburgh Alex decides to "help" Molly get the girl, while proving to her own flame that
she is not just totally selfish—but things do not work out as the two have planned.

Identifiers: LCCN 2021039742 | ISBN 9781534493797 (hardcover) | ISBN 9781534493810 (ebook)

Subjects: LCSH: Lesbians—Juvenile fiction. | Interpersonal relations—Juvenile fiction. |
Friendship—Juvenile fiction. | Dysfunctional families—Juvenile fiction. | Dating (Social customs)—
Juvenile fiction. | Young adult fiction. | Pittsburgh (Pa.)—Juvenile fiction. | CYAC: Lesbians—
Fiction. | Interpersonal relations—Fiction. | Friendship—Fiction. | Family problems—Fiction.
| Dating (Social customs)—Fiction. | Pittsburgh (Pa.)—Fiction. | BISAC: YOUNG ADULT
FICTION / Romance / Contemporary | YOUNG ADULT FICTION / Romance / LGBTQ

Classification: LCC PZ7.1.L568 Sh 2022 | DDC 813/.6 [Fic]—dc23

LC record available at https://lccn.loc.gov/2021039742

This one's for us
—R. L. & A. D.

SHE
GETS
THE
GIRL

CHAPTER 1

ALEX

Every single person in this room is looking at Natalie Ramirez.

The hipster dude clutching an IPA like it's his firstborn son. The girl wearing a faded Nirvana shirt that *screams* Urban Outfitters. Brendan, the bartender, too distracted to realize he's made not one but *two* rumless rum and Cokes. All of them have their eyes glued to the stage.

I finish wiping up a few water rings clinging to the counter and throw my white bar towel over my shoulder, craning my neck around the sea of people to get a better view.

The stage lights cast an odd purplish hue over everything. Her face is outlined in shades of lilac and violet, and her long black hair shines a deep burgundy. I watch as her hands move up and down the neck of the guitar without so much as a second glance, every fret memorized, the feel of the strings ingrained in her fingertips.

Because while all eyes are on her, Natalie Ramirez is only looking at me.

She gives me a small, secret smile. The same one that gave me butterflies five whole months ago, when her band first performed at Tilted Rabbit.

It was the best performance I've seen in the three years I've worked here. Being a small local venue, we've had our fair share of Alanis Morissette wannabes and weekend warrior cover bands. There was a guy just last week who tried to go full Neutral Milk Hotel and play a saw for an hour straight, the sound so screeching that everyone except my coworkers and his girlfriend left the building.

To be honest, between the iffy music, the weird hours, and the less-than-ideal pay, the turnover rate here is pretty high. I'd have quit ages ago, but . . . my mom needs money for rent. Plus, I do too, now that I'm leaving for college.

And I guess it's all right. Because if I had quit, I wouldn't have been there that night five months ago, and I wouldn't be here right now, catching Natalie Ramirez's gaze from behind the bar.

My stomach sinks as I realize this is the last time I'll hear her play for a while, and even though I try to push that feeling away, it lingers. It sticks around through saying a final farewell to the ragtag crew of coworkers that let me study at the bar on school nights, through waiting for Natalie to get done with her celebratory drinks backstage before her band goes on their first-ever tour next week, and through the two of us veering off to spend my last night here at home exactly how I want to spend it.

With her.

We're barely through the door of her cramped Manayunk apartment before she's kissing me, her lips tasting like the cheese pizza and warm beer she has after every show.

It's a blur of kicked-off Converse shoes and hands sliding up my waist as she pulls off my black T-shirt, the two of us stumbling across the space she escaped to after graduating last year from Central High, the public school just across the city from mine.

This place has pretty much been my escape all summer too, so I lead us effortlessly across the worn wooden floor into her room, dodging her bandmates' instruments and sheet music and scattered shoes. Her bedsprings squeak as we tumble back onto her messy sheets, the door clicking shut behind us.

The moment is so alive, so perfect, but that feeling I had earlier still sits heavy on my chest. It's impossible to not think about the bus that will whisk me away to college in the morning. The prickling nervousness I feel over leaving the place where I've lived my whole life. My mom, on the other side of the city, probably half a handle of tequila deep after spending the afternoon guilting me over "leaving her" just like Dad left us.

But, most importantly, I want to finally have the conversation

3

I've been avoiding. The conversation about how I want to make this work long distance.

I zero in on the feeling of Natalie's skin under my fingertips, her body pressed up against mine, working up the courage to pull away, to *say something*, when I feel her soft whisper against my lips.

"I love you."

I pull her closer, so wrapped up in her that I hardly register what she just said. So wrapped up in what I'm struggling to say that I almost say it back.

More than almost. My mouth forms around the words. "I lo—"

Wait.

My eyes fly open and my heart hammers in my chest as I jerk away, those three words bringing with them a flood of moments *much* different from this one.

Thrown plates and screaming. My dad stooping down to say "I love you" before he got in the car and drove away, into a new life.

A life without me. Never to be seen or heard from again.

I can't possibly say them to her now. Not like this. Not when *I'm* the one leaving.

I see the question in her face illuminated in the glow of the yellow streetlight outside her window, so I quickly disguise my sudden movement by reaching out to run my fingertips along the black strap of her bra.

4

"I, uh. I loved that new song you guys played tonight," I whisper, trying my best to cover the words that almost came out of my mouth. I kiss her again, harder now, the kind of kiss that usually ends any conversation. But what she said lingers in the air around us like a thick fog.

"Alex," she says, pulling her lips off mine. She studies my face, her eyes searching for something.

"Yeah?" I say, avoiding her gaze as I look down at her fingers laced with mine, the chipped black paint on her nails.

"Sometimes . . ." She lets out a long sigh. "Sometimes I wonder what exactly this *is* to you."

I lean back and squint at her, finally meeting her gaze. "What do you mean?"

"I mean my band is going on tour. You're leaving tomorrow for college. You're going to be all the way in *Pittsburgh*," she says as she sits back and pulls her black hair into a bun, a sign the moment is slipping away. *Fast.*

There's a long pause. I can tell she's still searching. Still waiting for me to say the words she wants me to say. "It's our last night, and I want to know what *we* are. That I mean something to you. That this is going to work long distance, and you won't just ghost me and see other people. That I'm not just . . ."

Yes. "Natalie." I scooch closer to her. "I wanted to talk to you about that. I—"

My phone vibrates loudly on the white sheets beneath us,

the screen lighting up to show a text from Megan Baker, littered with winky face emojis, and a message reading: HMU if ur ever back in the city!

Natalie squeezes her eyes shut, angry now, like she's found the answer, but it's one she didn't want. "Megan Baker? That girl that plays the triangle in that Fleetwood Mac cover band? For real, Alex?"

"Natalie," I say as I reach out for her. "Come on. It's not—"

"No," she says as she pushes my hands away and stands up, her jaw locking. I notice her hazel eyes are glistening, tears threatening to spill out of the corners. "This is so . . . typical. This is so *fucking* typical. I try to get close and you pull this. We've been seeing each other for *five* months, and I haven't been able to trust you for a single one of them."

"Natalie. Come *on*. We've been over this. I went on, like, *three* dates. Four, max. I thought things were ruined between us. I thought we were done." I swing my legs over the bed and stand, all of this feeling *very* familiar, in *exactly* the way I didn't want tonight to go. "And only one was with Megan. She means *nothing* to me."

"How can I trust you in Pittsburgh, when you're getting texts like this when we're in the *same city*?" she asks, glowering up at me.

"Texts like *what*?" I snort, and turn the phone to face her. "She wished me safe travels and *all* I said was thanks. Then she's the one that—"

6

"Just *admit* it, Alex. It's impossible for you to have a conversation without flirting. I saw you tonight talking to that girl at the bar during my set. It's why you said no when I asked you to change your plans and come on tour with us last month. Why you avoided every conversation about what happens when you leave. You would rather flirt around in Pittsburgh than actually have a *real* connection." She shakes her head, her voice breaking as she looks away, out the window. "You've never chosen me. Never really been all the way in."

A familiar wave of guilt washes over me. For those dates I went on at the very beginning, and the times I've maybe crossed the line between talking and flirting during my shifts at Tilted Rabbit.

But I *am* in. I didn't date anyone like this all through high school. I kept it casual with everyone because, well . . . I never wanted them to know the truth. The part of me I keep hidden. A wrecked home life and a mom too drunk off her ass to even take care of herself, let alone me.

But Natalie's different.

She's been different since she tried to surprise me with takeout after our third date and found my mom passed out on our porch. I ghosted her for two whole weeks out of embarrassment, going on other dates, sure she would never want to stick around after that, but . . . she didn't give up. She's the only person to get close enough to know the truth and stick by me anyway, baggage and all.

7

Now, though, her voice is cold when she talks next. Distant. "You may have a phone filled with numbers, but at the end of the day, without me, you have no one. You're *alone*."

I'm taken aback. We've had fights before, but I've never seen her quite like this. "*Alone?* That's ridiculous."

"Is it? Friends. Relationships. You push *everyone* away when they get too close. It's a miracle *I'm* still here! We've been together for *five* months and I haven't met *any* of your friends. Just your past hookups. Because that's all you have, Alex. *You don't have any friends.*" She turns her head back to face me. "I'm here, and I care about you. I've supported you through all the shit with your mom, when no one else *ever* would. I mean, you almost said 'I love you too,' Alex. I know you did," she says. "But you stopped yourself. *Why?*"

"I . . . I don't know. I just . . ."

I'm stumbling over words. I don't know how to say *because it was more than I was expecting.*

"All right, Alex," she says, crossing her arms over her chest. "I'll give you another chance. Actually tell me how you feel. Tell me you love me too."

She has me cornered, and she knows it. *Why* is she doing this? "Natalie, look, I . . ."

My voice trails off into silence.

"Wow." Natalie lets out a huff of air as she shakes her head. "Sometimes I think you really might end up just like your mom."

8

I stand there, stunned. She, more than anyone, knows that was a low blow. How nothing in this world scares me more than that.

I try to steady myself as the room starts to feel smaller and smaller, my chest tight when I try to take a breath as memories swim to the surface. My parents screaming at each other from across the house. The sound of glass shattering into a million pieces. The back bumper of my dad's car fading into the distance.

And for the first time in five whole months, I feel like running away, just like I always have.

I grab my T-shirt and angrily pull it back on. "You think you know *everything*, huh? You want me to tell you how I feel, Natalie?" I say, the fear and rage boiling to the surface. "I feel like you don't know shit about me."

"And whose fault is that?"

We stare at each other for a long moment, her chest heaving, the sharp lines of her collarbones intensifying.

"Get out," she says finally, her voice low.

I don't even fight it. *"Gladly,"* I say, plastering a smirk on my face, like I don't care. It feels familiar, and I hate it.

I push past her out the bedroom door and grab my duffel bag off the floor, pulling it onto my shoulder as I angrily jam my feet into my shoes. The heel folds in and gets caught under my foot, so I jimmy my ankle around, twisting it back into place while I yank open the apartment door.

I give her one last glare as I grab the handle of my suitcase, that small smile she gave me onstage tonight long gone, those butterflies from five months ago and every time I see her play certifiably crushed. Then, with all the might I can muster and enough force to piss off old Mrs. Hampshire two apartments down, I slam the door behind me.

My head spins as I jog down the uneven steps, my suitcase clunking noisily behind me. I push through the door and out onto the street, trying to *calm down*, but the warm late-August air only makes me angrier.

It's the middle of the night and the temperature still hasn't dropped.

I storm down the block and around the corner, almost running smack into a group of barhoppers as I turn onto Main Street, a blur of faces and shapes and colors. I look to the side and slow down as I catch sight of the small coffee shop we went to on our first date, where we talked about her band, the Cereal Killers, and my upcoming graduation, and our favorite places in the city.

Adjacent to the coffee shop is the diner where we would hang out every Saturday in the corner booth, stealing kisses between bites of pancakes bigger than our heads.

We'd have been there tomorrow morning before I left, but now . . .

I duck my head and look away, the anger giving way to

another feeling. *Loss.* For those Saturdays at the diner, for the night we could have had, and for the girl who stuck around even though she knew the worst parts of me. Even if she just threw them all in my face.

My chest is heaving by the time I get to the SEPTA station. I collapse onto a bench and pull out my phone. The screen lights up to show it's only . . . 1:00 a.m.

It's one o'clock in the morning? Shit. My bus isn't until eight.

And . . . I can't go home. I can't spend one more night scraping my mom off the floor while she berates me for leaving. I'm afraid I'll never leave if I go back.

So, where the hell am I going to—

My eyes land on the text from Megan.

It's . . . worth a shot. She's about to be a sophomore at Temple, and her new dorm is pretty close to the bus station.

I tap on the notification and then the call button, holding my breath as it rings.

"Hello?"

"Hey, Megan," I say, a wave of relief washing over me when she picks up. "Can I come over?"

"*Oh,*" she says, her voice changing ever so slightly. "I'd love it if you . . . *came* over."

I cringe. Jesus. No wonder Natalie was mad I went on a date with her.

"I mean, I, uh," I say as I shift the phone to my other ear. "I was just planning to, like . . . sleep since my bus isn't until eight tomorrow, but . . ."

But . . . *what have I got to lose?* Shit just hit the fan with Natalie. And Megan's clearly not looking for anything serious. Would it really be so bad to forget everything, just for a night?

"Oh," she says, jumping in before I have a chance to back-track. "You could, but, uh . . . my roommate is sick."

"Julie?" I frown. "I just saw her at Natalie's concert tonight. She was—"

"Yeah, I think . . . I think she must have come down with something after," she says. Her voice is muffled as she pretends to call out to her roommate, "What's that, Julie? You're throwing up? I'll be right there to help!"

Wow is this girl bad at lying.

"Alex! I think I've got to go," she says in an attempt to wrap up her one-woman show. "Julie just started—"

I hang up before she can finish, saving her from having to keep up the act for even a second longer.

Sighing, I pull open my contact list, scrolling through it as I search for someone else to call. The *A*s alone are about a mile long. Natalie may have been right about Megan, but that doesn't mean there aren't a million other people I know and can stay with.

My eyes glaze over as I pause on individual names: Melissa, Ben, Mike. Coworkers that never became more than acquaintances. People I've met working behind the bar or at school, each text chain I try to start left empty as I see how I just . . . lost touch with them, months passing since the last text as I ignored their questions or their offers to hang out, so busy with schoolwork and taking care of my mom I didn't have time for anything else.

But I also realize most of them are . . . hookups. Or, I guess, potential hookups, just like Natalie said. A lot of them. Girls I flirted with just to see what would happen, knowing I could never commit to more than just this moment. Knowing I could never have more than the temporary.

Some don't even have names.

Brown hair, Starbucks.

Freckles, pizza place.

There are *ten* like that. Maybe more. Just some generic description of a girl followed by where I'd met her.

I keep scrolling, until the screen bounces as I hit the bottom of the list. There's no one I can call at 1:00 a.m. Nowhere I can go except to the Greyhound station to sit and wait for seven hours for the bus to come.

You're alone. Natalie's face pops into my head, the pointed look in her eyes clouding my vision.

But, I mean, I had my mom to worry about. And I was *leaving.* For Pittsburgh. I was never going to see most of these people again. Of course I let the ties go. The casual acquaintances, the hookups, the friends I never really talked to outside of school, keeping my personal life tucked away in a little box.

The only person I really held on to was her. Until tonight.

I feel a rush of hot air as the train screeches noisily to a stop in front of me. Numbly, I stumble inside and slide onto one of the blue-carpeted seats. I rest my arms on my knees and squeeze my eyes shut as I rub my face, the words circling around and around in my head, the truth in them catching me off guard.

She was right. She saw me better than I saw myself.

She said "I love you" and I *stopped* myself from saying it back to her. She asked me to say *one* thing about how much she meant to me, and I couldn't.

I couldn't just tell her how Saturday mornings with her are the highlight of my week. How her lyrics speak to me like no other song has before, and watching her perform makes me feel . . . light, how for just those few moments, nothing is weighing down on me. I couldn't tell her how grateful I've been these past few months having someone to support me through all the shit with my mom.

I'm not sure I'd be able to get on the bus tomorrow morning if it weren't for her help.

But I didn't say that. I didn't say anything. I messed it all up because she asked for the moon, and I couldn't give it to her yet.

She's the first person I don't want to say goodbye to, and here I am running away.

What is *wrong* with me?

I swallow hard on a lump forming in my throat and rest my head up against the window, watching Philadelphia whiz by on the other side of the glass, knowing I need to make a change.

I'm not sure how I'm going to fix this, but I've got all the way to Pittsburgh to figure it out.

CHAPTER 2

MOLLY

Oof.

I wake up struggling for breath as my ancient, one-hundred-pound Lab hurls himself onto my bed, his big yellow paw jabbing me right in the kidney.

"Leonard, get down!" I try to lower my voice a few octaves, but it's no use. He only ever listens to my dad. For the next five minutes he attacks me with kisses and steps on every single one of my organs, until he finally hops down, satisfied with his work.

I will not miss waking up to *that.*

Well, at least not too much.

As I wipe the slobber off my face, I feel around on my side table for my phone, but my hand lands on the pile of five freshly labeled binders I finished preparing last night, ready for the upcoming school year. Nothing quite compares to a peaceful night, just me and my label maker.

I reach past them to tug my phone off the charging cord. And then for the ten thousandth time this summer, I search for Cora Myers's Twitter profile, careful not to accidentally tap the follow button.

I fell asleep at nine thirty yesterday just like I always do, so I missed her tweet from late last night: *Tomorrow I officially become a panther! #hail2pitt.*

A wave of nausea rolls over me, but a grin breaks out across my face too as I press the phone against my chest.

Today.

It's been three months since we graduated from high school.

Eighty-seven days since I've seen her.

Just to be clear. I am not *following* her to college. About half my high school gets funneled into Pitt. We both just happen to be part of that half.

And . . . if you ask me, it feels an awful lot like fate. Like the universe is *finally* doing me a solid after such a crappy four years.

I've really tried to keep my mind occupied with other things this summer, but when you meet a girl like Cora Myers, it becomes impossible to think about anything else.

Well, maybe "meet" is the wrong word, but I haven't been able to get her out of my head since she walked into ninth-grade homeroom wearing a vintage red velvet coat and a pair of oversize yellow combat boots that didn't match at all.

But I liked them anyway.

And I wasn't the only one.

Her energy was magnetic. People naturally gravitated toward her at the beginning of every class, in the hallways, and after school, but the attention never seemed to go to her head. She was never mean, never exclusive, and she was always exactly herself no matter who was around. It seemed like she could talk to anyone about anything.

Not that she ever talked to *me*, but you can hear a lot from two desks over.

It's not that I didn't *want* to talk to her. I'm just not good at opening myself up to people. I'm not good at making friends. When you spend as much time as I have worrying about what to say and how to say it and it still comes out wrong, it just becomes easier to not say anything at all.

This year, though, I don't have to be quiet Molly Parker with the crippling social anxiety. Things can be different at Pitt.

This is college. It's a fresh start, a chance to rewrite myself. People are always saying that things get better in college, and I have to believe that. This can't be all there is.

It *has* to get better.

I don't think I can make it through another four years of—

Crash.

A big box of something hits the kitchen tile downstairs, the sound carrying up through my floorboards.

Mom.

Even though I told her a million times last night that everything I need is already in the car, I just *know* she's packing more crap for me to take. If I don't get down there right now, she's going to have the entire house packed into the back of her SUV.

I take a deep breath before hopping out of bed and taking the steps two at a time. As I turn the corner, I find my mom flying around the kitchen, opening and closing every drawer and door within her five-foot-nothing reach. Her salt-and-pepper chin-length hair is half pulled back into a black clip.

"Where is that son of a bitch?" she grumbles, so focused on looking for who-knows-what that she doesn't even see me. I hear the rustle of paper and look over to see my dad's hazel eyes peeking over the top of the *Pittsburgh Post-Gazette* at me from our breakfast nook.

They crinkle at the corners just like they always do when he smiles.

"Glad you're up." He's already snickering at whatever he's about to say. "Thought we were going to have to come roll you over so you wouldn't get bedsores." An absolute *classic* Charlie Parker morning zinger.

"It's only eight thirty," I say, making a face. Laughing at his jokes will only encourage him.

"Molly!" An instant grin replaces my mom's frustrated frown as she finally stops her search and sees me. Flyaway strands of hair float around her round face as she rushes over to give me a hug. Two-handed, one arm over, one under, or she'll make me do it again, because it "just doesn't feel right." She's acting like I am going off to war, but even though she's crushing me almost as much as Leonard, it's hard to pretend like I won't miss this.

When she releases me, I walk over to the counter, closing a few cabinets and hip-thrusting a drawer back into place along the way. I certainly did not get my compulsion for organization from my mother. "*What* are you doing?" I ask.

"I told her not to," my dad interjects without looking up from his newspaper.

"Oh, just do your puzzles, Charlie." Mom waves her hand at him as she crosses the kitchen to open yet another cabinet. "I'm getting a few more things together for you. I just need a whisk and then I'm done, but I can't find my second one," she says.

"Mom," I say as firmly as I can. "I do not need a whisk."

"*Everyone* needs a whisk," she replies, as if we're talking about a toilet or something.

"What am I going to do with a whisk in a dorm room?" I ask her, hoping to bring some logic to the conversation this morning, but she just keeps rifling through every cabinet.

I lean down and open the flaps of the box she's packing up, feeling utterly confused at its contents: a roll of foil, the stapler from our junk drawer, a spatula, two can openers, a nonstick pan.

"Mom, I don't need any of this," I tell her, placing my hand on her arm to try to stop her from opening yet another drawer.

"But what if you do?" she asks, her voice shaking a little. "What if you need something and you don't have it? What if you get hungry in the middle of the night and . . ."

"Then I'll just have to figure it out for myself." I pull her away from the drawer, forcing her to face me. She looks up with tears coating her eyes.

"Please don't leave," she says, even though she doesn't mean it. At least she's trying not to.

"Mom, I'm going to be fine," I tell her. I try to sound more confident than I feel.

"But I'm not," she admits through a pathetic-sounding laugh.

I give her another hug because while I know it's lame . . . we're basically best friends. We've never explicitly called each other that, but when you're this close with someone, it doesn't need to be said. She's been my closest friend all through high school. My only friend, if I'm honest.

Now, somehow, I have to say goodbye to her, this person who has been by my side through all of it. It doesn't feel possible, but if things are going to change this year, I need to let go a little.

21

And I need her to let go a little too.

"Molly, we need to leave in about an hour. If we wait any longer, I'm afraid your mom's going to pack herself up in one of these boxes," my dad says, and my mom throws a kitchen towel at him.

An hour later we're officially on our drive to Pitt. My dad volunteers to drive my car down, so it's just my mom and I in her SUV, and I find myself regretting it as she points out seemingly everything familiar on our way. My old school, the movie theater, a roller rink off the highway where I spent so many nights skating with my brother, Noah. I tear my eyes away, the memories making this whole moving thing even harder.

Luckily, once we arrive, I pretty much can't think about any of that because campus is pure insanity. Every trunk in sight is hanging open, and mini fridges, bedding, and IKEA furniture spill out onto the street. The sidewalks are filled with parents trying and failing to round up their younger kids. A girl sporting a Pitt soccer hoodie loses control of her giant moving cart and watches in horror as it slams right into a parked car. Then *I* watch in horror as she just casually walks in the other direction. Just to be safe, we decide to leave Dad to guard the car after he parks mine in the student lot.

"Hi! Welcome to Pitt!" A guy with perfectly coiffed hair greets me as I enter the quad with my mom in tow. "I can help you get checked in," he says, leading me over to a table. I give him all the information he needs, and he hands over a welcome bag and my student ID card, featuring a horribly blown-out photo that was taken of me at orientation over the summer.

"How does she find out who her roommate is?" my mom asks, stepping up to the table.

"Oh." The guy furrows his eyebrows. "You should have gotten an email months ago."

But . . . I've been refreshing it religiously all summer, so there's no way I missed it. Right? My stomach sinks, but I don't want to be *that* freshman.

"Oh, okay, I'll take another look," I tell him.

"Well, is there any way you can look it up? She didn't get an email," my mom interjects, and instantly my skin prickles. Just once I wish she'd let me handle something for myself.

"Mom, it's fine," I whisper under my breath. "I'll figure it out when I get up there. Besides, Noah's on his way, right?" I thank the guy and tug my mom away from the table.

Thankfully, my distraction works.

"He said he was going to bike over and . . . meet us in the quad? Is this the quad?" she asks. I nod, looking around at the four identical dorm buildings for . . . *there it is* . . . Holland Hall.

"I'm just going to run up and see my room. I'll be back," I reply, but quickly realize that she's following on my heels anyway. "Mom, can you maybe stay here and keep an eye out for Noah?" I pick up speed before she can reply. I actually kind of want her with me to see the room for the first time, but I keep reminding myself that things have to be different. And for them to be different, I really cannot have my mom barging in behind me as I meet my roommate for the very first time.

Both doors have been propped open, and girls are flooding in and out constantly. The elevator looks pretty busy, so I take the five flights of stairs up to my dorm room, stopping right outside the door to catch my breath and get myself together.

First impression, Molly. New you. You've got this. All you have to say is "Hi, I'm Molly."

Deep breath.

I open the door expecting to see my roommate, but what I find instead makes my stomach sink straight to the floor.

"This is a joke," I whisper to myself as I look around the shoebox of a room.

One bed. *One* desk. Even though it was my last choice. Even though I specifically asked for anything *but* this.

It's a single.

Like it's not already going to be hard enough for me to make friends, now I get to live in solitary confinement. I step in, looking around my room as I listen to girls go by in the hall, talking with their roommates about what should go where and who gets which side.

"Hey, Moll, where do you want these?" a voice asks from behind, making me temporarily forget my predicament. I turn around to find a huge stack of boxes blocking the entire hall-

24

way, a pair of muscular legs sticking out the bottom, almost buckling under the weight of about every item I own.

"Hey, Noah," I say, feeling lighter at the sight of him. "You know they have carts for that." I hop up on my plastic mattress to make room for him to get by before he drops everything on the floor with a few thuds. He takes a second to catch his breath, hands on his knees.

"I've got two perfectly good carts right here," he says, slapping each of his biceps. I roll my eyes at him. "Besides, what else are older brothers good for?" he asks with an amused smile, coming over to give me a hug.

"Charlie, quit running over my heels!" My mom's voice echoes down the hallway, accompanied by a laugh that fills up all this empty space. We both turn to the door as our parents appear with a moving cart filled with another load of my things.

My mom's smile drops instantly as she scans my room.

"They put you in a single," she says, the corners of her mouth turning down.

"Lucky, right? Man, I would've *killed* for a single in college," Noah says as he sits down on my desk.

"Yeah, this is really nice, Molly. You've got your own little space here," Dad adds.

I meet eyes with my mom, the only person who could possibly understand what this means for me. The only person who knows that this was my one good chance of having a built-in social life in college.

I look away before she says anything, because talking about it will only make me feel worse. So I throw myself into the task at hand. Organizing. The thing I *love*.

Noah and Dad bring up load after load while my mom and I put every single thing in its place. I try not to think about everything I was looking forward to with my roommate. All the nights we were supposed to sit up in bed, gossiping about all the exciting things happening in our lives here, or the midnight trips to Market to get Pitt's famous waffles and ice cream that Noah told me about. I try not to think about how I was supposed to be putting this dorm together with her, not my mom.

"So I was thinking," my mom says as I sit down on the floor next to her to refold some T-shirts. "Why don't you order takeout and ask one of your floormates to hang out?" She tries to sound excited, but the look of pity in her eyes is too familiar.

"They're all going to be getting to know their own room-mates. And I don't *know* anyone to ask," I say, returning my gaze to the shirt I'm folding.

"What about Cora?" She nudges me playfully. "Maybe she's free."

"Can we not talk about this right now? Let's just fold," I say, but she can't let it go. Like any true best friend, she also knows how to get under my skin like *no* other, and it feels like that talent is on overdrive today.

26

"Why don't you send her a text to see if she wants to hang out tonight?"

"Mom," I say firmly, turning to face her. "I can't just ask her to *hang out*, okay? That's not . . ." I let out a frustrated sigh, picking up my phone to mime texting. "Hey, Cora. You don't know me at all, and I don't even have your number, but we went to the same high school and I'm practically in love with you."

"Why *can't* you do that? I mean, I'm sure someone you know would have her number. The last part might be a little strong, but . . ." She finally trails off, giggling. "What do I know?"

"Oh my God." I shove her onto her side, and she bounces right back up. "You honestly drive me crazy."

"I'm just trying to help. You know that, right?" she asks, and I nod. "Okay, so if it's a no on Cora, what if *I* come back down tomorrow and we go shopping or something?"

"Mom . . ." I pause to gather my thoughts, wanting to make sure I say all the right things. I hate that I want to say yes. And that tells me I *have* to say this. I just don't want to hurt her feelings too badly. "I *need* college to be different. Okay?" I look up to meet her eyes. "It's going to be hard enough now for me to figure that out. If you're showing up here all the time, I don't know if I'll ever be able to make other friends. And I cannot, I *cannot*, go through another four years like that."

She looks a little hurt, but mostly she looks guilty.

"I know. I know. I'm sorry." She wraps her arms around

27

herself and squeezes tight. "I'll give you some space," she says.

I narrow my eyes at her for a second, having a hard time believing that's something she's actually capable of. "I promise!" she follows up, extending her pinkie finger out to me, and I finally laugh.

"Okay. At least for a little while," I reply, taking it in mine.

"Well, that's everything," my dad announces, appearing in the doorway next to Noah. "What do you think, Beth?" he asks.

Now?

This all went by too fast. I was just talking about how much I want things to change. But . . . not right this minute.

Tears press against my eyes as the goodbye I've been dreading all day lingers in the air.

My mom pushes herself off the floor with a grunt as she straightens out her legs. "I think we're all set. Unless you want me to help you finish folding, Molly?" She looks down at me like she's trying so hard to do what I've asked, but it goes against everything she's feeling.

I will have a full breakdown if we extend this goodbye any longer than it needs to be.

"You can just go with them. I've got this," I say, motioning to the pile of clothes.

"Are you sure?" she asks.

Not even a little. But instead, I say, "Totally."

I give my dad a quick hug, knowing that he doesn't like

for me to see him get too emotional. But I can still tell he's struggling, widening his eyes so he doesn't cry.

"Good to have you in the city," Noah says with a smile, pulling me in for a one-handed bro hug. I *am* thankful that he lives nearby. "Call me when you want to hang out. And, Molly?" he says, already halfway out the door. "Open doors make happy floors." He swings my door all the way open before following my dad into the hall. As if making friends is as simple as opening a door.

But I guess that's because it has been for him. Everything has always been so easy for Noah—making friends, playing sports. He was somehow even voted prom king. I mean . . . name one other school in rural PA that named an Asian dude as *prom king*. That just doesn't happen.

I close my eyes and take a deep breath as my mom turns around to face me.

"I promise you it's going to get better," she says, resting her hand on my cheek. I step forward, wrapping her in a hug, and this time I'm the one holding too tight.

"Okay," I whisper, even though it really doesn't feel that way now.

"Okay," she says, her voice quivering as she lets me go and takes a step back into the hall. "Call me later. I love you."

"I love you," I say, biting my cheek until I taste blood. She disappears from the doorway, and I turn around to face my new home. My chest tightens at the all-too-familiar feeling of

29

loneliness, except this time I don't have my mom to fall back on. Here, I really am alone.

Just focus on the task. Unpack. Organize.

I take a deep breath, trying to ignore the lump in my throat as I unfold the flaps of the last cardboard box.

My vision blurs as I reach in and pick up a metal whisk with a note attached in careful handwriting.

Just in case ♥

CHAPTER 3

ALEX

I feel dizzy by the time I make it to Pittsburgh. My ten-minute nap on the Greyhound bus was nowhere near enough time for my body to reset, but I mean, who needs sleep when you can stare out a window for seven whole hours, regretting every decision you've ever made in your life?

No matter how hard I tried to think of a solution, I just . . . couldn't.

She really *knows* me. All the parts of me that I thought I was hiding from her. All the parts I was hiding from myself. And she actually *loves* me.

I've never had that before.

And I think that's why I really *want* to be in this with her. Fully. Instead of just running away and leaving her in the dust, like my dad did. Instead of keeping her at a distance and letting it fizzle out like the rest of my relationships.

I tap pause on "Pretty Games," the Cereal Killers song

that got them signed to an indie record label a few months ago, and check my phone for the millionth time, but there's still no reply to the **can we talk?** text I sent her when I got on the bus. No phone call. She hasn't even looked at my Instagram stories.

I really fucked things up this time. Her silent treatment has never lasted this long.

This is *way* worse than any of our other little fights, over flirting, or my "emotional unavailability," or whatever text lit up my screen at the breakfast table.

I mean . . . the things she said last night. The things *I* said. It's like ten girls giving me their number during a shift at Tilted Rabbit combined.

Sighing, I double-check Google Maps to see I have two more stops before I get off this swaying Port Authority bus, the weirdly patterned fabric of the seat prickling my thighs. I scoot forward and peek out the window to see a giant stone building looming in the distance, the bright afternoon sun turning the gray brick almost white.

The Cathedral of Learning, the forty-two-story centerpiece of Pitt's campus.

I'm actually here. Officially a college student. For a second, thoughts of Natalie finally recede.

I almost feel like I can breathe in a way I never have before.

I can't believe I did it. I can't believe I *actually* did it. I made it out.

This is what I wanted. To figure out how to do more than just scrape by. To worry only about myself for once.

Well . . . mostly.

Reflexively, I glance down at my phone to see my mom hasn't replied to the texts I sent her on the ride here. Which is nothing new. But I still feel queasy over it, since now I can't run home to make sure she's still breathing.

I pocket my phone as the bus jolts to a stop, and I grab my stuff before stumbling down the aisle. I thank the driver as I hop off at Atwood Street, supposedly four blocks away from my Craigslist-found apartment, squinting against the sun as I swivel my head from left to right.

Instantly, I'm struck by how different this place is from Philly. It's so *small*. I mean, I know it's not *Downtown* Pittsburgh, but . . . this is definitely going to take some getting used to. From the buildings to the number of people walking on the sidewalks to the stores lining the street, it's like someone took home and halved it. And then halved it another ten times.

I follow Google Maps down the block, past a Starbucks and a Rite Aid and a Mexican grocery store, horrified when I catch sight of my reflection in a window. I look like I got *hit* by a bus instead of riding in one.

My blond hair is pulled into a lumpy bun, baby hairs making a break for it everywhere I look. My T-shirt is so wrinkled it looks like I left it in the dryer for an entire year.

My normally perfectly even eyeliner is somehow completely missing from my right eye and is still somewhat intact on my left. How is that even possible?

I quickly pull out my hair tie, then comb my fingers through my hair and rub my still-lined eye as the light in front of me turns green.

My phone buzzes, and I almost fling it into the road as I fumble to pull it up to my face, hoping to see a text message from Natalie.

But it's my mom. She *actually* replied to one of my texts.

U there?

The queasiness instantly melts away, baby hairs and uneven eyeliner aside. One night down. I slow to a stop at the overflowing trash can on the corner when I see a bright red door, the number 530 tacked to it in rusting silver. The same apartment building that was in the PITT STUDENT IN NEED OF ROOMMATE ad posted a month ago.

Obviously, it was showing the good angles of this place.

My new roommate, Heather Larkin, *definitely* used the equivalent of the Snapchat dog filter on this thing, the hidden pores and under-eye bags now fully exposed in the form of peeling paint and crumbling brick.

It's not far off from my place back home, though, so I'm not too worried about it.

I text back, Yep. Just got here, then take a step forward and squint at the ancient buzzer tacked on the wall, carefully avoiding the exposed wiring while I press the button for what I hope is apartment 3A. There's a long buzz and then a staticky crackle, a muffled yet chipper voice pouring through the speaker.

"Be right down!"

I run my fingers through my hair a few more times and try to swipe off some more of the eyeliner, fixing a smile on my face as the door opens. I'm relieved to see the curly-haired Heather Larkin I was expecting from my social media creeping and not a literal ax murderer.

"Hi!" she says, holding out her hand. "You must be Alex."

"Yeah! Heather, right? Nice to meet you." I shake her hand and nod down at her carefully manicured nails. "I like your nails."

She gives me a grateful smile, and I follow her inside. Both of us struggle to fit together in the narrow entryway. The speckled carpet is worn and fraying, mail is overflowing out of the boxes, but . . . it doesn't smell like cat pee or trash. Which counts for something, I guess.

Besides, this was the only place I could find that was furnished *and* under $500 a month—much cheaper than on-campus housing and the only way I could afford to go to school *and* buy all of my overpriced "special edition" science textbooks.

We climb the steps up to the third floor, and Heather talks away while I try not to pass out on flight number two from lugging my massive suitcase.

"You're a freshman, right? You excited?"

"Yeah, I think so," I gasp out as we loop around the stair-case.

"Why'd you decide to come here?"

"Good premed program. In-state tuition." Did I pack bricks in this duffel bag? Jesus. "But still far enough away from home that it feels out of state," I add as I pull it up farther on my shoulder, taking Natalie's words to heart and opening up just a tiny bit more than I usually would.

"Girl, I get that." Heather looks back and rolls her eyes before coming to a stop in front of a bruised white door. "I wanted to go to the University of Colorado, but . . ." Her voice trails off, and she rubs her thumb against her middle and pointer fingers.

Money. Tell me about it.

She fits the key in the lock and pushes inside. "But Pitt's a good school. You'll like it here. My boyfriend, Jackson, is a transfer student, and he loves it *way* more than Penn State, so that's got to count for something."

She smiles at me as we step through the doorway, and I smile back, reassured.

The apartment is surprisingly nice. The wooden floors are a little scratched and worn, and there's an ominous brown patch on one of the white ceiling tiles that will probably leak by the end of this term, but Heather and her currently-backpacking-through-Europe roommate have really made this place feel homey.

36

There's a comfy-looking gray couch, an IKEA coffee table, and cute string lights looping from the ceiling and over the big windows. Pictures hang on the walls, some generic quotes in calligraphy, others shots from around the city, the Cathedral of Learning, Heather and a big group of friends.

Maybe, just maybe, I actually pulled this off.

"Your room is just past the bathroom," Heather says, pointing to a door at the end of a small hallway.

I'm barely past the small kitchenette and into the hall when the bathroom door flies open and I'm body-slammed by a still-wet, very shirtless, *very* hairy boy wearing nothing but a small white towel.

A *way too small* white towel.

I know that because as we go tumbling to the ground, it does not cover even a single ball. I can feel the entire outline on my leg like I'm back at my first middle school dance, and Matt Paloma is grinding his little heart out on me.

"Oh my God," I say, horrified, our eyes locking. I see him take in my face in a way I've seen hundreds of times over the years. It's the same look I've been getting since I hit puberty in seventh grade.

I grimace and push away as we both scramble to our feet. And . . . as if this entire situation couldn't get *any* worse, that's when I notice it.

He has a boner.

He tries to hide it with the tiny towel, but it's no use.

"Are you kidding me, Jackson? Really?" Heather says as she pushes past me to grab his arm. *Jackson.* Her boyfriend.

I press my back up against the wall as they slide past. She drags him across the apartment, and just before she slams the door to her room shut, she glares at *me*. Me! Like his boner is somehow *my* fault.

Great.

I lean my head against the wall and let out a long exhale. There goes that chance at a friendship. What a way to start my freshman year.

I push through the door at the end of the hallway and look around the room. There's a small desk. A tiny closet. A blue twin mattress by a curtainless window.

I drop my stuff and collapse onto it, rubbing my face with my hands.

I can't believe it. I've spent *years* just dreaming about getting away, but now . . . I wish I were back in Philly. I wish I were back with Natalie, at her apartment, rewatching *New Girl* while she plucks away at her guitar, always practicing for her next concert, her roommates clattering around in the background.

Natalie.

I pull my phone out of my pocket and sit up, tapping on her contact info. I hesitate, my finger frozen over the call button, the fear of an unsuccessful apology getting the better of me.

"Come on, Alex," I whisper. "This is what got you here in the first place." I force myself to press the green button, holding my breath as the phone rings and rings.

Just as I'm about to give up, she answers.

"Hi."

"Hey!" I practically shout, relieved she picked up instead of letting the call go to voicemail. "How are you?"

"Fine."

Curt. Angry. But . . . responding. That means we're maybe past the silent-treatment phase of her being angry at me.

That means I've got a chance.

"What're you doing tonight?" I stall, thinking of all the things we'd usually do on a Saturday night if I didn't have work and she wasn't performing. Flipping through vinyl at the record shop. Reading on a blanket at the park. Watching a movie together at her apartment.

"About to get some food at Steggy's."

"Oh." A pang of longing hits me square in the chest. What I wouldn't give to be with her in that grungy-ass hole-in-the-wall, picking at the absolute mountain of nachos they sell for seven bucks.

It's hard to imagine her there without me, and it . . . surprises me how much it bothers me. I keep picturing all the uneaten guacamole that'll be left on her plate at the end of the night. The guacamole *I* would always trade her my jalapeños for. The conversations we'd have about her band and how their

39

new album was doing. The way she'd hold my hand under the table while we waited for our food. How she wouldn't mind if I had to dip early to go check on my mom.

"You need something, Alex, or . . . ?"

"Nat, I . . ." I fight for the words to come out. *Come* on, *Alex.* "I just . . . I miss you."

She snorts, and I can practically see her shaking her head. "I thought I didn't know shit about you."

Oof. Not my best moment.

"I didn't mean that. I just . . ."

"Alex, we both know you're not calling because you miss me. You're calling because you don't have anyone else."

"That's not true. I mean . . . it *is* true I don't have anyone else—you were right—but I don't *want* anyone else. I've spent every second since I left your apartment thinking about you. About us," I say, trying to string all the thoughts I had on the bus together, trying to talk about my feelings even though it's tough. "Listen, I . . . I'm sorry about what happened. I'm sorry I pushed you away and ran when you tried to get close, just like when I ghosted you. I'm sorry I didn't make you feel like you were the only girl in my life. I'm sorry that when you said 'I love you' and asked me to be real with you, all I did was change the subject and close myself off." I take a deep breath. "But I don't want to run away this time, Natalie. Not with you."

There's silence on the other end. I pull the phone away from my ear to check that she didn't hang up.

"I meant it," she says finally. "I meant it, Alex. I love you, but . . . I just don't trust you. I *can't* trust you. Especially not when you close me out all the time." She lets out a huff of air. "Not to mention the fact Megan told me you called her last night after you left. I saw her at the diner this morning."

Fucking Megan.

"It wasn't like that! I called her because I had nowhere to sleep." I jump up and start to pace the room, back and forth. "Natalie. Come on. Please. Let me prove to you I can change. Let me prove to you that you can *trust* me. I want to make this work long distance. Really."

The thing I never got a chance to say to her last night.

"I don't know. I mean, you're not *here*. How will I know what you're even doing there? If you couldn't say 'I love you,' what's going to stop you from cheating? I mean, that's why I wanted you to come on tour with me." She takes a deep breath, her tone questioning when she speaks next. "We don't leave until tomorrow."

I squeeze my eyes shut and run my fingers through my hair. I look around the unfamiliar room, at my suitcase by the door, the roommate that already hates me on the other side of it. My mom back in Philly, who I probably shouldn't even be away from anyway.

But . . . I can't. I don't want to go. This is my chance to make my life different, and I can't pass it up.

"Natalie, I'll do anything," I say. "Anything but that."

41

She's silent for a moment before letting out a long exhale. "Listen. I was going to surprise you before all of this, but . . . I'll be in Pittsburgh for a tour stop on September thirtieth." I feel my heart leap. "I mean, I'm sure you'll have, like, four girlfriends by then, but if you don't, maybe we can talk." She pauses. "*Really* talk. About how you feel. About what you really want and if we can make this work long distance."

Yes. I can work with that. I can do that.

"Natalie. I don't want to be with anyone else. I *won't* be with anyone else," I promise, reassuring her. "I want to be with you. For real. Okay?"

"Well, I guess we'll see, won't we?" She pauses. "I hope you prove me wrong."

"I will," I say as I smile to myself, relieved.

Besides, I've always loved a challenge.

CHAPTER 4

MOLLY

After having a cup of severely undercooked microwave ramen for dinner last night and a brown-sugar Pop-Tart for breakfast this morning, I can't put off venturing out to the cafeteria for lunch any longer.

As I step out of the elevator and into the lobby, there's a lady standing across the hall from me in the doorway of the common room.

"You here for the event?" she asks, her pink lipstick popping against her skin.

"Oh, no. I'm just—" I point to the exit, but she's already talking.

"Come on. It'll be fun," she says, the natural smile on her face actually making me believe it.

I don't know what this is, but I guess it's probably better to try to meet people before I'm awkwardly looking for a table to eat lunch at.

Inside the room are about forty other people scattered around the floor and a table with a bowl of mints and a *ton* of bananas.

Odd refreshments combo, but okay.

I come up with a quick game plan to sit in the middle somewhere, but it fizzles out when I grab a banana from the table and someone snickers right beside me. Instead, I step around bodies and over legs until I'm all the way in the back corner by myself. *Excellent start.*

As the two women at the front of the room pull a big container of Ping-Pong balls out of a tote bag, I realize that I totally just walked into an icebreaker event. Not that I'm complaining. These things were literally made for people like me. It's probably the best way to force myself into some social interaction. Although, I'm not going to lie. I wish we were playing some actual Ping-Pong. *That* I can do.

As they're getting set up, I peel my banana and take a bite. But then I notice a boy staring at me from across the room.

I do a double take as I recognize his shaggy black hair and fitted jeans. Christopher Matthews, my workshop partner from AP English last year. I wave, and he whispers something to the guy next to him before standing up and carefully stepping across the room toward me.

Just be cool, Molly. Be normal.

It's Chris, I talked to him almost every day in workshop. This should be fine.

"Molly, what's up?" he whispers, sliding down the wall beside me.

"Not much," I reply, internally nudging myself to continue the conversation. "What's up with you?"

"My floormates dragged me to this," he says, looking over at a few guys along the side wall, laughing and shoving one another like they've been friends for years, not twenty-four hours.

"Yeah, I'm kinda looking forward to it," I admit, and he gives me a weird look. *Maybe admitting you're into lame icebreakers in college was the wrong move.*

It felt so different talking to him in the classroom, but it *was* different. There were talking points, rules, things I'm good at.

There's a lingering silence, so I take another bite of my banana to fill it.

"Uh . . . Molly?" I look over at him, midchew, and his eyes widen. "I came over here because I wanted to give you a heads-up. I . . . don't think those are for eating." The corner of his mouth pulls up into a smirk.

The women in the front finally turn around. One of them is holding a banana and a mint. The other one is swinging around a balloon stuffed *full* of Ping-Pong—

That's not a balloon.

And those aren't mints.

"Oh. My. God," I whisper, mortified as I watch the woman

roll a condom down over a banana, the one in my mouth suddenly making me nauseous as I try to choke it down.

"I thought we were going to play some games," I admit to Chris, who is struggling to keep his laugh quiet. "What the heck am I doing here?"

"Free banana?" He shrugs. "Plus, you'll always know how to properly use a condom."

"Yeah, I'm, like, *super* gay," I tell him. I'm so embarrassed, the words tumble out before I can even obsess over them.

He laughs, hard. Even though I'm still mortified, that laugh feels like a victory. It's like the anxiety that usually sits between me and the person I'm talking to doesn't feel as impenetrable as usual. Maybe I can save this.

"Oh, really? You never told me that before," he says. "Well, just a free banana, then."

"What are you doing after this?" I ask.

"Nothing really, well . . . until tonight. Do you remember Kristen Osborne?" he asks, keeping his voice low. I nod, picturing the redheaded captain of the danceline when Noah played football in high school. "She's a senior now, and her sorority is having a party tonight up by Sutherland Hall. You should come." He says it like it's nothing, like my mom inviting me along on a grocery run. But it's not nothing to me.

I haven't been invited to a party since I was in middle school, when kids were *forced* to invite everyone.

"Really?" I ask, not quite daring to believe he means it.

"Yeah. I'll send you the Facebook invite."

We watch the woman stuff ten more Ping-Pong balls into the condom. "If he ever says he's too big, ladies, now you know. It's bullshit." She tosses it across the room like a rock star throwing a guitar pick into the audience, and it lands in the hands of a girl who absolutely did not want to receive it.

"You think there'll be a lot of people from Oak Park?" I ask, digging for a specific name.

He shrugs. "Matt, Tim, Brie, Cora . . ."

My heart stops. The rest of his words are just a jumble of sounds as she infiltrates every section of my brain. It's been so long since I've seen her, and now . . .

Now I'm actually going to talk to her. At a party. That I was invited to.

This is my fresh start. It couldn't be more perfect.

After the women finish their PowerPoint, Christopher tells me he's getting lunch with his floormates as my stomach growls. Instead of inviting myself along with them, I part ways with him and eat in the farthest corner of the cafeteria so I don't accidentally run into him.

Back in my dorm room, as I wait for the invitation to come in, I find myself thinking about what I did wrong today. All the things I should've said but didn't and the things I maybe should have kept inside. Like when I admitted I thought I'd walked into an hour of icebreakers. Earlier the party sounded *perfect*, and I truly felt like I should go, like I *could* go. But it's starting to just feel like a lot.

Like maybe I shouldn't press my luck by going.

Like maybe I should just stick to my normal weekend-night routine and stay in. Make a good cup of tea and rewatch a few episodes of *Wynonna Earp* on Netflix.

Without having a roommate like I had planned, I need to adapt. I need to come up with another way to put myself out there. I can't just stop trying. So I decide to pop over to Noah's apartment to talk to him about it, hoping he might be able to give me a few tips so I don't have to embarrass myself tonight—*if* the invite ever even comes in.

It's a ten-minute drive to his rental house in Lawrenceville, which rivals East Liberty for the most gentrified neighborhood in Pittsburgh. You can pick up a rock from a crumbling row house and throw it across the street into the private pool of a twenty-million-dollar apartment building. His place is something in between, a slightly updated two-bedroom.

He opens the door, holding an entire half of a pepperoni pizza in one hand and a bottle of honey in the other. He's wearing his Little League baseball T-shirt, which somehow finally fits him now that he's a grown man, and a pair of gray Nike sweatpants. One of the perks of working from home.

Right after he graduated college last year, Noah landed a job at one of the coolest start-ups in the country, based right here in Pittsburgh. He's always writing code for something awesome: a robotic monkey for an Old Spice commercial, an installation of interactive flowers for a Google event, a secret sliding bookcase for my parents that opens up to a safe only when the correct number of books are moved in the correct order.

I watch as he drizzles a bit of honey on the corner of the pizza, his almost-black eyes focused on creating the perfect bite. He sinks his teeth into it and nods a "what's up" at me.

"I thought CrossFitters were supposed to eat healthy. Chicken and rice and protein shakes," I prod.

"Don't put me in a box," he replies, making me smile. "You want some?" He rolls the hot bite around in his open mouth. "I've got the other half in the oven." He drizzles more honey and takes another bite before he even gets a chance to swallow the first one.

"Yeah, I'll take it," I say, following him into the kitchen. He doesn't hand me the entire half like he's eating it. Instead, he cuts it into three slices and slides the pan closer to me.

"Have you made any friends on your floor yet?" he asks. I shake my head, taking a bite out of the crust. "You know, Molly, you're like . . ." He struggles to find the right words. "You're cool. I mean . . . you're cool to hang out with. Other people would think so too if you just gave them a chance." His words catch me off guard.

When have I not given people a chance?

But then I think of Christopher. I kept eye contact with him in the common room, and I ended up talking to him more than I had in a whole semester at Oak Park. As much as I hate to admit it, maybe Noah's got a point.

I take a deep breath.

"I got invited to a party later, but I'm kinda scared to go," I tell him.

"Go!" he says without hesitation, then stops himself. "I mean, I don't want to tell you what to do, but . . . college parties are a means to an end."

"What do you mean?" I ask.

"They're, like . . . disgusting, but that's how I met Dave and Nick. I even met Kendra at one of them."

"Kendra cheated on you sophomore year and broke your heart," I remind him, but the look on his face tells me that he didn't need reminding.

"Molly, that's not the point. My point is that I met some of my best friends at some of the trashiest parties. So if I hadn't gone . . ." He shrugs, his point made.

I let out a loud groan. "Cora's going to be there."

"Molly. You *have* to go. Are you kidding me? How is this even a question?"

I can already feel the anxiety crawling across my skin at the idea of going, but I know he's right. "I know. *I know.* Fine." I let out an exasperated sigh, collapsing dramatically into one of his dining chairs.

"Awesome, but one thing." He points an authoritative finger at me. "No drinking and driving."

"Okay, *Mom.*" I laugh. "I probably won't even do any drinking."

"Well." He shrugs, giving me a look. "Maybe do a little drinking."

My phone pings on the table as he shoves the rest of his pizza in his mouth. The party invite from Christopher lights up the screen along with a private message. Hey molly, hope to see you there!

My pulse quickens at the uncertainty of what might happen. But I know what happens if I stay home. Nothing changes. Cora won't magically reach out to me. I have to give myself a chance. I have to give *them* a chance, just like Noah said.

CHAPTER 5

ALEX

I try to refresh the Cereal Killers Instagram for the hundredth time today, but my data speeds have been reduced, and the picture they just posted refuses to load beyond an amorphous blob of shapes and colors.

Fuck.

I wanted to get the Wi-Fi password from Heather this morning, but she's been giving me the cold shoulder since the boner incident with Jackson yesterday, glaring angrily in my direction every chance she gets.

I thought I was maybe being a little paranoid, but when I got back from a Target run this afternoon to buy toiletries and a sheet set, she made a whole show of turning off the TV and storming into her room like an angsty middle schooler.

Sighing, I roll onto my back and send a check-in text to my mom, since she didn't reply to me this morning.

I try to fight the nerves that inevitably follow, but they

get the better of me and my thumb swipes into my contacts. I hesitate over the cell number for our next-door neighbor, Tonya, holding my breath as I stare at the green call button. Somehow I manage to stop myself from pressing down.

She already agreed to check in on her twice a week, and I don't want to bug her too much.

I toss my phone down next to me and stare up at the ceiling. The empty room feels somehow incredibly crowded. Itchy. The longer I lie here, with absolutely nothing to distract myself, the more my ears begin to ring. I can feel the weight of it all, tightening its grip on my lungs, until it's so heavy it's hard to draw even a single breath.

Even though I'm finally gone, it suddenly feels like I'm right back in the house I left behind. Just *waiting*. Waiting for Mom to come home.

My mind would always get the better of me. I couldn't stop obsessing over where she was. Who she was with. How much she was drinking. How much she was spending when we had a whole stack of bills on the kitchen table.

After our electric shut off one night, getting a job at Tilted Rabbit three summers ago was the only way to silence all of it. The only way to take a little bit of control back. I convinced the owner, Stew, to let me do dishes until I was old enough to work behind the bar.

But now that's gone just like I am. And I don't know what she's going to do.

Add in this mess with Natalie and the fact I'm officially starting college tomorrow, and I can literally feel all of it crushing me, getting heavier and heavier by the second.

I need to get out of here.

I jump up and grab my wallet off the desk before sliding into my white Converse and heading down the hall as fast as I can. I throw open the apartment door and jog down the steps, feeling the pressure slowly give way with each floor.

By the time I'm outside, I feel like I can breathe again. I inhale slowly as I glance up at the sky, the color a deep, dusky blue, the sun just disappearing below a string of houses-turned-apartments, lopsided porches and worn brick and Pitt flags pinned to crooked windows. I turn left and head down the street, dodging around girls in tiny black dresses and boys with water bottles filled with vodka, screaming their way to some party. And it's this sight, of people with a purpose and a place to go, that makes me realize . . . I have no idea where I'm headed.

Back in Philly, this night would look *completely* different. Yeah, I'd still leave home with no idea where I was going, but I'd always end up exactly where I needed to be, at one of Natalie's concerts, working an extra shift at Tilted Rabbit, or flirting my way past a bouncer to get into some club.

Nights out changed after we started dating, though.

Less sneaking into clubs, more dinner dates and movies. I didn't want Natalie mad at me over some flirtation, real or imagined, so it was best to just avoid it altogether.

But here . . . I don't even have that.

It's not that there isn't a wealth of options, even if this is an unfamiliar city. I mean, it would be *easy*. I could just tag along with one of these groups to a frat party. Find a grungy bar to hang out at. Sneak into a concert and disappear into the crowd after someone buys me a drink.

In another world I'd do it in a heartbeat. But in this one, even with the distance between us, I'm trying to keep on the straight and narrow. I promised Natalie I would, and I want to keep that promise.

Still, I can't help but feel like a washed-up old man, reminiscing about his youth. The good ol' days.

If I could roll my eyes at myself, I would.

I head down an unfamiliar side street, determined to not turn back yet, and the pothole-filled road eventually gives way to a convenience store, a red-and-white sign reading SNACKZ buzzing just outside. The bells atop the door jingle noisily as I step inside. The guy behind the counter looks up from his phone to nod hello to me. "Carl" is scrawled sloppily on the name tag pinned to his chest, and I see him do a double take, pushing his glasses farther up on his nose to look at me.

For a fraction of a second I wonder what snacks I might be able to get for free, but my eyes land on the Flamin' Hot Cheetos that Natalie always gets.

Right. Natalie.

And now that there's no benefit to his double take, I just feel . . . annoyed.

I roll my eyes and walk past a pile of newspapers and magazines to get to the Cheetos, pulling out my phone to snap Natalie a quick picture of the bag and write thinking of u below it. I turn toward the wall of windows, holding my phone up to the sky for better service, the message finally sending.

Pocketing my phone, I turn down another aisle to see two girls at the very end stopping midconversation to glance over at me.

The taller one looks away almost instantly, her black curls bouncing as she squints shiftily at the front door, but the shorter one holds my gaze for a long moment, hazel eyes peeking out at me from under a pixie cut. She's wearing a pair of parachute pants. Vertical stripes. Very, *very* bright.

Not exactly my thing, but . . . she's making it work.

"He said he would be here," her friend hisses, and the pixie-cut girl finally shrugs and looks back at her.

I pretend to eye some chocolate bars, casually scanning the nutrition facts on a Hershey's while I listen in, a million scenarios naturally falling into place in front of me.

I could say I like her pants. I could stroll over and get one of the packs of gum on the shelf just behind her head. I could make a joke about how the person I'm waiting for isn't here yet either.

"Brie is already there, and she says there's only a keg. And like . . . Fireball."

Ew. Gross. My mom is a certified alcoholic, and even she won't go near that stuff.

"Well, is there anyone else we can call who can buy something for us?" Parachute Pants asks her friend.

There's silence. Clearly they're about to be doomed to a night of choking down cinnamon-flavored whiskey. A fate I wouldn't even wish on Heather Larkin's boyfriend.

Before I realize what I'm doing, I drop the Hershey's bar back in the box and head down the aisle, running my fingers casually through my hair.

"What do you want?" I ask.

They both turn to look at me, surprised. Pixie-cut girl gives me a once-over, the corner of her mouth ticking up in a smile.

"You're twenty-one?" she asks skeptically. Up close, I see she has a nose ring. Silver. Cute.

I lean casually against the shelf next to us, the metal cool under my arm. "Depends on who's asking."

She laughs, rolling her eyes. "So that's a no."

"Well. What about you?" I say, leaning closer until her face is inches from mine, her hazel eyes widening as she looks up at me. "If you were behind the counter, would you give it to me?"

She shakes her head, but I can tell it worked. We both

know she would. I doubt I'd even have to show off my acting chops.

I feel a small rush from a win like that and open my mouth to say something, my eyes still locked on hers, when Natalie's words pop into my head.

How can I trust you in Pittsburgh, when you're getting texts like this when we're in the same city?

Instantly the rush fades as quickly as it came. *Come* on, *Alex. Focus.* It hasn't even been forty-eight hours.

I pull away, determined to turn around and go back to my snack hunt, but then she swipes a crumpled twenty from her friend's hand and holds it up. "Whatever. We're desperate. We need a six-pack. Mike's Hard, preferably. But we'll take Seagram's. A cider variety pack. As long as it's fruity."

I hesitate before holding my hand out for the money. "All right."

It's a good deed, after all. And besides, aren't I supposed to be making friends to eventually introduce Natalie to? She hands it to me, and her fingers linger in my palm before slowly sliding along my fingertips.

Oof. Uh, maybe not.

I clear my throat and nod to the candy bars behind me, trying to make my expression all business. "Buy something so it's not suspicious. I'll meet you outside."

I move past them and around the corner to where the alcohol is, scanning the refrigerated section two times over, looking for the familiar black-and-yellow packaging, as I hear the cash register dinging behind me.

There's no sign of it. Just rows and rows of IPAs and light beer.

Not wanting to give up after talking a big game, I stroll casually up to the checkout counter and lean on it, the two girls' eyes boring holes in the back of my head as they creep toward the door. The clerk drops his phone, his cheeks turning bright red as he straightens up.

"Hi, Carl," I say, giving him a flirty smile as I brush my hair behind my ear.

"Uh, hey," he says, fumbling around on the counter for his phone, and then a pen, and then his phone again.

"You wouldn't happen to have any Mike's Hard, would you?"

He jumps up, eager to help. "I think . . . in the back . . ."

As he shuffles off to get it, I hear the bells on the front door jingle somewhere behind me, letting me know the two girls have finally left the store. I glance casually to the side to make sure they aren't just waiting at the front windows, peering through the glass.

Thankfully, they've gotten out of sight.

Carl reappears with a six-pack, nearly dropping it as he slides it onto the counter.

This is going to be easy.

"Can—can I see your ID?" he asks as he scans it.

I put the twenty on the counter and make a big show of checking my pockets before letting out a long, frustrated sigh and covering my face. "Oh my God. You've got to be kidding me. I left my wallet at home." I can feel the tears welling up in the corners of my eyes as Carl begins to panic. "I just got broken up with *completely* out of the blue last night and now *this.*"

That's . . . technically true.

I look up as I will a single tear to roll slowly out of my right eye. A look of horror fills poor Carl's face as he watches it make its way down my cheek.

The Academy should be giving me a call later for this performance. Move over, Meryl.

I sniff loudly and wipe it quickly away as I reach for the twenty. "I'm sorry. I'll just—"

"Hey, you know what?" Carl says, getting to it first, our hands gently grazing as he scoops it up. "Don't worry about it."

The cash register swings open with a ding, and he quickly counts my change.

"Really?" I ask, careful to keep my eyes dewy and glistening.

"Yeah. I'm, uh, sorry about your breakup," he says, handing me my receipt and a handful of dollars and cents.

"Thank you *so* much." I take the money and the six-pack and give him a small, grateful smile, squeezing his hand before delivering my last line. The finale, if you will. "Hopefully, I'll find a guy as nice as you, Carl."

It could *not* land any better. He beams at me as I head out of the store, and I'm careful to keep a sad slump to my shoulder until I make it to the back corner of the parking lot, where the girls are standing below a blinking streetlight.

"You did it!" Pixie Cut says to me as I hand over the alcohol and the change, straightening up as I finally retire my acting career.

"Are you *crying*?" her friend asks.

"It's all about the commitment," I say with a grin. There's a long pause, so I fill the silence. "I'm Alex, by the way. I'm a freshman at Pitt."

"Us too. I'm Abby," the girl with curly hair says.

"Cora," Pixie Cut says when we lock eyes. She takes a step closer to me, slowly. Confidently. "I don't know if you have plans, but . . . this girl I know from high school is having a small get-together at her place tonight, if you want to come. As a thank-you."

"Uh." I pause, quickly swallowing the yes that was about to escape.

A small get-together.

I mean . . . that's not a party.

I'm sure Natalie wouldn't be thrilled if I went to a party with two girls I just met, but if it's only a small get-together, that's not *really* tipping the scale.

Besides, I can't just sit in my room alone and claustrophobic.

This is my *freshman year* of college! This is my chance to . . . I don't know. *Make friends.* Make some real connections, like she told me I was *seriously* lacking.

She can't be mad about that, can she?

I just have to be careful about . . .

Cora smiles sweetly up at me, her hazel eyes bright.

About *that.*

"Sure," I say, looking past her to Abby as I lean ever so slightly away.

I follow them both to the bus stop, the unfamiliar streets all blurring together. I check my phone battery, relieved to see I still have an 82 percent charge, because I'm *definitely* going to need to GPS my way back.

As we walk, I find out Abby's a mechanical engineering major, and Cora is doubling in history and English.

I guess after their name everyone at college just introduces themselves by their major.

"Everyone tells me there's no money in an English major, but I just *love* books," Cora says, turning to face me while we wait below a blue-and-white bus sign.

I do too, but I don't want to tell her that. In fact, I would've probably majored in it if it weren't for that singular fact.

"Oh, cool," I say as I glance down the street for the bus instead of jumping into a conversation about our TBR lists. Probably safe to avoid having too much in common with Cora now that I'm running a one-woman convent.

"What about you?" she asks as I lean up against the sign-post. "What are you here for?"

"I'm in premed," I say, watching as the bus comes swinging around a corner, a group of students scattering out of its way.

"Oooh," Abby says, wincing. "You're braver than I am. I couldn't handle all that blood and stuff."

"Eh, that's no biggie," I say, but I can't deny the queasy feeling that swims into my stomach. Luckily, there are a few things that outweigh that.

Job security. A fat paycheck. Not having to struggle to pay rent and keep food in the fridge.

What's a little queasiness when you get that much of a payoff?

The doors hiss open, and we squeeze inside. Abby opts to stand, but Cora slides into the seat next to me, smiling at me as her leg grazes against mine. I clear my throat and pull my leg away, glancing out the window.

This night has already been *quite* the test. Harder than I thought it would be. And it's only my second day.

I can't help but see that Natalie was right about more than just me not having friends.

I'm so hardwired to flirt that I never even realized how much I was doing it. How what I thought was harmless really wasn't.

But Natalie did. For five months. The guilt creeps back up, but I can't let it swallow me.

Instead, I decide tonight is actually a good thing. It's a test. A chance to make an actual change.

And now I'm that much more determined to prove that I can.

CHAPTER 6

MOLLY

As soon as I step inside, the hallway is plastered with people
I've never seen before, and I can feel my hands clam up.

The urge to bolt is strong, but I remind myself, *Stick to the
plan.* Get a drink. Pretend like I belong.

Find Cora. Then . . . hope that she's alone too and looking
for a familiar face to hang with. I mean, it's been a day. She
can't have made that many friends yet, right?

I keep my eyes peeled as I squeeze through the crowd,
taking note of the bathroom in case I need a second alone. I
find my way into the kitchen and grab a red Solo cup off the
stack. I hold it against the ice dispenser attached to the fridge
and peek back at the drink selections: a keg of beer, a half-
empty six-pack of Mike's Hard, three handles of Fireball, and
some cans of Coke, so it takes me a minute to realize no ice is
coming out.

"That's busted," a big sweaty boy says, coming up beside

me with a cup filled with a brown liquid that's probably not soda. "Here. You gotta . . ." He rips the freezer door open with his free hand, and I jump out of the way as he pulls an actual *hatchet* out of the back. I watch with horror as he hacks away at the ice, his drink sloshing out of his cup and all over my arm before I can dodge it.

Yep. Definitely not soda.

"Uh, thanks," I say as he bare-hands a chunk of ice and drops it into my cup. He grunts, throws the hatchet once more to the back of the freezer, and then lumbers away like nothing happened. I make my way over to the "bar" and pour myself a can of Coke. No one needs to know there's nothing else in it. Probably not the best moment for my first drink.

I head through the other doorway out of the kitchen, where a plastic beer pong table is set up in what should probably be a dining room. I always heard Cora was a killer pong player, so this seems like the best place to keep an eye out for her while also blending in. I find an open spot against the wall and try to pretend like I'm riveted by the four guys tossing a couple of balls back and forth into the cups. It actually hurts to see them doing it, when they *could* be using them for what they're *really* meant for. The beautiful game.

I glance over at the boy standing next to me, and his face is familiar.

"Hi," I say, looking into the blue eyes of Jason Shober. It's weird that I've never said a word to him, but here, so far from home, surrounded by strangers, his presence manages to calm my nerves a bit.

"Hey. I'm Jason," he introduces himself like I didn't sit in front of him for four years of homeroom.

I'm about to say "I know," but I swallow it. "Molly," I say instead, feeling like I just took a blow to the gut.

And then it gets worse.

As I turn my head back to the game, there's a blur of white coming right at me.

I could duck.

I could put my hand up and block it.

But I do absolutely none of those things. Fifteen sets of eyeballs watch a Ping-Pong ball bounce directly off the center of my forehead and drop into my Coke.

"Sorry," a guy shouts from across the table.

My face immediately fills with heat, and I know it must be redder than the cup I'm holding. The room explodes with cheers and claps as a boy in an unbuttoned polo shirt takes my drink and chugs the whole thing, then spits the ball out onto the floor, barely missing my beaded sandals.

"Is this just Coke?" He scrunches his face up at me, and I go into full panic mode.

"What? No. It's—" He burps, handing me the cup back before I can come up with something. I don't look at him or anyone else around me. I just make a beeline for the bathroom that I passed earlier.

I close the door and click the lock behind me.

"Molly, what the hell . . ." I run my fingers through my hair and drop my elbows onto either side of the sink. I should've stayed home.

I'm in a new place, surrounded by new people, but the truth is . . . I haven't changed a bit. I've just been lying to myself, pretending like I could be someone different here. It's becoming abundantly clear that no matter what changes happen around me, I'll always be the same Molly Parker. No friends. No life. No chance in hell that Cora would ever even talk to me, let alone *go out* with me.

I raise my chin to face myself in the mirror, absolutely horrified to see my eyeliner and mascara smeared around my eyes. *Shit.* I don't wear makeup enough to remember the rules about touching your face. As in, don't do it.

I look down, and without much hesitation, start rifling through the drawers. Normally, I would *never*, but now is not the time to be worried about invading people's privacy. I've got an emergency on my hands, or I guess my face. *Bingo.* I find a small makeup bag in the bottom drawer. Thank you, Kristen.

I wash my face off, scrubbing away with the hand soap until the black smudges are gone. I reapply the mascara but nix the eyeliner, because it took me almost half an hour to get a clean line the first time around.

I inspect myself in the mirror. My skin looks slightly

blotchy after the full scrub down. So I flip open her foundation and dust the powder all over my face.

Oh my God.

My reflection's eyes go wide in the mirror as it becomes obvious to me now that Kristen is about two, three . . . a million shades paler than me. I lean closer to the mirror and cringe. It's like I'm straight out of *Memoirs of a Geisha*, except I'm half Korean, and only a quarter as attractive.

I quickly wash all the makeup away *again*, then plop down on the lid of the toilet with a sigh, dropping my face into my hands.

Maybe the universe is trying to tell me something.

Maybe some people are just meant to be alone.

I pull out my phone to call the only person in the world I want to talk to right now.

"Hey, baby," my mom answers as I close my eyes. "How are you? How's the dorm? What are you up to?"

"Hey, Mom. I'm okay. I'm just . . ." I laugh, looking around me. "I'm hiding in the bathroom at a party."

"Why are you hiding?" she asks.

"Cora's here," I tell her. "I don't think I can do it, though. I can't talk to her. I couldn't even just stand in a room without . . ." I let out an exasperated sigh.

"Molly—"

"I don't want to be here anymore," I whisper into the phone, wishing I were at home with her instead. I should never have told her I wanted space. Not when she's the only person I'm ever going to have to talk to.

"Listen to me," she says. "You've been going on about this girl for a long time. Now she's right on the other side of the door from you. This is the perfect opportunity!"

"She's not going to like me."

"Well, you have to give her the chance to, baby," she says. Noah's words from earlier today resurface in my head. It's hard to deny them now, when I'm locked in a bathroom. That's pretty much the definition of trying to keep people out. Maybe they're both right. It's not like Cora was in the room when everything went down out there. I really could still have a fresh slate with her. It's not too late.

"You're right, Mom. I'll call you later. I gotta go."

"Remember, no drinking and driving!" she shouts just before I hang up. *Oh my God.* Noah is going to be so mad when I tell him they're pretty much the same person now.

I tuck my phone away in my pocket and stand up off the toilet to pace the tiny room and make a new plan.

I'll go find her, and instead of trying to just bump into her, I'll walk up and say hi. I'll talk to her about her classes this year, ask if she's taking another fiction writing class like the one we took together last year at Oak Park. I already know the answer, because I saw her schedule when she posted it to social media over the summer. She'll say yes, and then I'll tell her about how I'm next on the waitlist to get into one of the other Intro to Fiction sessions. It's the perfect conversation topic, because it's something we're both interested in.

That's it. And then see what happens.

It's not much, but it's a more realistic plan. I can work with that.

I'm just about to try to reapply the makeup when a loud pound on the door scares the crap out of me, and the mascara flies out of my hands and under the cabinet.

"Just a second!" I yell, dropping down to my hands and knees to fish it out, then popping back up to the mirror to see my familiar face looking back at me.

Actually, it feels a lot better without makeup. At least I feel like me.

There's another heavy pound on the door.

I throw everything back in the bag and stuff it back into the drawer before opening the door. I barely make it all the way out before a boy runs in and slams the door behind him.

With my heart pounding in my chest, I wipe my palms on my olive-green shorts and go back to the kitchen to pour myself a fresh Coke. Cup in hand, I'm careful not to let anyone in the pong table room see me as I slide back into the hall.

A handful of people are hanging out on the stairs, so I guess the second floor is not off-limits. Maybe that's where Cora is. I head up, squeezing past a couple making out at the top like it isn't the most inconvenient spot to be doing that in the entire house.

Laughter carries down the hall, so I head toward the last room on the right and peek in. I see a few people scattered around in groups, some on the bed, some by the window, and—

My breath hitches in my chest as I spot her on the floor wearing the absolute coolest pants I've ever seen.

She looks exactly the same as I remember. Pixie cut, nose ring, and a smile that could make me ascend into the heavens.

She looks perfect.

All of a sudden I feel like I'm going to throw up, so I step out into the hall and press my back up against the wall, taking a few deep breaths. I remind myself of my plan, the talking points.

Give her a chance to like you.

I take another gulp of my Coke, then slowly wander into the room, walking . . . right past her and over to an orange milk crate of books on the floor. Because *of course* she's with a group of people like usual, and my talking points plan did not include an audience or a group I'd have to break into.

I peek down at her from my peripheral as she lets out a big laugh and squeezes the arm of a tall blond girl who is . . . well . . . a lot hotter than me. She couldn't be any more my opposite, dressed in head-to-toe black, with rings hanging off most of her fingers. She also doesn't seem to be having *any* trouble at all making conversation with Cora.

Talk about a nice confidence booster.

But then the girl grabs her drink off the floor and sits back against a dresser out of Cora's reach, like maybe she doesn't want to be touched. But who wouldn't want to be touched by Cora Myers?

I'm so caught up in that thought that I forget to look away. Cora must feel my gaze, because her eyes flick up to mine so fast that I know I don't look away in time. A hot panic crawls up my back as I try to focus on the books at my feet.

"Hey, didn't you go to Oak Park?" I hear her ask, but I don't turn around. She could be talking to anyone. There are a lot of people here from our high school, including Chris. Maybe she's talking to someone else?

"*Molly*, isn't that you?" she says, and well, there isn't much arguing my way out of that one.

But also, suddenly I realize what that means. SHE KNOWS MY NAME. Cora Myers *knows my name*.

And it's that that gives me the confidence to slowly, very slowly, turn around. She's staring right at me. I open my mouth, but nothing, none of my carefully planned talking points or conversation starters, comes out, because I'm basically an awkward puddle on this shaggy tan carpet.

"It is Molly, right?" she asks, but when I don't say anything, she palms her face. "Oh my gosh, don't tell me I got that wrong. I'm so sorry!" she apologizes as my heart explodes through my chest.

Speak, Molly. SPEAK!

"Uh, no." I clear my throat. "Sorry, yeah. Molly, that's me." I shake my head at myself.

She smiles at me, relieved, and her hazel eyes glow in the light from above her. God, she looks good. "You wrote that story in English class, right? About the two girls who ran away?"

"Yeah. I . . ." *She. Remembers. My. Story.* "That was me," I reply, trying my best to fight off the blackout that's seeping into the corners of my vision. "Are you taking any more writing classes here?" I ask, clasping my hands around my Solo cup as tightly as I can without crushing it.

"Yeah, I decided to stick with it," she says, then gestures to her two friends on the floor with her. "Hey, we were just about to get a game started. You want in?"

"Okay," I reply, feeling a boost in confidence at the idea of getting to show off my board game chops, which have been perfected by hundreds of nights in with my family. I take a deep breath as I sit down next to Cora, folding my legs under me.

What is happening!?

"This is my roommate, Abby Williams." She points to a girl with curly black hair and glasses, who offers me a smile and a wave. "And this is Alex . . ." She holds the last syllable and cocks her head at the blond girl leaning against the dresser.

"Blackwood," the girl finishes.

Cora furrows her eyebrows and laughs, warm and velvety. "Your name is . . . Alex . . . *Blackwood*?" she asks, impressed. "Jeez, could you be any cooler?"

"I'm not that cool," Alex says with an unconvincing smirk as she sips on a bottle of Mike's Hard. I try my best not to roll my eyes at her.

I wait for someone to break out Monopoly, but instead everyone just starts chatting while we all sip on our drinks. I try *so* hard to add something to the conversation, to pepper in one of my talking points, but each time I've worked up the perfect thing, they've already moved on to another topic entirely.

Finally, Abby starts telling us how she and Cora were supposed to be put in Sutherland dorm instead of Nordenberg. It's the perfect opening for me to bring up getting stuck in a single, which will hopefully get me a second invite to hang with them, but as I open my mouth to speak, Alex changes the subject *again*.

So I basically just sit there with a smile plastered onto my face, nodding, and laughing along with everyone else.

But despite that, I'm doing it. I'm sitting here right now at a *party* talking to Cora Myers . . . or at least listening to her talk. To me.

"Well, it's been, like, twenty minutes since we sent Rosie to find a deck of cards, so she must've gotten lost at the pong table. What else could we play?" Abby says. A perfect opening for me to join in on the conversation, to suggest a game for us, but then—

"Never Have I Ever?" Alex suggests. *Oh. That kind of game.* Of course she wants to play the game where she can show off all the "cool" stuff she's done.

"Think you could beat me?" Cora asks in a tone that sends a pang of jealousy through me. Who even is this girl?

Alex shrugs. "One way to find out." She holds up her hand, five fingers outstretched.

The rest of us follow suit, but my head's not really in the game. I'm distracted by how close Cora's leg is to mine on the carpet and hoping she looks at me the way she's looking at Alex.

When my turn comes around the first time, I try to come up with something not extremely lame but also not embarrassing, like . . . well, basically anything relating to sex, drugs, and alcohol, because (SURPRISE!) Molly Parker has never ever done a whole lot of . . . stuff. And from what information I've gathered from our first few rounds, these people have. Because there are already more than a few fingers down around the circle, but my five are still in the air.

"Uh. Never have I ever . . . smoked a cigarette," I say, because everyone knows cigarettes are gross cancer-causing death traps. They're not cool. Of course, Alex drops a finger, but at least no one else does. A point to me at last.

More people join in, and the rounds get longer as our circle grows. I know it's not the game, though. Just like in class, Cora's magnetic pull is already at work without her even noticing.

People get bolder with their statements as the night goes on, and still fingers go down, which makes me even more nervous because the dirtier they get, the more likely it is I'll win, and in this game, even I know winning is losing.

Which apparently I'm pretty good at because I "win" three in a row. It's different here, though. I didn't go to any parties in high school for obvious reasons, but I have a feeling they would've been much different from this. Lots of whispers and snide comments. Here, no one seems to care about what I haven't done, though I can feel Alex's eyes on me as she takes another gulp of hard lemonade.

"Never have I ever ridden a motorcycle," a guy with a thick beard and Pirates cap says halfway through the next round. Finally! I finally get to put a finger down. As I'm sipping my drink, I share a smile with Cora.

"You have?" she asks, knocking her shoulder into mine.

"Yeah." I nod, my cheeks feeling flushed. "My uncle restores antique Harleys." She looks back at me, slightly impressed.

This could not be going any better.

Then Alex's turn comes around, and she looks dead at me. I notice for the first time how very green her eyes are as she smirks across the circle at me.

"Molly, how old are you?" she asks.

"Eighteen," I say, sweat creeping down my back as I wait for the punch line.

"Never have I ever been a virgin at eighteen," Alex finishes. I gasp and look back at her, trying to process if she

77

really just said what I heard. Her forehead is on her knee, and her shoulders are shaking.

My reaction was too obvious to try to lie. Not that anyone would buy it anyway. I drop my finger, but this time it doesn't feel like a win at all. I raise my cup to take a sip, and I look across the circle at Alex as she lifts her head, a big grin smeared over her face.

My vision blurs, and I take another sip to hide it.

Don't cry. Don't you fucking cry, Molly Parker.

I swallow hard on the lump in my throat and force myself to laugh with the rest of them. Every single person in the circle is laughing at me.

All except one.

Cora sends a glare in Alex's direction. "That wasn't funny," she says, swatting Alex on the shoulder, solidifying everything I thought I knew about Cora. She's a good one.

"They thought it was pretty funny." Alex shrugs, motioning with her bottle to the people around her. "You're up, boss," she says to her.

"Never have I ever illegally bought alcohol for a stranger," Cora says, narrowing her eyes at Alex, who laughs, clinks her bottle against Cora's even though she doesn't extend it, and then downs the rest of her hard lemonade to end the game.

"I gotta get a refill," Abby says.

"Me too." Alex springs up off the floor to follow her, and my heart leaps. *Finally.* But then Cora loops her finger into the laces of Alex's high-top Converse shoe, annoyance seemingly forgotten.

"Will you get me a refill, pleeease?" she asks, flipping her empty bottle around in her hand. "I think I'm drunk enough to stomach some of Kristen's Fireball."

Alex hesitates, but takes the bottle and then stops to look down at me. "Molly? Anything?" she asks.

Wow, so nice of you.

I shake my head. "I'm good." I take a deep breath as my eyes finally start to dry up. Thank God.

When they're out of the room, Cora shuffles around to face me, her bright striped pants dragging across the carpet.

"Hey, you know she was just joking, right? You don't have to be embarrassed." She puts a hand on my shoulder. Cora Myers is making sure *I'm* okay.

"I'm not embarrassed." I shake my head, trying my best for a real genuine laugh. "That was funny as hell." I can feel the heat of my skin under her hand. This is all I've wanted for so long, but not like this. Not like I'm this pathetic person she has to comfort. I check my phone, hoping my cheeks aren't as red as they feel. "I should probably head back to my dorm soon, though."

"Oh no, you should stay, seriously!" she says, and that makes me want to cry too, but for a totally different reason. "Maybe when they get back, we can track down that deck of cards and play Kings instead."

She wants me to stay.

"Okay. That would probably be way more fun than watching Alex lose all night," I reply, and I get a genuine laugh out of her that makes me melt.

I settle back into place next to her as she brushes her bangs cutely out of her eyes.

If only she knew I'd stay here all night if she wanted me to.

CHAPTER 7

ALEX

"That was *way* bigger than a small get-together," I say to Cora as we sit on the bench at the bus stop while Abby squints at a bus schedule on her phone. It's just after 2:00 a.m., and the streets around us are dark and quiet except for the fellow students who stroll by, giggling couples clinging to each other, a group of friends championing a box of pizza.

"Maybe just a bit," Cora says, laughing as she grabs my arm and leans into me, the cinnamony scent of Fireball moving over me in a wave.

I fight the instinct to pull her closer and scoot a little farther down the bench. Abby lets out a long sigh and circles over to where we're sitting, plunking down right in between us.

"Well, we're fucked," she says as she pockets her cell phone. "Last bus was twenty minutes ago."

I peer past her at the enormous hill we rode up on the way here. I don't even have to open up Google Maps to know it's at *least* a mile back to my apartment, the route winding and poorly lit. I grimace and turn back to meet Cora's gaze over Abby's curly hair.

This isn't Philly, and I am *not* a fan of strolling around after midnight in a place I am not even a little bit familiar with. Especially when I've hit my self-imposed two-drink limit and am *definitely* a bit buzzed. Then again, what woman is?

"We can call an Uber," Cora offers.

An Uber would . . . definitely be out of budget for me. Bus rides are free for Pitt students. An Uber at this time means surge pricing.

I bite my lip and try to psych myself up for the impending walk as a small white sedan chugs to a stop in front of us. The window slowly rolls down to reveal warm brown eyes, identical to the ones I sat across from for most of the night at the party.

Molly. I've never been happier to see someone that awkward in my life.

"Hey," she says, pushing her long dark-brown hair behind her ear. "Do you guys need a ride?"

The words are barely out of her mouth before we're all tumbling into her car, singing her praises.

"You're an actual lifesaver!" Cora says, and Molly's cheeks turn faintly red over all the attention.

We buckle in and tell her where we're heading. Cora and Abby are roommates at Nordenberg, the bougiest of the freshman on-campus housing. I saw the pictures online when I was applying—vending machines in the lobby, a flat-screen TV in every room, air-conditioning. It's the Ritz-Carlton to my Econo Lodge over on Atwood Street.

I somehow get cramped in the back seat for the ride home, even though I'm at *least* a head taller than Abby, who snagged shotgun. I rest my forearms on my knees, enjoying the darkness of the car and the song playing through the speakers and, admittedly, the way that last bit of alcohol is making me feel. Normal, for the first time since I left.

As we drive down the treacherous hills into South Oakland, I pull my phone out and check my Snapchat, refreshing it a few times just to be sure it's not my low-speed data telling me that Natalie *still* hasn't replied. She opened my Cheetos Snap *four* hours ago and didn't send anything back.

Great.

I glance up as the car starts to slow, and I see the multi-floor, gleaming glass and brick building that *must* be Nordenberg come slowly into view for the first time. Even with the beer cans strewn along the walkways, the pizza boxes overflowing out of the trash cans, it looks like an actual palace. I think I can see a girl on the fifth floor in a hoodie and a blanket, the AC nice and crisp even in the late-August heat.

Molly slides into an open space and puts the car in park, and Cora looks dead at me.

Oh no.

Her hand slides onto my leg. "You can come up if you want," she whispers as she leans toward me.

I freeze, looking down at the ignored Snap and then back into Cora's hazel eyes. Everything about her is open. Inviting. My skin begins to prickle under the weight of her hand, the promise of a night of not having to think about anything and the comfort of having someone close just waiting for me to reach out and take it.

I could just lean in and kiss her. I've done it before, and I know it would be that easy.

But . . . I don't want to take it the easy way. The superficial way, without feelings and real connection. Not anymore.

Not when it leaves me more alone than when I started.

I give her a small smile and shake my head. "I, uh . . . I've got a girlfriend."

"Oh." Cora nods and pulls away, looking surprised. "Lucky girl." She opens the door and slides out of the car. Then she ducks her head back in, beaming up at the driver's seat. "Thanks for the ride, Moll."

As the door swings shut, I catch sight of Molly, in the rearview mirror, a longing expression plastered on her face. I follow her gaze to Cora, then turn back to her, my head swiveling back and forth a dozen times before my tipsy brain can fully process what I'm seeing.

"Ohhh my God," I say, doing my best to squeeze from the back into the front of the car, accidentally elbowing Molly in the boob before landing in a heap on the passenger seat. "Molly. Ask her to use the bathroom."

"God, how much did you drink?" she says, making an incredulous face and rubbing her chest where my elbow landed.

I frown at that, those exact words usually coming out of my own mouth and directed at my blacked-out mother.

"Besides, I don't even have to go to the bathroom," she continues.

"I *know* that," I say as I glance out the window at Cora. Her time is running out. Cora's almost at the front door. "But *Cora* doesn't! Ask to use it so you can go in. Shoot your shot. I can walk home."

I can practically see the sign for Atwood Street from here, and the bus stop I got off at this morning is just down the block. We're super close to my apartment.

I meet Molly's eyes and see she's hesitating, debating. She turns to look out her window at Cora again, who is now scanning her key card . . . now opening the glass door . . . now going inside. . . .

"It's too late," Molly says finally as the door shuts behind them, wrapping her hands around the steering wheel, her grip tightening.

"Only because you waited so long!"

"Where do you live?" she asks, ignoring me.

I point in the direction of my apartment. "That way—530

Atwood Street." I grin and lean my back against the door. *"You like Cora,"* I sing as she puts the car in drive and rolls her eyes.

"And you clearly don't, so I don't get why you were stringing her along for most of the night."

I feel myself sober up and grab ahold of the "oh shit" handle to pull myself into a seated position. "Hey, it's not my fault you didn't make a move."

"Kinda hard to do that when you get called out for being a virgin," she says, her dark eyebrows jutting angrily down.

"Kinda hard to when you're making excuses before you even try," I fire back.

Her light-brown eyes widen in surprise as she glances over at me, and I know I struck a nerve. It's, admittedly, not the first one of Molly's nerves I've struck tonight, but I'm not going to let her just keep judging me, like she did for most of the night from across the circle at the party.

I wait for another sarcastic comment, but it doesn't come.

"You're right," she finally admits, turning onto Atwood Street.

And all at once it dawns on me that she wasn't *judging* me. She was just . . . frustrated. That she couldn't find a way to get close to Cora.

I think about our game of Never Have I Ever. All the rounds Molly was left sitting there with five fingers. All the rounds she got us all out with all the things she hadn't done, from never smoking a cigarette to never pulling an all-nighter to never going to a concert.

And now I feel like the biggest asshole in the entire world for what I said. Especially because she's sitting here doing the one thing I can't. Being *honest*. Being vulnerable about something, even when it's a sensitive subject. Even when it's hard.

I bite my lip as I realize this is a pretty damn perfect example of what Natalie was saying yesterday. How I completely disregarded Molly's feelings, just like I've done to Natalie for *months*. How this night *still* took a precarious turn, Cora's hand sliding up my thigh only a few moments ago.

It would've been so easy for me to get with Cora. And for Molly? Who has *real* feelings for her? Like climbing a mountain.

And that's when the idea hits me.

"I . . ." My voice trails off as I double-check myself.

I study Molly's face, my eyes narrowing thoughtfully as she gives me an uninterested glance.

I mean . . . she so clearly couldn't be *less* attracted to me. I think repulsed could even make its way onto the table.

Plus, in this case, my intentions are actually pure. For once.

"I can help you," I say, grabbing her arm in excitement. "I can help you get Cora to fall for you."

This is *perfect*. I mean, if I help Molly, I can stay out of trouble *and* have something real and tangible to show Natalie in a month that will prove I *am* different.

Not only will I have a friend to introduce her to, proof I'm not the "emotionally unavailable" asshole she thinks I am, but I'll show her that something *good* can come from my flirting. From me. Without all the . . . other stuff.

Maybe then she'll see that I mean it when I say that I want to be with her. That I'm someone worth being with. Across the distance and even with the baggage in my personal life.

Molly looks over at me, clearly not amused. "What? How?"

I point to the red door of my apartment building, and she slows to a stop, then shifts the car into park.

"Well, she's into me, so I know what she likes."

Immediately I know that . . . definitely didn't make my case.

She rolls her eyes and unlocks the car door, not saying anything. The conversation is clearly over.

I nod. Cool. Great start.

"Thanks for the ride," I say as I slide out of the car.

Molly doesn't say anything. She doesn't even look at me as she steps on the gas and drives away, leaving me standing there on the curb, watching until her white bumper fades from view.

But I'm not giving up. Not when this idea is perfect.

I just have to show Molly what I can do.

CHAPTER 8

MOLLY

A biology class at 8:30 a.m. on a Monday would not have been my first pick, but when Cora posted her class schedule on Facebook last month, it was the only one I could find with open seats left. So, I guess I'm interested in living organisms now.

I take a deep breath and adjust my hair over each of my shoulders before pulling the heavy door open and heading into the lecture hall.

I scan the rows. There are a few quiet-looking kids sitting alone in the front, groups of friends talking about their summers in the middle, and a crew of Pitt athletes in the back of the room with their legs hanging over the tiered tables.

There's not a single person who doesn't look bleary-eyed from a presemester party. It's a look I recognize all too well from after prom weekend and ski club Sundays.

But for the first time, I actually understand how they feel.

I'm exhausted too. I feel a pang thinking of the short story class I gave up for this. But despite biology being mostly a premed weed-out class at Pitt, it also covers one of my science gen eds. It's saving me a science class on my schedule in a future semester. So I'm not *just* here for Cora, I tell myself yet again.

I make my way into the room and finally catch sight of her brown pixie hair. She's talking to Abby and wearing a smile that warms me all the way down to my bones. I think she's the only person in here smiling.

I grab on to the straps of my backpack and walk up to the third row, where she's sitting a few chairs in. Abby is now tapping away on her phone, and I take half a step closer until I could wrap my hands around the back of the empty swivel chair beside Cora if I wanted to. We hung out last night. Sitting together is totally normal.

"Anyone sitting here?" I ask from behind, trying to sound . . . I don't know . . . flirty or something? But it comes out as basically a stage whisper. Between that and the jocks goofing around in the back, she doesn't hear me. I look over my shoulder at the girl sitting in the next row back as she flips her fiery-red mane of hair and throws me a glare like, *Just fucking sit down or move.*

I clear my throat, about to ask her again, but simultaneously, Abby says, "Cora, look at this!" And Cora turns her chair away as Abby holds up her phone to show her something on Instagram. I turn the other way and hesitate, meeting eyes

90

with the salty redhead, then ultimately decide to just slip out into the aisle and find a seat in the back before either of them can notice me just standing there.

Great job, Molly. Way to follow through.

I release my death grip on the straps and let my backpack slip onto the floor as I plunk down into my seat, trying my best to brush it off and instead focus on class. I pull out my binder and mechanical pencils, getting everything set up in front of me.

Everything is so fresh and new and *ready.*

It's exactly the way I like it to be, but still, I can't shake the uneasy feeling in my stomach every time my eyes flick down to Cora and the empty seat that could have been mine.

Just as the professor is adjusting the microphone on the podium to his height, the door swings open, and in walks none other than Alex Blackwood. Late. No backpack. Just a book tucked under her arm and a half-eaten 7-Eleven sandwich in her hand.

I duck my head and pretend I'm really interested in the syllabus clipped into my binder, praying she doesn't see me. I watch her out of the corner of my eye as she stops to say hi to Cora and Abby, who actually see and hear her, of course, but then she skips right up the steps and squeezes behind five people to plop down in the empty chair . . . right next to me.

She takes a big bite of her sandwich and leans on the shared table in front of us, eyes trained on me. I keep mine down, but she just keeps staring at me, chewing loudly in my ear.

"You know your girl's sitting down *there*," she practically shouts, pointing her sandwich toward the front of the room.

"Shhh!" I look over at Cora to make sure she didn't hear, but she's talking away to Abby. The chair on the other side of her is still empty.

"Why didn't you just sit by her?" Alex asks.

"Why don't *you* go sit by her?" I ask. "Or literally *anywhere* else." I motion to the smattering of empty chairs across the lecture hall.

"Oh yeah, shit, I forgot." She snorts. "You don't need my help."

I glare at her silently as she takes another bite of her sandwich, then turn my attention back to the professor, who is just introducing himself. He starts going over the syllabus, letting us know that he will not be taking roll, because this is not high school. If we do not come to class, we will fail. If we do not spend thirty hours a week studying, we will fail. If we do not do these things, we can plan on retaking this class next semester.

Seems a little dramatic.

As I start taking notes, I see a hand reach across the pages of my binder.

"Hey." I smack Alex's hand away, and she recoils, twisting her face up at me.

"Jesus! I just need to borrow a pencil and paper," she whispers.

"Oh my God." I roll my eyes and rip out a blank piece to hand over. Why wouldn't she bring something to take notes with? This is college, not kindergarten. I roll a green mechanical pencil across the table to her and notice the book she brought in with her isn't the bio textbook but a copy of *Anna Karenina* by Tolstoy.

I didn't peg Alex Blackwood to be a reader of the classics.

Not that I've spent that much time thinking about her or her stupid offer at all.

I glance down at Cora again as class goes on, thinking about the car ride, the glass doors of her dorm closing behind her. And then today, pathetically asking to sit next to her when I could have just *sat next to her*. I look over, watching Alex scrawl notes on her paper in messy handwriting, as the professor goes on about our four exams and the final at the end of the semester. I already have the dates in my planner, but I bet Alex is too busy stringing girls along to have even looked at our syllabus before now. I sigh, trying to focus on the class, but my brain won't let it go. Alex just doesn't get it.

"If she was into *you*, it's not like she'd ever go out with *me*, anyway," I whisper finally, leaning on the table.

"Not if you don't ask her," she says, still writing.

"She barely knows who I am. I can't just ask her."

"I would," she says as we both pretend to look at our notes, "and I just met her last night."

"Well, we can't all be as cool as you. We can't all just snap our fingers and get whatever and whoever we want."

"You think I'm cool?" she asks, an annoying smirk stretching across her face as she looks over at me.

"I was being facetious." I roll my eyes. "That means—"

"I know what it means, but the word you're looking for is 'sarcastic,'" she says, cutting me off, just as I realize my misuse of the word. Fuck.

"Anyway, cool has nothing to do with it. I have social skills," she digs, hitting exactly where it hurts. "Maybe if you did, you wouldn't need my help."

"I never asked for your help!" I say a little too loudly. A few people turn to look at me, and I think this is the first time I've ever caused anything close to a class disruption. I sink down in my chair.

"Yeah, not yet." She makes a show of whispering but then focuses back on the professor and the rest of her sandwich. I clench my fist around my pencil, silently fuming as I wait for the moment I can put any amount of distance between me and Alex Blackwood. Just being next to her makes me want to scream.

Class finally ends after we finish covering the syllabus, and I quickly slip out the other aisle, leaving Alex somewhere behind me, hopefully for good. I manage to dodge between two football players and make it to the door just in time to squeeze in right behind Cora in the bottleneck of people trying to funnel out of the room.

I swallow hard and take a deep breath. I don't need help for this. I don't.

Just say hi.

We're almost out the door when a long arm reaches over me and taps Cora on the shoulder with the tip of *my* mechanical pencil.

I spin around just in time to see Alex duck back farther into the line of people, disappearing out of sight, and when I turn back, Cora is looking right at me.

"Molly, hey!" She smiles that smile that makes my feet go numb. "I didn't know you were in this class."

"Yeah." *Speak, Molly, speak!* "Knocks out a science gen ed," I force out quickly, nodding hello at Abby as the three of us make it out into the hall. Together.

"Yeah, I thought that too, but I'm just figuring out that this might be a weed-out class. I think I made the wrong choice." She huffs out a laugh. "Science is not my subject."

I know, I want to say. *You're really good at writing.* But I start to worry that she'll think I'm agreeing that she's bad at science, and soon my opportunity fizzles out.

"Well, we're headed down," she says as we reach the stairwell. "I'll see you around, Molly."

"Okay, bye," I reply as they turn into the stairwell. I hang back even though that's actually the way I was going too.

"See what happens when I'm around?" Alex pops up beside me out of nowhere, poking me in the arm with my pencil.

"Just stay out of it!" I say, exasperated, ripping my pencil out of her hand before stuffing it into my pocket. I storm off down the hall, even though it's out of my way.

It takes only a few long strides for her to catch up with me. "Why don't you quit being so stubborn and just let me help you?"

"I don't want your help, so just drop it. Cora doesn't like me like that. She's never going to like me like that. So what's the point?" I hiss at her.

"Molly." She tugs me aside into a nook in the hallway, letting people flow by us. "I saw how many rounds you were left with all five fingers up. If you spend your life focusing on the *never*, then you'll never actually *do* anything. You gotta cut it out with that self-pity shit. You think you're this little victim that no one is ever going to like, but how is anyone supposed to get the chance if you won't even speak above a whisper?" she asks as I cross my arms.

"I don't . . ." My voice trails off. She smiles, sensing the cracks starting to form, as I uncross my arms and look to the wall beside us.

I'm shocked and a little hurt, but maybe also slightly impressed by her unapologetic honesty. She's not interested in sugarcoating things for me. Her words are like the harshest mix of what my mom and Noah have been saying. But they feel different coming from someone my age, someone I don't even know, someone who I hate to admit . . . has a lot more experience in this department than I do.

What I really don't get, though, is why a girl like Alex Blackwood would even *want* to do something like this for me.

"What's in it for you?" I narrow my eyes at her.

"Just out of the goodness of my heart," she says with a shrug, her voice leaking with sweetness.

"Bullshit," I say flatly. "You don't strike me as the type of person to do anything out of the kindness of your heart. Again, what's in it for you?"

She lets out a big sigh and breaks eye contact with me. "I need proof."

"Proof of what?" I ask, watching her eyes look everywhere but at me.

"Proof for my . . . kinda, sorta girlfriend that I can be . . . a semidecent person."

I unsuccessfully stifle a laugh, and her attention is immediately focused back on me, her face looking slightly hurt.

She's serious.

Do I really trust Alex Blackwood enough to let her into this part of my life, the part I've hardly shared with my mom, when I can't even trust her with a mechanical pencil? Well, no. I mean, she just admitted she's barely a decent person.

But . . . she does have a point. If the past couple of days

have taught me anything, it's that college hasn't magically changed me like I thought it would. So I could risk spending four more years pining after Cora alone, hoping for a miracle. Or . . .

I picture how it could be, me and Cora together, walking to biology, holding hands, talking about all the things I've never gotten to talk about with anyone, a group of friends waiting for us when we arrive. I even think about kissing her. A first kiss with Cora Myers? I think I'd put up with just about anything if I could have that.

I don't want to be the reigning champion of Never Have I Ever for my entire life.

I fill my lungs with air and look up at Alex. Her piercing green eyes are already making me want to jump out a window. Maybe it'll be the worst decision I could ever make, but I have to do *something*. "Fine."

She grins and holds an old iPhone with a shattered screen out to me.

"Why are you handing me this crappy phone?" I ask, taking it.

"Oh my God, Molly. We have so much work to do," Alex says, rolling her eyes and dropping her hands to her sides. "Put your number in it."

And even though I regret it with every single digit, I do.

CHAPTER 9

ALEX

I head down the winding stone steps of the Cathedral of Learning, dodging students as I smirk at my "crappy phone," Molly Parker's freshly added contact info staring back at me.

This'll be easy.

Selflessly help Molly get with Cora. Show Natalie I am practically Mother Teresa, and not an emotionally unavailable asshole with an inability to get close to people. She gets the girl. We get back together. Everyone wins.

Whistling, I duck outside, turning my head right and left as I try to center myself, searching for a spot to get a jump on some job applications before my chem class, so I can actually afford the month of rent that I just spent on the textbook.

But . . . nothing looks familiar.

I squint around at my surroundings. Big trees. Weird

little fountain thing. Grassy park across the street filled with students sunning themselves.

Seems like my best bet.

I shrug and head in that direction, my phone buzzing noisily in my palm. I pull it up and see an incoming call from *my mom* lighting up the cracked screen.

She *never* calls.

Unless something's wrong. And I didn't hear from her all day yesterday.

Like it always does in these moments, my stomach sinks, and I tap accept.

"Mom? Is everything all right—"

"Aleeex," she slurs cheerily through the speaker, cutting me off. "How's school? Your . . . classes. Are they good?"

I pull the phone away from my ear to check the time. It's not even 10:00 a.m.

Nothing happened, but something's still wrong.

She's completely shit-faced on a Monday morning. Great.

Still, it's nice to pretend for a second that she's calling just to see how I am. Like I'm a kid again, and we're as close as we used to be, and she is actually interested in how I'm doing instead of when her next drink will be. I let out a long sigh and kick at the curb as I wait for the walk sign. "Yeah. I just had my first one. It's pretty good so far—"

"Roommate! How's your roommate?" she asks, clearly trying to speed the conversation along to get to the *real* reason for her call. The illusion evaporates.

I crane my neck back to look at the Cathedral of Learning, squinting against the sun. "Not great," I say with a grimace. "But it's fine. I've been trying to keep busy. Stay out of the apartment."

I look down to see the walk sign ushering me forward as silence stretches on the other end. There aren't going to be any follow-up questions. Might as well get this over with.

"So what's up, Mom? Why are you calling?"

She's silent for a long moment, readying her pitch. "Listen, baby," she says, while I circle slowly around the grassy park, students lying out on brightly colored blankets or kicking around a soccer ball, clinging to the final days of summer. I wish I were one of them instead of dealing with whatever *this* is. "I was going to go grocery shopping this afternoon, and I . . . just don't think I've got enough to get much past eggs and milk."

Much past a handle of vodka, I want to say, but I press my lips tightly together, taking a moment before I speak.

"You don't have to worry about groceries. I set up delivery. Twice a week. All the essentials."

There's a long pause as she takes that in, calculating her new angle.

"Well, could I maybe still borrow just a couple of bucks?

I was thinking about finally going in to see Rhonda this week about a job at that diner over by the train station, so I'd be able to get it back to you for *sure* this time. Would be good to get some new clothes before I do."

"Mom, I—I don't know." I swallow and shift the phone to my other ear, tallying up my expenses this past weekend, trying to figure out if I have *anything* to spare. "It's just . . . I gave you money last week, and you . . . well, you clearly didn't spend it on the right things."

I can practically smell the alcohol through the phone.

Her sobs echo through the speaker, making me wince and stop short. I look up to see I'm in front of an enormous sign reading CARNEGIE LIBRARY OF PITTSBURGH. My eyes travel past the sign to the beautiful stone building, with columns and intricate wooden doors.

I haven't even stepped inside yet, and I can feel the calm I need begin to settle over me, the safety of shelves and shelves of books and the silence calling my name.

"Alex, this time will be different," she chokes out, pulling me back to the conversation. "I mean, I thought you wanted me to get this job? I don't know why—"

"Of course I do. It's just . . ."

"You know what? Forget it. I'll just give Tommy a call and see if I can maybe—"

"Do *not* call Tommy." I try to keep my voice level, but I can feel my blood pressure skyrocket straight through the atmosphere into the damn sun. Just like every time she asks me for money, this is the card she knows I can't resist.

Tommy is the shithead she dated for a couple of years after my dad left. He always smelled like cigarettes and armpit, the scent so strong that even the cheap body spray he kept in his glove box couldn't mask it.

A montage of moments from their dumpster fire of a relationship runs through my mind. That time he yelled at her for not making dinner the two awful months he stayed at our house. The rowdy friends he'd bring over on Tuesday nights, like I didn't have school in the morning. The bar tabs he'd have her pick up with money she didn't have, the two of them only really getting along when they were both piss drunk.

Dating him was the tipping point in her relationship with drinking.

She's silent on the other end of the phone because she knows she has me now.

Hook, line, and sinker.

I let out a long sigh and pull my phone away from my ear, tapping open my white-and-blue banking app, my stomach falling when I see I've barely got a hundred bucks in there. My trip to Pittsburgh and textbook-buying has used up most of what I saved from Tilted Rabbit.

I am . . . officially fucked.

I've got rent to pay in a few weeks. More school supplies to buy. A mom that does . . . *this* every other week.

I go to transfer half of it to her, my thumb hovering over the accept button. I hold the phone back up to my ear. "I'll send it on one condition," I say, taking just a tiny bit of power back. "You need to text me. Once a day, just so I know you're doing okay. None of this no-replying bullshit. Deal?"

"Yes! Absolutely. Once a day," she repeats.

I let out a long sigh and tap the accept button. "I just sent it."

"Oh, Alex. Thank you! I'll get it back to you. I really will."

Sure. And I'm going to solve pi and become the youngest president of the United States.

"*Please* . . . spend it on the right things this time, Mom," I say, leaning against the metal railing of the steps. "Or no more."

"I will. Really."

It's a lie, and we both know it.

"And *please* don't do anything stupid if you happen to spend it on anything else."

I'm relieved I sold her car last summer after she got a DUI. She was pissed at me, but it covered more than a few months of rent and groceries. It was a ticking time bomb, and I still kick myself for not just doing it sooner.

"I won't. I promise."

I really hope *that* at least is true.

When she hangs up, I clamber up the stone steps and through the heavy wooden door into the library, like it's a lifeboat and I'm stuck in the middle of the ocean. My blood pressure instantly lowers as I wind through the stacks, my fingers trailing lightly along the shelves, the spines smooth under my fingertips. It's beautiful in here, *much* better than the small library a few blocks from my house. Hallways with intricate tile. Stone staircases with a dip in the center of some steps, the marble weighed down by a hundred years' worth of footfalls. Big, arched windows.

I head upstairs and settle into a spot at a computer, the wooden chair squeaking under me as I sit down.

Moving the mouse, I stare at the Google search box with my hands hovering over the keyboard.

Now I *really* need to find a job. And quick.

The morning fades into the afternoon as I send in application after application, to every fast-food place and coffee shop within a five-mile radius. McDonald's, Chipotle, Starbucks. But with every generic confirmation page, it begins to feel more and more hopeless. I don't even know if half these places are actively hiring.

Needing a distraction, I lean back in the chair and pull open Instagram, aimlessly scrolling and liking my way through my feed. A cool picture of a sunset. A teacup carefully placed next to a plateful of scones. A selfie of this girl I hooked up with a year ago after a concert I worked.

I pause and scroll back, quickly unliking it.

Eyes on the prize, Alex.

I head to the Cereal Killers Instagram to see a newly posted picture of Natalie and her bandmates, A.J., Paul, and Ethan, standing outside the Bluebird Theater in Denver. The baby-blue marquee over their heads has THE CEREAL KILLERS on it in thick black letters, the 8:00 p.m. start time just below it.

It's already got a couple hundred likes. They're definitely getting more hype since the album came out in July.

It looks . . . pretty legit. It's cool to see her out there, making it big, living her dream. I remember her excitement at the diner the Saturday she found out about the tour, and refreshing the Spotify page together to see how many streams there'd been of "Pretty Games" after its release. How she always hoped to take a picture exactly like this one.

But I can't help feeling like the space between us is even bigger. Here she is on this awesome adventure, and I'm still barely scraping things together, just in a different city.

Wait a second.

I zoom in on the shirt under Natalie's leather jacket to see she has on a faded black Led Zeppelin T-shirt.

My faded black Led Zeppelin T-shirt.

All at once the worry I felt is washed away.

I've got a fighting chance.

Smiling, I tap the paper airplane emoji and send the post to Natalie, adding nice shirt 😊 below it, before pausing to look at the picture again.

I forgot how good she looks in my T-shirts. How unexpectedly happy it makes me feel to see her in one, even though we're apart.

I check the time to see I have half an hour until my chemistry prereq starts, in a building that I have . . . absolutely no clue where to find.

As I log out of the computer, I feel a pang of longing. For the time we'd spend together before her shows. Helping her band set up. The TikToks we'd watch together to quell her nerves. The tea with honey she'd drink before getting onstage.

And then I think of the phone call I just had, and how she's the only one I want to talk about it with.

I miss that. Having someone I could be there for. Having someone who could be there for me.

I guess I . . . wish I'd realized sooner how right she was about all of it. How closed off I can be. How bad I am at saying how I feel. How no one else would possibly support me through all this shit with my mom.

It makes me want to set things right just that much more.

I grab my stuff and head down the steps into the lobby, swinging around the banister toward the exit. As I pass a bulletin board filled with papers, I catch sight of a poster for the Cereal Killers concert next month.

No way.

As I go to send Natalie a picture, a mustard-yellow sheet of paper sticking out from just underneath it catches my eye. I

107

lower my phone and gently push the poster aside to see FOOD TRUCK HIRING, CASH, written sloppily in Sharpie across it. There's an email address scrawled just at the bottom, and I take a photo of that instead.

I smile to myself. It's like Nat led me right to it.

I mean, I don't know shit about food trucks, but cash is cash, and it doesn't sound like this person is too picky.

And, honestly, how hard could it be?

CHAPTER 10

MOLLY

She's late.

Of *course* she's late. Probably still sleeping after flirting her way into another party last night.

I pull out my phone and type up a text.

You know YOU asked ME to meet now.

But before I can hit send, Alex's head appears at the top of the staircase leading up to the coffee shop inside the campus architecture building. She plops down in the chair opposite me, and I roll my eyes.

"What?" she asks.

"You asked me to meet you here. At *two*."

"Yeah?"

She follows my eyes to my phone lit up on the table. *2:13.*

I take a deep breath and let out an audible sigh. "Forget it."

"It's thirteen minutes."

"What if I have class soon?"

"You don't."

"How do you know?" I shut my bio textbook and slide it off to the side of the table.

"Molly, it's a Friday afternoon, and you wouldn't have *come* if you had class." Alex drops her chin and gives me a deadpan look. I swear it feels like her green eyes are looking right through me. I can see how she might actually be good at something like this. She's pretty good at reading people, at understanding what makes them tick . . . at least with me.

Not that I'd *ever* admit that to her.

"Why are we here? Is this step one in your big plan?" I ask. Her confidence falters just a little. "You do have a plan, don't you?"

"The plan . . . is five steps. It's a five-step plan." She motions her hand through the air like she's reading off a marquee above my head as she announces, "How to Get the Girl."

My whole body recoils. I can barely even get the girl to notice that I exist.

"I know that title's pretty cringe. Sorry. But each step is about getting Cora's attention until you guys can *get* in a relationship," she says, totally mistaking my unbridled anxiety for judgment of her title. "Anyway, step one: *get* her number. So we're not leaving until you successfully get someone's number."

I start choking on absolutely nothing. "Phone number?" I finally manage to cough out.

"No, Molly, their social security number."

"Alex, you can't just go up to someone and ask for their phone number! And what the heck am I going to do with some stranger's number anyway?"

What if this is just another attempt for her to humiliate me like in Never Have I Ever? Maybe this has nothing to do with proving herself to her *kinda* girlfriend. Maybe Alex is just bored and she's only looking to ruin my life. It was naive of me to think she was actually capable of doing something nice for me.

"I'm not doing this." I shake my head and stand up from my chair.

"Yes. You are." Alex slaps her hand down over my bio textbook, pinning it to the table. "Sit down." When I don't, she continues. "It's not *just* about the number. It's about having the confidence to be able to go up to someone and ask for it. Or the confidence to sit down next to a girl you like in class."

"Give it to me." I hold my hand out palm up, even though that sort of makes sense. She slides the book even closer to herself. "Alex," I say in a firm voice. I can see the wheels turning in her head as her eyes flick around the room before centering their attention on me.

"Look, I'll go first. Pick someone. Anyone in this place

without a wedding band. If I can't get their number, you can go." She pauses, a smile spreading across her face. "But if I *can* get it, you have to stay and do this. Okay?"

I snort out a laugh, letting my hand drop back to my side as I scan the café. I still don't think asking someone random for their number gets me *any* closer to Cora, but what's the harm in watching Alex fall on her face? I filter through the people, looking for the perfect mark. There's a guy close to our age, swinging a lanyard of keys around and around on his pointer finger. A strawberry-blond girl tapping away on her phone as she waits to pick up her drink at the end of the counter. Another, younger person next to her with short-cropped hair and pink glasses.

I need someone who wouldn't possibly give their number to her, someone like . . . *there.*

Standing next in line at the register is a woman with her hair pulled back into a bun so tight that she *must* end the day with a splitting headache. She's wearing a gray fitted pencil skirt with a matching blazer and black heels. Maybe mid to late twenties. I lean to my left to get a better view of her hand clutching the handle of a briefcase stamped with Pitt's business school logo. No ring.

I laugh, happy that I've got a front-row seat for this epic crash and burn I'm about to witness. Sitting back down into my chair, I meet eyes with Alex across the table, before flicking them up to the woman. Her scowl is telling me that the absolute last thing she wants right now is to be hit on, *especially* by someone like Alex.

I watch as Alex glances behind her and then back to me. There's *no way* she can do this.

"Power suit?" she asks. "*Psh.* No problem." She gets up from the table without a second thought and goes to stand behind the woman. I laugh to myself as she combs her fingers through her hair a few times and readjusts her Sylvan Esso shirt so the front is tucked in a little neater.

I wait for Alex to make a move, tap the lady on the shoulder, compliment her tight bun or maybe her tight *buns.* But she just waits. As the woman's ordering, Alex finally leans forward like she's going to whisper something, and I hold my breath waiting for it, but instead she just . . . stands there. The woman swipes her card and then steps aside to wait for her drink at the end of the counter.

She choked. Alex Blackwood actually choked. She couldn't even *try.* It wasn't as entertaining as I'd hoped, but at least she couldn't get the number, which means I don't have to.

I pull out my phone to send her a text as she places an order.

Guess I'll see you later.

Three dots blinking in a bubble and then . . .

Stick around, Parker.

I look up from my phone and catch Alex winking back at me. She flips her wavy blond hair to the other side and goes to stand at the pickup counter.

"I've got a nonfat, iced skinny mocha with light ice and whipped cream," the barista calls out. To my surprise, Alex and the woman both reach for it at the same time. Their hands almost touch as they stutter around each other. There's no way that's Alex's drink order.

As Alex motions for the woman to take the drink, she stands a little straighter, her movements slightly more refined than usual, her smile less cocky.

I lean forward, trying to hear what she's saying, but I can't pick anything up.

Whatever it is makes the woman *giggle*.

This woman in the power suit with the briefcase *actually* giggles at her.

Even though she already has her order and is ready to go, she doesn't leave.

And then . . . *no way*.

Alex holds out her phone, and Briefcase takes it, typing something in. As she hands it back, Alex holds on for an extra second, before taking the phone. When she comes back to the table, I try not to let my jaw hit the floor. I can't lose this bet. So I pivot.

"There's no way *she* gave *you* her real number."

She snickers and presses call on the number, holding it up

for me to see. My eyes flick over to the woman as she walks out the door. She's juggling the drink and her briefcase as she digs around for her ringing phone in one of her pockets.

"How . . . ?" I shake my head. "That woman was obviously straight."

"Well, nobody is *obviously* anything," she says as she ends the call, totally unaware of the woman almost spilling her drink to answer it. "Admit it. You're impressed."

I don't say anything, and the silence stretches between us until the barista calls out, "*Another* nonfat, iced skinny mocha with light ice and whipped cream."

Alex bounces back to the counter and returns to her seat, popping the lid off the drink.

"So, what? You just ordered the same drink as her and then magically ended up with her number?"

"It's not magic, Molly. It's a science," she says. "And nothing is magically going to happen between you and Cora without you initiating something. You know how I got Power Suit's number? *Confidence.* I'm telling you, it's everything in flirting."

"But I have none of that," I reply before I can even realize what I've admitted. The reality of the situation starts to settle in on me as I look across at Alex, who is loudly slurping all the whipped cream off the top of her coffee like a vacuum cleaner.

"Yeah, I'm well aware. I've seen you try to function in public. But that doesn't mean you can't get some. It's like . . . *biology.* If we tried to take the final right now, we'd all fail because we haven't put our thirty hours a week in. We haven't taken the smaller exams leading up to it. But if we go to class, study, most of us are going to make it through. That's why we're *here* doing this first. This is a practice exam. And Cora? She's the final. It doesn't matter if you fall on your face today. You never have to see them again. Low stakes."

When she puts it like that, it actually does make some logical sense. I rub circles into my temple and look right at Alex as she snaps the lid back over her cup and pushes it aside, apparently already having finished the only part she wanted.

"Molly, come on. You got this. Chill. It's just another homework assignment." She looks around the room until her eyes stop on someone behind me. "There," she says, pointing over my shoulder. I glance behind me to see a boy sitting at a table by himself, reading a fantasy novel thicker than the Bible.

"Umm . . . he's a guy," I say as I turn back to face her.

"Oh my God, Molly!" She leans across the table toward me. "I'm not asking you to suck his dick. Just ask for his number. This way you *really* won't care what happens."

Yeah, right. I shake my head. Just because it's a guy, it doesn't feel any easier on my end.

"Fine. Her then." She points at a girl coming up the stairs, who I might think was pretty cute if my mind weren't occupied by Cora 100 percent of the time.

"She's . . . definitely straight," I say, trying to stall, well aware that she's got a beanie and a flannel on in eighty-degree weather, but it's not like she's got a Pride symbol tattooed on her forehead, so . . .

But Alex just points straight ahead as the girl walks up to the counter and . . . a Pride pin comes into view on her backpack. "Come on. I won the bet. Go," she insists. "I'm telling you, Molly, if you can do this, it's a big step closer to Cora."

I let out a big dramatic sigh and wipe the sweat off my hands, but eventually I force myself to stand up and get in line behind Beanie Girl. *Here goes nothing.*

"I'll take a small vanilla latte," she tells the cashier.

And then it's my turn. "Hi, could I please get a small vanilla latte?" I ask. So far so good. Just like Alex did.

I follow the girl to the pickup counter, playing out the scenario in my head while I wait for the barista to call out her order. When the moment comes, I'll step up and reach for the drink at the same time she does. Eye contact. Smile. Say something to make her laugh, like . . . *I see you're a basic bitch too.*

No. Not that.

Okay, maybe I shouldn't go for humor. That's not really my schtick. The problem is . . . I don't really know what is. If I'm just going to be myself, I'd never talk to her in the first place.

"Vanilla latte." The barista slides it across the counter, and it's go time before I'm ready. I try to time it perfectly, but I come in *way* too hot, trying to catch up with her, and my hand knocks the cup over, sending coffee *all over* the pickup counter.

117

"Are you kidding me?" she asks, obviously annoyed. "That wasn't even yours."

What am I doing?

"Sorry. I'm so sorry," I tell her. The barista carefully sets my drink down on the other side of the mess before going to sop it up, and I grab the cup. "Here, you can take this. It's exactly the same. Sorry." I hand it to her and quickly make my way back to our table, avoiding her gaze.

"Wow. That was fucking hard to watch," Alex says. I don't look up at her. I just slink down in my chair a little more. "First of all, I can't believe you just tried to pull the exact same move I did. And second of all, Molly . . ." She stops midsentence, seeing my distress. "It's fine, okay? For real. Like I said, you never have to see these people again. It doesn't matter, so just let it go." She takes a deep breath and leans across the table. "I think that was my bad. I should've given you more direction. Listen, you've gotta sorta play it by ear. The same thing isn't going to work for everyone in every scenario. Maybe with this girl, you could've complimented her Pride pin, right? Go with what you feel from them. Show the part of yourself you think they'll relate to. You know?" she asks, like she's talking to someone with any amount of game.

"Alex, I tried. Okay? I can't do it. I'll never get Cora's number. Let's just call it here." I reach out for my biology book, but Alex knocks her elbow into it, sending it flying off the table and onto the floor. "Wow. Real mature."

As I lean over to reach for it, another hand scoops the book up and holds it out to me. I follow the arm up to his face and find a muscular boy with a buzz cut and familiar brown eyes looking down at me. Jeez. I know half my school comes here, but I didn't expect to be running into them at every corner. I prepare myself for a similar interaction to what I had with Jason Shober by the beer pong table. But he surprises me.

"Hey, Molly," he says, actually remembering my name, but while I recognize him, I . . . can't remember his. "Dustin." He puts his hand over his chest. "You saved my butt in—"

"Oh, *anatomy*, sophomore year. Right, I remember," I say quickly, his face finally snapping into place.

"If you hadn't lent me your notes, I totally would've bombed that final," he says with a laugh, scratching at the back of his head. Almost like he's a little nervous too?

"Glad I could help." I offer him a smile as I take my book from his hand. "Thanks." There is something about Dustin showing some nerves that calms mine.

Just then something kicks me in the shin under the table and I wince, sending Alex a death glare. She widens her eyes at me in response.

Ohhh.

"Uh, Dustin." I turn my attention back to him, remembering how much trouble he had in that class. "If you ever want to meet up to study or . . . just want to meet up or whatever . . . we could. Or whatever."

He lights up. "Oh, that would actually be really dope."

Alex kicks me under the table again, and this time I kick her back as I turn to her and mouth, *I got it.*

"Here." I hand him my phone. "Add your number in and I'll text you." I'm not sure this constitutes getting someone's number in the way she means, but technically I *am* getting his number. Dustin hands my phone back to me, thanks me, and then heads up to place his order.

"Dude!" Alex says when he's out of earshot. "You did it! Feels *good*, doesn't it?" She's practically buzzing with excitement, but I really don't feel much different.

"I guess so. I don't know." I shrug, meeting her green eyes. "He only gave me his number because he needs help with school. It wasn't like he wanted anything more than that."

"Molly." She gives me a deadpan look. "He wanted a lot more than that."

"Oh my God," I whisper, my cheeks burning hot. "Shut up. He did not."

"Uhh, I have eyes, and he *did*," she says. "But all that aside, you got out of your head and you got that little hottie's digits. So now when it actually matters, *with Cora*, you'll *know* you can do it."

"But like . . . how? I'm not you."

"You don't have to be. You were *yourself* with him. You found something you knew about him and used that to work your way in. That's all it is. I just want you to be more *you*, instead of a little ball of quiet anxiety in the corner of the party."

I swallow.

"Getting her number doesn't have to be so formal or charged. Ask her to study, or ask her *and* Abby to do something. And then, once you have it, you can flirt her up over text, which I assume would be a lot easier for you. Yeah?"

I nod. She doesn't have me totally convinced, but she's making too many good points to completely ignore. Getting Cora's number . . . doesn't seem completely out of the realm of possibility now.

"What's next, then? Do we finish all five steps like this? And then I apply it to Cora? Or do I get her number now, and—"

"Jeez," she interrupts me. "You've got a real kink for being in control, don't you, Molly?"

"Well, it *is* a plan, isn't it? So shouldn't you tell me the rest of it so I know what's going on?" I ask.

"You don't need to know the full layout right now, or you're gonna spiral out. Just . . . focus on talking to her. Focus on building confidence, and get her number when it feels right. Okay?" she asks.

I let out yet another big sigh. I don't like to be kept in the dark, but . . . "Fine."

"Okay," she says, slapping one hand down on the table and sliding her chair backward. "I gotta go. I've got a job interview at two forty-five to get to."

I try to picture Alex in a workplace. Pushing people around in wheelchairs at Presbyterian, the hospital on campus. Helping kids find books at the library. Somehow I can't see her doing either of those things.

"What's the job?"

"Food truck."

Food truck.

Farmers' markets, summer pop-up events, late-night breweries. Something different every day.

"That's cool," I reply honestly.

It suits her.

"Here. You can have the rest of this." She slides her coffee over to me. The one that I just watched her slurp all the whipped cream off.

I look at her, disgusted. "I don't want your germ coffee."

"Okay," she replies, like I offended her. "I was just being nice." She grabs the coffee and starts toward the stairs, and I feel a little bad about leaving things like that when she did actually help me.

"Alex," I call out, and she turns back to me. "Maybe . . . don't be *so* yourself for the interview."

I'm not sure that made it any better, but she laughs. "You givin' me advice, Parker?"

I shrug and nod, and both of us are grinning as she disappears down the stairs. I pick up my phone, the screen lighting up with the time. *2:44.* One minute before her scheduled interview time.

Oh my God. I can actually feel my anxiety kicking up *for her.*

Why am I trusting this girl with my love life when she lives her actual life by the seat of her pants?

CHAPTER 11

ALEX

I hop off the bus to find that I have . . . officially discovered the creepiest place in Pittsburgh.

A ginormous, run-down storage facility sits in front of me, with enough rust and broken windows to convince me that no one should actually think their belongings are safe here.

It looks abandoned.

Tumbleweeds of old plastic bottles and snack wrappers roll across the empty parking lot, graffiti lines the garage doors, and an out-of-service train track runs parallel to the building, with overgrown grass and brush covering the metal rails.

Is it abandoned?

I double-check the address Jim, the owner of the food truck, sent me just this morning, cross-referencing it with the building standing in front of me.

Surprisingly, it's correct.

If I die here, all twenty-six dollars in my bank account belongs to my mom. Which, I guess, means it really belongs to Lydia's Liquor Store, just past the gas station two blocks away from our house.

That thought, surprisingly enough, pushes me forward.

Here goes nothing.

I chuck the empty cup from my overpriced mocha into a trash can that probably won't be emptied for another thousand years and follow the numbers around the building to unit 134.

Who knew being a good person was so expensive?

I slow to a stop when I see a wide-open garage door and let out a sigh of relief when I peer around the corner to find a black food truck with JIM'S EATS painted on the side. Sitting next to it is a huge guy wearing a sweat-covered red bandanna and a stained gray T-shirt.

The legend himself, I presume.

"Uh, Jim?" I say as he throws a cardboard box of hoagie buns into the truck.

He slams the back door and straightens up to wipe his hands on a dirty rag as he sizes me up. "Alex?" he asks, a cigarette dangling from his lips.

When I nod, he grimaces. "You're late."

"I was helping a friend with something. It won't happen again, I promise. I—"

"You don't look like the right fit for this job." Jim cuts me off, scratching his stubbly chin as he squints at me. "It isn't

125

all sunshine and rainbows and shit. Y'know, not just sitting around looking pretty."

I bite back a snarky response *and* the desire to roll my eyes, Molly's words of advice from earlier ringing in my ears.

"Well, I have a lot of experience not sitting around. Dish-washing, kitchen work, cashier. You name it, I've done it," I say as he grabs his keys off a table littered with Heinz ketchup packets. I became a bit of a jack-of-all-trades at Tilted Rabbit, jumping to whatever job I was needed at over the course of my three years there.

"I dunno. It's tough work," he says. "No AC or heat. No bathroom breaks. Long shifts."

I shrug. "Great. Sounds like my childhood."

He scoffs and yanks open the passenger door, heading up the metal steps.

But I'm not going down without a fight. I *need* this. I haven't gotten any bites on any of my other applications.

"Plus, since you think I'm a pretty face," I say as he slides into the worn leather driver's seat, yellow stuffing poking out the bottom, "think of all the tips you'll rake in."

Jim rolls his eyes, not taking the bait, and I change tacks immediately.

"What if you just give me a shot? No harm in that. You're clearly heading somewhere tonight," I say, taking a step toward the truck. "And it seems like you're going to be stuck working both the window *and* the grill."

He lets out a long sigh and chucks his cigarette out the window, his face thoughtful.

I keep going, knowing I struck the right chord this time.

"If I suck, you don't have to pay me. I'll just go. No harm, no foul."

He rubs at his stubble, squinting his bloodshot blue eyes at me.

I squint back.

We stare at each other for a long moment, neither of us blinking.

"Hop on." He nods to the jump seat, which is hanging on by a literal thread. "You got one shot. Don't fuck it up."

I step aboard, the seat creaking as I pull it down and slide onto it. I look left and right, but there's only the bare metal wall.

"Is there a . . . ?"

"Seat belt?" he finishes, shaking his head with a snort. "Nah."

Oh good.

He turns the key in the ignition, and the truck barely has time to rumble to life before he guns it out of the garage, banking a hard right turn, the boxes of hoagie buns sliding around in the back, the metal cooler bouncing from wall to wall.

If I didn't believe in God before this drive, I sure as hell do now, because a miracle is the only way I'm making it wherever we're going in one piece.

The drive is only about five minutes long, but Jim still manages to flip the bird to two separate cars for "cutting him off" as he swings the truck across three lanes of traffic, his cigarette arm slung out the open window for use at a moment's notice.

We end up at a local brewery, with picnic tables set up under circular string lights. The warm afternoon has brought out a sizable crowd of people, who are craning their necks at us with interest.

After Jim lights the fryer, he shows me how to work the cash register and gives me a quick rundown of the super-basic menu. Burgers, cheesesteaks, and three different varieties of fries (plain, cheese, and bacon-cheese, naturally). Then he looks at me seriously.

"Now, listen to me. You can give *one* to each customer," he says as he pats the pile of brown paper napkins right next to the register. He points to a huge bin of cheap plastic forks sitting just next to them. "And the forks are for the bacon-cheese fries *only*. If someone else asks for a fork, don't give it to them."

I squint at the giant container. There have to be about a thousand forks sitting there, easy. "Why not?"

He holds one up. "Each one of these costs me *seven cents*. I'd be out of business if I gave every damn customer one of these."

I nod like that makes sense, even though this man is charging fifteen dollars for a burger, a bottle of soda, and fries.

He scoots past me to eye the fryer, nodding his approval,

and just like that, the truck window swings open and we're ready for business.

At least I hope I am.

At first it's a bit overwhelming. The line of people, the cash register, Jim grumbling behind me while he cooks.

Soon, though, we're moving like clockwork, my three years at Tilted Rabbit taking over. Take the customer's order, hang it on the ticket holder, serve it when he's done cooking.

Repeat a million more times.

Jim wasn't lying. The grill and the hot sun turn this metal box into an absolute sauna in minutes, and sweat lines my brow after only a half hour.

Plus, shockingly, Jim isn't very talkative, even though he had a hell of a lot to say back at the storage unit.

He mostly just grunts or talks smack under his breath when a customer asks for a substitution.

Even a few hours in, when the hectic start to gives way to a slow patch, he stays silent. So I let my mind wander as I gaze out at all the people, enjoying their evening at the brewery. I catch sight of a girl with long black hair sitting at a table with her friends, her head thrown back with laughter in a way that reminds me so much of Natalie it makes my heart hurt.

I let out a long sigh and lean against the counter.

I wonder what Natalie will think of Molly. I mean . . . they couldn't be more different. The way they act, the way they dress, how they carry themselves.

Although, I guess they do have one glaring similarity: they both call me out on my shit.

Molly maybe even more than Natalie. And honestly? I was completely full of it today.

Okay, so . . . I admit, I was *maybe* talking out of my ass at the coffee shop earlier with the whole "five-step plan" thing. But Molly really seemed to need one, and, I mean, it can't be hard to come up with four more.

Not when I've done this a hundred times. I just have to break it down and *actually* think about it.

Especially now that I've realized that what works for me . . . probably isn't going to work exactly the same for Molly.

Which is the *key* in all of this. Having it work for Molly.

I grimace as I picture her knocking over that girl's drink today and the awkward exchange that followed.

I didn't show my hand to Molly, but after that happened, I thought this whole thing had the potential to be flushed down the drain. Or at least, it would be a whole hell of a lot harder.

I thought that just showing her what to do would be enough. Like . . . I don't know. Exposure therapy or something. Giving her the tools and letting her use them in a safe, consequence-free environment.

But I didn't account for that small vanilla latte. Or, well . . . Molly. The second the drink mishap happened, I realized I'd fucked up.

I could practically hear Natalie saying I'd "thrown her to the wolves" and that I "wasn't helping anyone."

But then . . . Molly's small smile when she succeeded. The look of shock in her brown eyes when it *actually worked*. The fact she thought Dustin was only interested in *studying*.

I shake my head, smiling at the thought.

That's what it's about. That's what I've got to focus on when I put "the plan" together.

Molly has to find the parts of herself that Cora will love and—

"Order!" Jim calls, and I snap back into action, grabbing the red-and-white-striped paper tray and a single napkin to hand out to the waiting customer.

"Thank you," I say to the backward-hat-wearing frat boy, giving him a flirty smile as he takes the food.

He shuffles the tray around awkwardly and, like I hoped, pulls a few dollars out of his pocket and stuffs them into the overflowing tip jar, which I will hopefully be getting at least a small portion of.

When the dinner rush dies down, one of the bartenders swings by the window, and Mr. Seven-Cent Forks surprises me by handing her a free cheesesteak. "Y'all want anything from inside? Beer? Cider? Cans to go?"

"Nah," he says, and I shake my head too, even though showing up to my next party with craft cider would probably make me a local celebrity. The bartender thanks Jim for the cheesesteak before heading back into the brewery.

"Sounds like a pretty good perk. Don't drink on the job?" I ask him, and he snorts.

"Drinking on the job was all I did for about twenty years," he says as he flips one of the burgers. "Recovering alcoholic."

It's the most he's talked all shift, so that's something.

But I look away, my stomach twisting. I want to ask Jim more. About what made him stop, how he did it, but a group of people stroll up to the window, and I plaster a smile on my face, ready to take their orders and hopefully get a few more bills in the tip jar.

When we close up shop for the night, the clock is ticking close to midnight. Jim hops off the truck for a smoke break while I wrap up the cheese and the vegetables, guessing on where to put them in the prep cooler. I glance outside to see him pull the menu down, the ground shaking under me as he closes the window. He circles the truck a few times before stamping his cigarette out in the gravel and climbing back on to count the money. I hold my breath.

"Pay is ten bucks an hour," he says, holding out a wrapped cheesesteak and a wad of cash. "You keep half the tips."

I think about negotiating on the tips, since this "pretty face" certainly did rake in a lot of cash, but I can tell Jim is not easily swayed. Not even by me.

So I reach out and take it, relief flooding through me. *I got the job.*

"You can go." He points out the window to a bus stop just down the street. "I've got your number. I'll text you the schedule tomorrow morning."

I head for the back door, then stop to grin at him. "Did pretty good, didn't I?"

He shakes his head, chuckling as he zips up a worn bank bag filled with tonight's earnings. "Get the hell off my truck before I change my mind."

Don't have to tell me twice. Laughing, I hop off, calling a "See you!" over my shoulder before closing the door.

It's a welcome relief when I make it onto the air-conditioned bus and even more of a relief when I get back to my apartment and count the money I made tonight.

One hundred sixty-four dollars in cold, hard cash.

I divide it into two jars, one for me and one for my mom, just like I've done since high school.

I hesitate, though, before dropping the second half into my mom's jar, my hand frozen in midair as I hold the bills over the opening. Even now, all the way in Pittsburgh, I'm *still* doing this.

Eighty-two dollars.

That's all my paperback books, used, for my English class. That's almost a *quarter* of my rent. That's a *lot* of food, if you're not buying mochas from the school coffee shop.

And probably enough for a week's worth of booze for her.

But I can't let her go back to Tommy. I can't.

I let out a long sigh and drop the money in before collapsing onto my bed.

I'm absolutely exhausted. My legs ache from all the hours of standing on the steel floor of the truck, the heat at the start of the shift taking it out of me.

As my eyelids begin to close, my phone buzzes noisily on the comforter next to me as a Snap comes in from Natalie.

Natalie. I stopped messaging her two days ago when I wasn't hearing anything back. I *knew* if I gave her some space she'd finally reply. I force my eyes open and reach out to grab it, tapping the screen to open the message.

She's still wearing my faded black Led Zeppelin T-shirt, her long hair over one shoulder. I smile sleepily when I see the text at the bottom: concert in Texas was great tonight, think this shirt may be lucky.

And it's a *good* reply. A flirty one at that.

Like old Natalie.

Talk about progress.

I tap the camera button, snap a photo, and add a ton of heart-eye emojis. My thumb slides sleepily over the send arrow as I drift off, Natalie's smiling face dancing beneath my eyelids.

CHAPTER 12

MOLLY

The following week I'm waiting in line for a snack and a hot tea at the coffee stand on the main floor of the Carnegie Library when a lanky figure with a black hood pulled up over their head cuts *right* in front of me.

I stare, burning holes in the fabric of their sweatshirt as they reach into the display cooler to snatch an orange juice and a cinnamon bagel wrapped in plastic.

Hey, pal, there's a line.

I open my mouth to say it but decide to just let it go. There's no point getting into a fight over it, especially in the middle of the library.

"You're just gonna let me cut like that?" the hooded figure asks in a voice I somehow know all too well.

"*Oh my God.* Don't you have anyone else to bother?" I ask as Alex turns around to face me.

"You know, you can quit pretending that you don't like

me." She pulls her hood down, giving me that grin like she thinks she's so clever for making an entrance like this.

"Noted," I reply dryly, selecting a shrink-wrapped sugar cookie from the wicker basket on top of the cooler. "What are you doing here? Other than getting on my nerves."

"Ouch." She cringes, placing a hand over her heart before showing me the book that's tucked under her arm.

"What's it about?" I ask, turning my head sideways to inspect the one-thousand-plus-page fantasy novel.

"Don't know yet." Alex shrugs as she places her OJ and bagel down on the counter in front of the cashier. "I just grabbed one off the shelf on the top floor."

"You just grabbed a random book off a random shelf, and you're going to read it without any idea what it's about?" I ask, incredulous.

She shrugs again. "Isn't the point to read it and find out for yourself?" She hands over a few bucks and steps aside, making room for me to check out.

"Could I have a medium Darjeeling tea, please?" I ask the cashier, then turn my attention back to Alex, who is unwrapping the bagel with her front teeth like an animal. I look down at the book again, with its faded cover, knights and mythical creatures all twisted together under a green sky. It seems like something my brother would be into, but *definitely* not me. "Looks . . . interesting."

"Didn't your mom ever teach you not to judge a book

by its cover?" she asks. "Speaking of, have you gotten Cora's number yet?"

"Why 'speaking of'?" I ask, looking quickly around as I take my tea from the barista. I drag Alex into a quiet corner. "What do your weird reading habits have to do with Cora? And can you *please* stop shouting her name in public!"

"Well, you like her because she's got a nice cover," she says like it's the most obvious thing in the world. She must notice my blank stare because she finally follows up with "She's hot, right?"

"No. I mean yes, but that's not . . . I like *her*, everything about her."

"Well, you don't really *know* that. I mean, you've barely said two words to her."

"Yes, I have." I can feel myself getting upset. "I've been in school with her for *four years*."

"Yeah, but did you ever even talk to her during those four years?" she presses.

I decide to ignore that. "I still heard plenty about her. Besides, I sat by her all night at the party. We both want to be writers. We have tons in common." I catch myself smiling at the fantasy future I've spent a lot of time thinking about. We both become writers and spend nights in, watching reruns of *Wynonna Earp*. Then we move back to the suburb where we grew up to be close to our families and . . .

"Well, I mean, you know her about as well as I know . . .

Olivia Wilde. I know what I see on Instagram, what she puts out to the world. I know that we both like indie music, but I don't know *her*. Just like you really don't know Cora. At least not yet."

I take a deep breath, reminding myself who it is I'm talking to. This is *Alex Blackwood*, the person who flirts with random girls who *aren't* her girlfriend. Of course she thinks looks are what matters. "Look, you just wouldn't understand. Okay?" I swing my backpack around and slip my cookie into the front pocket for later.

"And why wouldn't I understand?" she asks. I laugh, brushing her question off as rhetorical because it seems so obvious. "No, why wouldn't I understand?" she repeats.

"Well, you clearly don't feel as strongly toward your girl-friend, or else you wouldn't be flirting around with Cora at a party." I shrug. "If you felt the way I do, you wouldn't have even *wanted* to, because you'd already have everything you could ever want."

She watches me silently for a few seconds, the look on her face shifting from anger to hurt to indifference.

"Okay, maybe you're right," she says finally, her face hollowing as she bites the inside of her cheek. I can tell it's not really what she wants to say, but she moves on anyway. "So, did you get her number yet?"

"No." The truth is . . . I have been trying *all* week. Every time I see her, I come up with some game plan to talk to her, to work up the confidence to maybe ask her for her number. But getting out of my head is much harder when I'm dealing with Cora Myers and not just some dude from my high school. I haven't gotten any farther than a smile and a wave. Unless you count this past Wednesday when I saw her outside of Market. I was about to tap her on the shoulder to say hi when I tripped over absolutely nothing and fell flat on my face at her feet. Not exactly the best time to ask for her number. "I still haven't found the right moment," I tell Alex, but I know I sound defensive.

"You know every day that you don't get her number is a day she could be giving it to someone else," she says, and takes a sip of her orange juice while my heart plummets into my stomach. *She's right.* I need to get this done. And soon.

"Can't you help me?" I beg, looking up at her, but her face isn't showing any sign of sympathy.

"First you insult me, then you pull this?" she asks, but her face softens. "Molly, I already helped you. At the coffee shop."

"I need it to be more direct. Can you help me at least make the moment happen? You're the mastermind behind all this, aren't you?" I ask. "Isn't there something in your plan?"

She huffs out a laugh. "Of *course* it's in my plan. The plan is airtight. Solid. Like concrete."

A text pings in from my mom, a picture of Leonard wearing a yellow raincoat. My eyes dart to the time at the top. I sigh. "Shit."

"What?" Alex asks, ripping off another giant bite of her bagel with her teeth.

"I'm going to be late for class. Someone dropped Intro to Fiction, so I got into the open slot, but it's all the way on the third floor of the Cathedral." I pocket my phone. "Tell me about this solid concrete plan later?"

"Yeah, yeah. Sure."

I try to remember which way the building is from here. As I turn toward the south exit, Alex grabs my shoulder and turns my body in the complete opposite direction.

"Cathedral is . . . thataway, Parker."

"I know," I lie.

I walk as fast as I can through the door and across the street, trying to leave everything she said behind. All that bullshit about how I don't really *know* Cora. I didn't ask for any sort of opinion from her. She's only supposed to be around for the plan, to teach me how to do these things that I've never done before. That's all I need from her. If she can just give me that, everything will work out in the end between me and Cora.

I check the time on my phone again. I shouldn't have let Alex distract me like that. Now I'm probably going to be late to a class that I already missed the first week of.

Awesome.

CHAPTER 13

ALEX

The second Molly said "Intro to Fiction," I knew she was in my gen ed class.

I smile to myself and stretch out my legs, tapping my pencil against my notebook as the teacher—or as he wants us to call him, *Jon*—starts to rattle off the attendance from the front of the classroom.

And she was giving *me* shit for being late.

I half raise my hand as he calls out my name, and a girl with faded red highlights from two desks in front of me glances behind her to give me a once-over, like she does every class.

I look away so I won't even be tempted to so much as wink at her, my eyes flicking to the wooden door as Jon calls out, "Molly Parker?"

But there is no Molly Parker to be found.

"We got a Molly?" he tries again, the knob twisting as if on cue to reveal a familiar, disheveled shape.

"Here! Sorry," Molly squeaks from the doorway, smoothing down her brown hair and fixing her shirt, her eyes widening as they land on me.

I grin at her, patting the empty chair next to me.

And, naturally, she gives me a murderous look that was worth sprinting up the three flights of stairs on the opposite side of the building to beat her here.

"Take a seat, Miss Parker," Jon calls, peering at her overtop his glasses. "Class starts at eleven o'clock."

Molly mumbles an apology, scanning the room for another seat option before plunking angrily into the one next to me.

"Why didn't you just show me where to go if you *knew* I was in your class?" she hisses at me when the teacher turns his back.

"*Molly,*" I say, crossing one leg over the other. "I can't fix your love life *and* your internal GPS. I'm only one woman."

She rolls her eyes and pulls out a binder and a worn copy of *Twelfth Night,* one of my favorite Shakespeare plays and also the assigned reading for the first two weeks of class.

As Jon starts the lecture on the themes in the pages we read, her words from the library come back to me.

Well, you clearly don't feel as strongly toward your girlfriend, or else you wouldn't be flirting around with Cora at a party.

I can't even enjoy this lecture on my *favorite* freaking play because I can't get over how much they bothered me.

I mean, she's probably never even kissed anyone before—what does she know?

I shake my head and glance out the window to see students milling about on the other side, my skin prickling as I see Molly's reflection in the glass.

"And what about you?"

I blink, my eyes deglazing as I glance up to see the professor looking at me, a few heads turning in my direction. He's got his glasses pulled down almost completely off the tip of his nose, and he's looking over them at me with that teacherly arrogance that is just the *worst*.

Molly raises her eyebrows at me, absolutely *loving* this.

I clear my throat and fix a confident smile on my face. "Who?" I look left and right. "Me?"

"Yes." He could not be more smug. "You."

His condescending look borders on pity. Like I haven't read this play a hundred times. Like my lesbian ass hasn't *religiously* watched the movie adaptation with Helena Bonham Carter a thousand times more than that. "I asked what points *you* thought Shakespeare was making about romance."

"Well," I say, grabbing Molly's book off her desk and flicking to act 1, scene 5. "'How now? Even so quickly may one catch the plague?'" I read, repeating the character Olivia's comparison to love being a literal illness.

"Romance, love . . . It's like the plague," I say with a shrug, returning the smug energy he gave me a moment ago. "If you're feeling as dramatic as Olivia is, at least."

I close the book and slide it back onto Molly's desk. "Then

again, she *just* met the person she's talking about, so dramatic is kind of her thing." I cross my arms over my chest and lean back in my chair. "So, I guess you could say Shakespeare's making *two* points. Love is suffering, probably because you fall in love with someone you hardly know. *And* plenty of people are in love with love and not the actual person."

Molly snorts. "Maybe you're projecting," she says, tapping her fingers on the cover of the book. I wonder if she even realizes she's speaking to the whole class. "I mean, it works out in the end, though, doesn't it? For all the characters. Olivia, Viola, Sebastian, Duke Orsino. Everyone rides off into the sunset, completely content with their happily ever after, in whatever shape it takes. No one is suffering. The love they felt was enough, when it was felt for the right person."

Her cheeks turn red as she talks, both of us knowing this is about more than just some characters in a Shakespeare play.

"Yeah, but who knows what happens after they ride off into the sunset?" I ask, and Jon nods from the front of the class.

"That's a fair point," he says, and I feel a smile creep onto my lips. "I mean, who knows how long infatuation will keep the train running for."

"Listen, I'm not saying it will," she concedes, a small victory after that moment in the library. Still, her face turns even redder, the fight far from over. "But why does it *have* to be bad after that?"

I open my mouth to say something, but . . . she's right.

Why does it have to be bad? Why do I automatically assume that it *will* be?

For myself. For Molly and Cora. I guess that's my problem. I guess that's why I'm always so scared to jump in.

Maybe Natalie is the "right person."

Maybe *I* can be the "right person" for Natalie.

And maybe Cora is the right person for Molly, if I can help her get there. She's like my own personal Duke Orsino, struggling to confess her love to the person she's head over heels for.

The professor turns back to the board, scribbling on it in chalk before continuing on.

But Molly and I stay staring at each other. Finally, I nod and look away at the lines on my notebook, conceding for the second time today, but this time I mean it. "It doesn't have to be."

When class comes to a close, Jon mumbling about our assigned reading for next week before sending us on our way, Molly is packed and out the door before I can even close my notebook.

I fumble as I grab all my stuff, then dodge the other students as I chase after her, grabbing on to her arm to stop her before she gets pulled into the crowded staircase. "Molly."

"What's up, Alex?" She sighs, turning around to look up at me. "I have to get to class."

"Next bio class, we're sitting next to Cora, okay? That's the plan."

I mean, she can't stay at step zero forever. She needs to get Cora's number, or she can't . . . I don't know. *Ride off into the sunset* wearing matching rainbow parachute pants.

"We should probably try to be on time, though." I let go of her arm and give her a big smile. "Not a lot of time to talk if you show up late."

She narrows her eyes at me, but I can see the smile fighting its way out. "See you at eight twenty-five a.m.," she calls over her shoulder before disappearing through the doors into the stairwell.

I smirk at her back, surprised when her head pops back through the doors to meet my gaze.

"And, Alex?"

I study her face, a tiny crease forming between her eyebrows as she wrestles with something.

"Thanks," she says, her brown eyes softening. "And I'm sorry. About what I said in the library."

"No worries." I nod, but it does make me feel better. I catch up and we push through the doors, the two of us clomping down the steps together.

I pull out my phone as we go, tapping on Snapchat to see

that Natalie has opened and not replied to yet *another* Snap, still upset that I fell asleep after my food truck shift.

Apparently, I drifted off before hitting send, which she absolutely didn't believe when she called me the next morning, going on a rant about how I was probably "up to my usual shit" and couldn't be bothered to reply to a text or call her. Never mind the fact that *she* hadn't replied to any of my messages for at least three days before that.

But I remind myself that she wouldn't be acting this way if I hadn't given her reason to feel like this in the first place.

I shove my phone back into my pocket, frustrated, but my fire to help Molly doubles in size.

The sooner she gets Cora's number, the sooner I'll have something real to show Natalie when she comes here later this month.

Proof. That I'm not up to anything. That what we have doesn't *have* to be bad.

My stomach growls as we push through the exit doors outside, and Molly holds out a piece of the sugar cookie she got at the library earlier.

I take it, and she nods to the right. "I've got a history class at Posvar next. I'll see you later," she says before turning to head in the direction she just nodded, her brown hair catching the breeze as she walks blissfully away.

"Molly!" I call after her.

She skids to a stop, looking back at me. "Wrong way?"

she asks sheepishly, and I nod, unable to hold back a smile.

I point to the right building, watching as she changes course and fades slowly into the distance, her enormous backpack disappearing from view.

Alex Blackwood and Molly Parker.

Not quite friends, but . . . maybe we're getting there.

CHAPTER 14

I just have to walk in there, pull the chair out, and plop my butt down.

Sounds easy enough, but the problems come *after* I sit down, when I have to actually hold a conversation with her.

Luckily, Alex will be right there beside me, feeding me things to say when my conversation well runs dry.

Even though she makes me want to rip my hair out most days . . . she's also the only person I've ever met and not been related to that I can be completely myself around, without buckling under the weight of my anxiety. I haven't totally figured out why yet.

Though maybe it's because I genuinely do not care what her opinion is of me.

As I look down the hallway for any sign of her, my phone buzzes in my pocket.

"I've been trying to give you space, but I've also been *dying* to know what happened at the party!" My mom's voice crackles through the speaker as I answer, *very* chipper for so early in the morning. She's probably already guzzled down her daily vat of coffee.

"Oh, uh." I pause, realizing that we haven't talked in over a week. Texted about small things, yes, but *talk* talked? No. Normally I'd be gushing to my mom about every little thing that happened, but now I find myself wanting to keep most of it to myself. At least for now. This could be my first relationship. I don't really want to jinx it. "The party was good. We played some games, and I ended up staying pretty late. It was a lot of fun," I tell her, leaving out all the details and what happened after, my plan with Alex. I don't think she'd be too psyched about that. "Nothing much new. Just about to head into bio."

"Leonard misses you," she says, but I have a feeling it's not just Leonard.

"Thanks for the pics." I smile, my heart hurting as I think back to the photo she sent last night of him curled up on my empty bed.

"Tired of the cafeteria food yet? Maybe I can take a ride down soon and we can grab a quick lunch?" she asks, her voice filled with hope. It *would* be nice to see her, and it's just a lunch.

"Maybe sometime next week?" I look up to see Alex dragging her feet down the hallway toward me, her cheeks full of the tiny powdered donuts from the package clutched in her hand. "Do you *live* at Seven-Eleven?" I whisper, tucking the phone into my neck.

"Like I could be so lucky," she huffs, stuffing another one into her mouth before offering the tube to me.

"Molly?" My mom's voice pulls my attention back to my phone as I slip one out of the plastic.

"Sorry. Yeah. Next week. I'll text you."

"Well, wait. I want to catch up. Tell me about your classes," she says.

"They're good, Mom. Sorry, one's about to start," I reply, trying to be short with her without being too obvious.

"Okay, okay. I get it. I'll let you go," she says, and I try to ignore the sadness in her voice.

We say our goodbyes, and I slip my phone into my back pocket.

"Ready?" Alex asks as I carefully place the donut into my mouth.

"You've got . . . uhh . . ." I motion to the white powder outlining her lips. "A bunch of shit on your face."

"Oh." She licks her lips, which does absolutely nothing.

"Still there."

"Can you get it?" she asks, squatting down to my level. She gives me a closemouthed smile, her cheeks still full. I roll my eyes, but instead of turning away, I dig a tissue out of the travel pack in the front pocket of my backpack and hand it to her.

"Thanks," she says, looking the slightest bit surprised at my gesture, before I turn to face the classroom.

Stay out of your head.

I push through the door, determined not to think, but the second I lay eyes on her, my brain revs up and I revert right back to high school Molly. I look behind me as Alex walks in, wiping her donut fingers on her (thankfully) white T-shirt with a screen-printed black rabbit on the chest pocket. She nods at me and flicks her eyes forward.

I can do this.

I start up the stairs. Cora and Abby both have their heads down, scrolling through their phones, and they don't wave to me like I hoped, something I could pretend was an invitation. By the time I make it to their row, my hands are shaking.

I can't do this.

I take another step, headed for our old seats, but Alex gets her hand around the top loop of my backpack. In one fluid motion, she tugs me back down a step and shoves me, almost stumbling, into their row.

Cora looks over at the disturbance and I hold my breath, but her face lights up when she registers it's me, which makes me smile too.

"Hi," I say, still reeling from literally being thrown into her. I send Alex a death glare behind me, but she's not even looking at me.

"Hey, guys," she says. Abby leans forward in her chair to nod a hello at us.

"Wow," Cora says, looking between Alex and me. "I did not foresee you two hanging out together."

I laugh nervously.

"Me neither, but I just can't seem to stay away," Alex replies coyly. I think it's supposed to be a joke, but her eyes widen as she realizes how it sounds. Cora looks even more shocked.

"Even though all I want is for her to stay away," I say quickly. "We're just friends," I add, trying my best to make it abundantly clear that in no world could I ever even *think* about Alex in that way.

"Okay." Cora squints at us and then returns to her phone.

As we sit down, I swing my backpack into Alex, before letting it drop to the ground.

"Ouch! Watch where you're swinging that thing," she whispers.

"Are you kidding me!?" I reply under my breath.

"What? I was *trying* to hype you up to Cora," she says, defensively.

"Are you regretting this eight a.m., or is it just me?" Cora asks from the other side of me. I drop the annoyance plastered all over my face before spinning my chair to look at her.

"Yeah," I say, trying to form a reply. "I—I could've used an extra hour of sleep today."

"I didn't even get to eat breakfast. I'm starving," she tells me, drooping in her chair.

"Me too, dude," Alex chimes in, leaning all the way onto my area of the table.

"You *just* plowed through a pack of donuts," I whisper to her as the professor starts speaking a few rows in front of us.

"Empty calories, Parker. They don't count," she whispers to me, sliding back to her side of the desk.

We all fall into the lecture, scribbling notes down on paper. Even Alex has a notebook and pens now, but every time I glance over, the pages are jumbled up with fragmented notes and cartoon doodles. I try my best to ignore her on my left and Cora on my right and just focus on class, but it's not easy. For very different reasons.

About halfway through the hour-long lecture, Alex slides her notebook between us with a note written at the top in pink ink.

Talk to her.

I can't talk to her in the middle of class, I write back.

She tears the bottom of her paper off, the professor's eyes flicking over to her and then back to the board. After writing something down, she slides it over to me, her rings scraping against the desk.

I unfold the note, deciphering her messy scrawl. *You guys want to grab breakfast after class?*

I look over at her, confused, but I *am* pretty hungry.

"Sure," I whisper, giving her a shrug. Her entire face drops into a straight line.

"Give. The. Note. To. *Cora*," she whispers.

Ohhhh.

That's actually not a bad idea, but I *cannot*. I shake my head and hand the note back to Alex, who lets out a huff of air.

"Fine. I'll do it," she whispers, but as she grabs for it, I quickly reach out with my pencil and add *at Market* at the end of her note. As she picks it up off the table, her mouth drops open, her lip curling with disgust.

"Molly, I don't have a meal plan, and I am *not* paying twenty dollars to eat cafeteria food," she whispers, but we're so close to the front that the professor still sends her a glare. I straighten up in my seat, waiting for him to turn back to the board.

"Relax. I'll swipe you in," I whisper out of the corner of my mouth, looking dead ahead.

Folding the note in half, and then again, she leans across the table and slides it all the way to Abby. I see her show it to Cora out of my peripheral.

I turn my attention back to the board, wiping my palms off on my legs.

Just breathe. If she says no, it's not a big deal. It's fine. It's just a group breakfast. It won't be a rejection. It didn't even come from me.

Soon Cora's painted nails reach in front of me, leaving the note on my binder.

I unfold it, beaming as I slide the note over to Alex. She holds her fist out to me under the desk and I high-five it. *"Oh, sorry,"* I say, readjusting and bumping a fist into it.

"You kill me, Parker," she says, trying to suppress a laugh. But even though she's making fun of me, I know she's psyched, too.

I don't know why I'm surprised to see that she's happy for me, but I am. And the weirdest part is that knowing that somehow makes me even happier.

CHAPTER 15

ALEX

There is no better food than free food.

I gaze in awe at all the different stations planted all across the dark, patterned carpet, the smell of eggs and sausage and French toast wafting over me in a cloud.

Where do I even begin? Should I do cereal and *then* eggs? A bagel with cream cheese? Maybe some fruit after my powdered donuts this—

"You're holding up the line," Molly says as she nudges me forward, the group of hungry students behind her giving her a grateful smile.

I follow after Abby and Cora, my head on a swivel as we make our way around the room, collecting food on worn white plates as we go. I veer off when I see a coffee station, nearly dumping my perfectly crafted cream and two sugars all over my white shirt when Molly appears out of thin air, grabbing on to my arm.

"Jesus . . . ," I say, and she gives me a sheepish grin.

"Sorry, I just . . ."

"Didn't want to be alone with Cora?" I finish, her silence letting me know I hit the nail on the head.

"Molly. The *point* of this is for you to talk to her alone." I juggle my armful of plates to take a quick sip of my coffee. "I mean, here I am, *sacrificing* my free time to help you get her number. . . ."

She raises her eyebrows at me as I jimmy a piece of bacon off one of my plates and into my mouth, crunching noisily on it.

"Yeah, seems like quite the sacrifice," she says, before her face glazes over with a familiar look of panic. "What do I even *say* to her?"

I shrug. "Ask her about her day! How school is going. What her *freaking phone number is* in case you have a bio-themed emergency." I pause, midchew. "You have had a conversation before, right? With another human being?"

Molly rolls her eyes at me, pouring herself a cup of coffee.

Tone it down, Alex. Baby steps.

"Listen," I say, nudging her shoulder. "This is super casual, okay? We're just eating some food and hanging out." I let out a long exhale, and even though it puts a pause on *my* plan, I say what I know she needs to hear if *any* of this is going to work. "If you get her number today, you get her number. If you don't, we'll figure something else out, okay?"

Molly looks relieved. "Really?"

"Yeah," I say with a shrug. "No biggie. But, I mean, you know, *try*."

We head over to a maroon-colored booth in the corner, Abby and Cora already digging in.

"Oh my gosh, I was *starving*," Abby says as she takes an enormous bite of a pancake.

Cora points a fork at Molly's plate. "No way. They have omelets?" she asks.

"Uh, yeah. Over by the . . ." Molly's cheeks turn red as she points to a station by the door, where a small line of students stand, waiting to give their omelet order.

There's a space for her to say something else, but . . . she doesn't, and an awkward silence settles over the table. Just the pleasant sound of cutlery hitting plates.

Molly shoots me a nervous look while I take a sip of my coffee, clearing my food-filled airway. What have they got in common that I know about?

"Hey, Cora," I say, putting the cup down. "Are you taking Intro to Fiction this term?"

"Yeah," she says, the bagel she's holding pausing halfway to her mouth. "I have Jon Davidson. He's . . . all right."

"Ugh." I point between me and Molly. "We have him too! We're in another section."

"He's clearly a fan of the classics," Cora says with a groan. She takes a big bite, chewing noisily. "*Twelfth Night*? I mean, come *on*."

I want to practically explode with all the reasons that's a bad take, but I bite my tongue, not wanting to ruin this for Molly.

I mean, I love *all* books, but the classics are what got me through my childhood. There's something reassuring in books and stories older than you are. Still talked about long after they've been written and long after their writers die. When the world around you is on fire, there's a certain kind of comfort in that.

Also, the classics section was always the quietest part of the library. And I *needed* quiet. I used to go there to escape my parents' fighting back home, and in the silence it almost felt like it had never happened.

Through my internal monologue I hear Molly find her voice, her words pulling me back into the conversation. *Thankfully*, she doesn't just agree. "I'm hoping Intermediate Fiction is a bit better."

"You're an English major too?" Cora asks, excited now. Everyone at Pitt is required to take Intro to Fiction. Intermediate and above is typically for majors only. "We should try to get some of the same classes next semester! That would be so fun."

"Definitely!" Molly says, her face lighting up.

When Cora looks away, I nudge Molly under the table, shooting her a thumbs-up.

She glares at me, but I can tell it's half-hearted.

I mean, it was *for sure* a missed phone number–exchange opportunity, but . . . at least it's progress.

Abby cuts in, talking about how she *wishes* she were just reading books, since her engineering classes are *so hard*.

I honestly tune her out, focusing instead on clearing every last crumb from my plate while she lists what feels like her entire physics syllabus, start to finish, groaning about how she has three tests scheduled for next week.

My phone buzzes in my pocket, and I pull it out to see it's a check-in text from my mom.

Groceries were just dropped off ty

She's actually kept her promise and texted me every day since our last phone call. Tonya even said she seemed to be in good spirits when she swung by to check on her yesterday.

Which is maybe why I decide to push it just a tiny bit.

NP. Any news about that job at the diner?

I know there isn't any, and I know she'll probably ignore this particular text, but it's worth a try.

Either way, it's nice to hear from her more than when she just . . . needs something.

"Anyway, Cora," I hear Abby say as I smile to myself and slip my phone back into my pocket. "I don't think I can possibly come Friday. Not with all the studying I have to do."

I jerk my head up, and Molly *kicks me* right in the shin before I can nudge her.

"What, uh. What's happening on Friday?" she asks while I bite my lip, trying not to react to the pain.

Holy crap. That's gonna bruise.

"Club rugby tryouts!" Cora says, beaming with excitement as we all scoop up our plates and head toward the dish drop-off.

"Oh, cool!" Molly says.

Since she practically left a dent in my shin back at the table, I figure she knows to take advantage of this, so I drift on ahead, dropping my stuff off before strolling casually over to the toasters, my eyes on an unopened loaf of white bread.

I lounge against the counter, nodding hello to one of the Market workers busy cleaning off the tables, my fingertips creeping closer to the bag. When their back is turned, I grab the loaf and stuff it into my shirt, spinning around and almost running smack into Molly.

She raises her eyebrows at me.

"*That's* new," she says, giving my newly acquired D cups a poke.

"Where's Cora?" I ask, slapping her hand away, my eyes scanning the students just past her head. "Did you get her number?"

"She had to go to class," Molly says as I catch sight of Abby and Cora heading out the door. I wave goodbye through the glass, and they wave back before disappearing up the steps.

"And . . ." She lets out a long sigh. "No."

"You'll get it next time. Without a doubt," I reassure her, trying not to sound disappointed.

For both of our sakes, I hope I'm right.

We leave Market and go our separate ways. I head for my boring chem class up the hill, not looking forward to sitting through another hour lecture with a professor so monotone, half my class is asleep by minute ten.

As I slide into my squeaky wooden seat, feeling slightly frustrated, I remind myself that I have to be a little more patient with Molly. I mean, sure, did moments present themselves today? Absolutely. But we're looking for the *right* moment.

I have to move at a Molly pace.

But . . . that doesn't mean I can't pull an *Alex* to force her hand a little.

CHAPTER 16

MOLLY

I've spent the last hour trying to keep busy, cleaning and reorganizing my dorm room, refolding my clothes and color-coding the shirts hanging in my closet. It usually calms my nerves, but this time it's done little to nothing to help get my mind off whatever Alex has planned for this evening.

I received a mysterious text from her earlier.

Meet me on the Cathedral steps at 6:20.

She wouldn't tell me why or what we are doing. The only thing she said was to "dress comfortably." I'm not sure what that means, but to be honest, it's Alex, so it must be about Cora. I decide to wear something on the nicer end of comfy.

I slip on my sneakers and head out into the quad.

Across the street, the Cathedral glows in the golden light from the sun, hanging low in the sky. As I get closer, I spot Alex sitting on the upper railing, legs dangling over the side. She's got on a shirt with chain saws popping out of a cereal bowl, and her usual skinny jeans have been swapped for black running tights.

"What the hell are you wearing?" she asks, looking down at me. "I told you to dress comfy."

I look down at myself, jean shorts and the same shirt I wore to the party, but in a different color. I even have on a pair of sneakers. "I am comfy," I call up to her. She swings her legs around to the other side, hops off, and jogs down the steps to meet me.

"I meant comfy like shorts and a T-shirt," she says, her eyes darting down to my chest and quickly back to my face. "A sports bra at the *very least*, Molly!"

"Well, you should've been more clear," I say, turning back toward the quad. "But it's fine. I'll just go change."

"There's no time. We're gonna be late," she replies, checking her phone.

I don't even have time to reply. I practically have to jog to keep up with her long strides.

"Late for what?" I ask as I catch up. I look down as we head around to the other side of the Cathedral of Learning, and that's when I realize her wrists and fingers are completely bare. She always wears her rings. "Is this the step in your plan where you tell me I need to get in shape and then we hit the gym? Because I have to tell you, I'm not big into exercise, and—"

"What?" She stops walking and looks over at me, her facial

expression all twisted up like I just offended her big-time. "No. Why would I ever tell you something like that?"

"Seems exactly like something you'd say," I reply, shrugging off her overreaction.

"You know what, Molly? I know I'm fucking pretty, and yeah, I like to flirt maybe a little too much, but I'm not the self-absorbed, shallow *bimbo* that everyone thinks I am. That *you* seem to think I am."

"Okay," I reply, taking a step back. I've never seen her show any . . . real emotions before. I didn't even know it was possible to offend her.

"I actually thought that you and I could be real friends, but if you think I'm such a jerk . . ." She pauses. "Molly, I've never said *anything* about your physicality *ever*, because there's nothing wrong with it. So don't put words in my mouth."

"Okay," I say more firmly, realizing maybe *I'm* the one who's being the jerk this time. Who's judging her. "I-I'm sorry. Really."

I didn't mean to treat her like that.

She takes a deep breath and for a second I'm scared she's going to leave, but then she keeps moving, leading me down the back steps.

"So then, why are you dressed like that?" I ask, hoping we can get past this.

She doesn't answer me and instead veers off the concrete path and onto the grass. "Are you going to just keep ignoring

166

me?" I ask as I follow after her, stepping around pockets of mud from yesterday's rain while I try to keep pace.

When she finally stops, I look up, and just ahead of us in the open field is a group of about twenty-five girls. Most of them have their hair pulled back into high ponytails, and their feet are sunk into brightly colored cleats. A few of them stretch in a circle, while others toss an oddly shaped football around in a . . .

My stomach sinks into my butt as I realize what exactly it is I'm looking at.

Rugby.

"Alex!" I whisper loudly, grabbing for her arm, but she pulls out of my grip. "Alex, please," I plead. My eyes dart around, looking for someone who I know *has* to be here.

"Cora, hey!" Alex shouts from in front of me, waving down a rainbow-sweatband-wearing Cora Myers, who looks so cute in her rugby clothes that I have to take a second to just breathe. I think about all the threats I could scream at Alex, but it's too late for that because now Cora is standing right in front of us.

"Hey, guys!" She greets us with a perfect smile spread across her face. "What are you doing here?"

I stand there trying not to *totally* clam up, while Alex answers for both of us.

"We're here for tryouts," she says, throwing her long arm over my shoulders.

Tryouts?

"Oh, awesome! I didn't know you guys were interested at all," Cora says, her attention lingering too long on my inappropriate outfit, but she doesn't say anything.

"Well, I can't play for shit, but Molly here . . ." Alex pats my arm, drawing me in closer. "She *loves* rugby."

"Yeah?" Cora smiles at me, her eyes lighting up with excitement, turning my entire body to mush.

"Y-yeah," I stutter. "Can't get enough of it."

"Why didn't you play at Oak Park? We honestly could've used a few more bodies on the field, especially after Mariah, Skeggs, and Anna all broke a limb in the same week."

"Uh." I pause, thinking about how much I treasure each of my limbs. "I'm more of a fan of the sport than anything, but . . ." I give Alex a sideways glare. "I . . . figured I could try now."

My lie must be at least somewhat convincing because Cora smiles. "Well, can't wait to see what you've got. Sign-ups are over there," she says, pointing to a folding table set up in the grass.

"Thanks," Alex and I both say as we walk past her. The second she's behind us, I shrug Alex's arm off my shoulders and jab her ribs with my elbow.

"*Oof.*" She laughs, wrapping her arm around her stomach to rub her side. "Save that for the pitch, Parker."

"I'm going to *kill* you." I take a step toward her, lowering my voice. "I don't even know what rugby is."

"Don't be so dramatic," she replies, taking the pen from the table and signing both of our names on the clipboard.

"Alex, I don't think you understand." I follow her past the table and over to a nearby tree, where she drops her phone and wallet on the ground. I enunciate each of my next words as panic creeps up my back. "I. Know. Nothing. About. Rugby. Okay? I'm not one of those sporty lesbians you hear about. I literally could not hit the broad side of a barn with *anything*."

"Well, luckily, I didn't bring you here to impress her with your Olympic abilities. I brought you here to get her number, because clearly you can't do it on your own, and you can't text her without it. It's been two days since we went to Market, and you haven't spoken to her at all." She pulls her foot up, stretching out her quad.

"That's not true. I waved at her yesterday from across the quad!" I snip.

"You *waved* at her!? Wait . . . what . . . what is that?" She cups her hand around her ear like she's listening for something. "I think I hear . . . church bells?"

I turn and walk away. It's not too late for me to save myself from this. If this is what I have to do just to complete step one, I don't even want to know about the other *four*.

I'm just about to step back onto the concrete path when I hear Cora call out my name from behind.

"Molly! Go long." I turn to find her winding up, and

before I can tell her not to, she hurls one of the weird-looking footballs through the air in my direction.

Catch it, Molly. Please for the love of God, catch it.

I step left. I step right. I take a step backward, get my hands up and ready. It's all lined up perfectly as the ball comes spiraling through the air toward me, and then . . .

Bonk. It slips right through my waiting hands and bounces off my chest.

I am acutely aware of them both watching me as I chase the ball around in the grass. "She's better at defense," Alex says, and Cora winces.

"Just saving it for tryouts, I'm sure." Cora gives me an encouraging smile.

Great.

With the option of leaving firmly behind me, I slog through the beginning of tryouts. They actually don't seem too bad, even if I am the most ridiculously dressed girl on the field. We spend about fifteen minutes just throwing the ball back and forth to each other, and I finally get the hang of it. The ball kind of starts to spiral through the air over to Alex, even though her passes to me are still flipping end over end the whole way into my hands. I start to believe that *maybe* I can fake my way through this.

But then we get into the second half.

"All right," a stocky girl wearing the captain's band says. Everyone stops throwing as she steps into the center and sweeps her arm right down the middle, splitting up each set of partners. "This half, grab a pinny. Let's scrimmage for the next twenty minutes."

Scrimmage?

Cool, so I'm supposed to take part in a scrimmage when I genuinely don't even know what the point of the game is. I mean, do we do touchdowns? Goals? Throw the ball through one of three hoops?

I send Alex a look across the field but quickly change my expression to a lighthearted, *I'm having the time of my life* smile when I meet eyes with Cora. They both grab a pinny from a saggy cardboard box next to the sign-up table, because they're assigned to the same team. Of course.

Over the next few minutes, the captain gets us all in our positions, and I manage to pick up the nickname Jean Shorts.

Cool. Cool. Cool.

As I'm standing there, I spot Cora again, now closer to the opponents' goal. Our eyes meet, and she smiles with a thumbs-up, which is enough to stop me from running off the field.

Then, out of nowhere, a whistle blows, and everyone around me takes off, like they know exactly where they need to be, probably because they in fact do. Even Alex is somehow expertly playing it off like she's supposed to be here.

I whip my head around to the side when I hear a scream over my left shoulder. A girl on my team with red French braids has the ball, but she's getting tackled from behind, two sets of arms violently taking out her legs. On her way down to the ground, she desperately looks around, and at the last second she picks up my eyes and flips me (*ME*) the ball.

Crap.

I don't know what to do now, but it doesn't matter. Before I can even get my fingers wrapped securely around the ball, there's a girl, a wall of muscle, crashing into me with all the force of her full-on juggernaut sprint.

I don't even have time to register that I'm not standing anymore before my body feels like it's in pieces.

"Molly! Are you okay?" a voice asks from somewhere nearby as I'm pressed into the mud. I can barely hear it over the sound coming out of me, violent breaths, loud and tight and dragging because I can't get any oxygen. "In through your nose, out through your mouth."

I do as the voice says, and soon my breath comes back enough for me to open my eyes. I look up to find Cora crouched right over me, her hazel eyes filled with worry for *me*. "You think you can walk?" she asks. Dang, her eyes are nice, and her nose and her mouth and . . .

"Molly?" she asks, and I blink my way back to reality.

"Sorry, um, yeah. I think I can. . . ." I roll onto my side, already extremely aware of the pain that's spreading across my ribs right now. As I push myself up, Cora slips under my right arm and wraps her left hand around my waist, where my shirt pulled up a little.

Suddenly my ribs don't hurt at all, because all I can feel is my bare skin warm under her fingertips. My pulse skips into double time as she walks me off the field and over to a big oak tree surrounded by backpacks.

"That was a *hit*," she says, setting me down super carefully. "Jeez. You think you're okay?" She helps me sit up against the trunk of the tree, her hand coming to rest behind my neck. I swallow hard, trying not to stare at her too much.

"I think so," I say, rubbing my side.

"Is it your ribs? Can I see?" she asks, and I nod. She reaches out and lifts my shirt enough to reveal a graphing-calculator-sized red mark across my ribs that is *sure* to age into a bruise. She winces like she can physically feel my pain. I watch as she studies it, her tongue sticking cutely out of the corner of her mouth as her fingers poke and prod their way across my skin.

"Am I gonna live, Doc?" I ask. Holy shit, I give myself an internal high five for being smooth. I actually got a joke out in her presence, and best of all, she laughs as she lets my shirt fall back down.

"Probably could use some . . . ," she starts, but before she can finish, Alex comes buzzing around the tree, *completely* out of breath. You'd think *she* was the one to get the wind knocked out of her. She can't speak yet, but she holds up a white plastic bag filled with ice. I have no idea where she found ice, but it must've been pretty far away for her to be huffing and puffing like that.

Cora takes it from her and holds it up to my ribs, our hands overlapping as she passes it off to me.

"Thanks." I smile up at her as Alex huffs and puffs off to get a drink from the orange Gatorade dispenser sitting on the table.

"Hey, Molly, I wasn't going to say anything, but now that we're here . . ." Cora scans my outfit again. "What's up with your, uh . . . getup?" she asks. I obviously can't tell her the *real* reason, so I make up a lie on the spot. Something about the shock of getting plowed seems like it's keeping me from getting too far in my head.

"Oh, I . . . I left a box of my stuff at home," I reply. "All my athletic clothes."

"You should've called me," she says, knitting her eyebrows together. "I could've lent you something."

I should've called her!? I have to dig my nails into my palm so I don't audibly gasp. It's literally the perfect opening.

"Really?" I ask stupidly, instead of pouncing on the opportunity.

"Totally. Anytime." She shrugs, peeking behind her at the scrimmage. "You think you're okay? You want to try to get back in there?"

Get back in there?

"Ohhh." I grab my side and wince. "No, I . . . I don't think I can." *There is no way in hell I am stepping back out on that field.* "You should go, though. I'd hate for their soon-to-be star player not to make the team because she was playing doctor." I laugh, wincing as a sharp pain shoots through my ribs.

"Well, if you need any other medical advice, you just call me," she replies, a smirk pulling at her lips. *The universe giving me a second chance.* I look right into her hazel eyes. *This is it.*

"Can I get your number?" I ask, my heart racing like I'm still running around on the pitch. "So I can call you? Or maybe text you?" *Of course it's to call or text, Molly. What else do you use a phone number for?*

I wait for what feels like a lifetime for her to answer.

"Yeah, of course," she finally replies with a smile as I try to stay conscious.

I left my phone with Alex's across the field, but luckily, Cora takes a pen from the outside pocket of one of the backpacks around us and holds her hand out to me. I look around for a notebook, some paper, a sticky note, but . . . I can't just start digging through backpacks. I turn and look again, maybe a leaf? I can't believe she was going to give it to me and now it's not going to happen because I have no way to take it.

She lets out a breathy laugh and gently takes my hand in hers, stretching my arm out between us. I hold my breath as her pen drags across my skin, and she writes out her phone number like we're in a teen movie or something. This stuff just doesn't happen in real life.

Not to me.

"I should get back out there," she says, returning the pen to its pocket and standing up.

"Sorry about tryouts," she adds, cringing.

"I think I'll make a better audience member anyway." I laugh.

"I hope so," she says, before jogging away.

She hopes so. She wants me there in the stands.

I meet Alex's eyes over the paper cup she's chugging water out of, and I'm so happy I forget to be mad at her. I give her the tiniest nod, but with a huge smile across my face. She drops her jaw open and does a little dance over to me.

"Dude! Are you *kidding* me?" Alex says. I hold my good hand up to her, and she pulls me onto my feet.

"I don't know what happened. I was so . . . so *smooth*! It was like you said at the coffee shop about just getting out of my head. I think getting flattened actually helped, like maybe the anxiety got concussed right out of me!" I say as she turns my forearm up, both of us taking in the neat scrawl of Cora's phone number.

"Molly! Step one complete!" She pulls me into a hug, her body knocking into my bruised ribs, making me grunt.

"Oh! Shit. Sorry," she says, but immediately she shoves me playfully in the shoulders. "Dude! This is huge. We *have* to celebrate." She waves for me to follow her across the lawn.

"They'll know why I'm leaving, but shouldn't you tell the captain or something, before we just take off?" I ask.

"*Psh.* I don't give a shit what those people think of me." She laughs as I jog to catch up, wincing as pain radiates along the length of my rib cage.

"How did you know that would all happen? Me getting plowed. Cora coming over to help me. It was weirdly perfect," I say.

"I paid her to lay you out," she admits, and my jaw drops open.

"You did not!" I yell, incredulous, and Alex busts out laughing, shaking her head. I shove her the best I can with my injured side.

"Honestly, I was just thinking you'd be so focused on trying not to make a fool of yourself in the game that when it was over, you wouldn't be so in your head when it came to Cora," she replies. "I had a feeling she'd want to look out for you, but I think we got a little lucky, too."

"Lucky!?" I ask, reliving my near-death experience with a shudder.

"Well, it *worked*. Didn't it?" she asks, and she *is* right. I think I might actually owe her for this one.

"Come on. We're getting frozen yogurt. My treat," I say. It feels like the least I can do for her, and the guilt from earlier comes rushing back. "And umm . . . I'm really sorry about earlier, what I said to you. I never meant to—"

"Don't sweat it," she replies easily, but I can tell by the look on her face that she appreciates it. I grab on to her bony shoulder for some support as I lead her across campus to Tutti Fresh Yogurt.

From the party that first night to this whole mess of a tryout that somehow ended with me getting Cora's number, things haven't gone as planned very much, but they also feel better than they have in a long time . . . maybe better than they have ever. I think Alex has actually had a big hand in that, which is something I never really saw coming.

This semester is finally starting to shape up into the college experience that I've been hoping for.

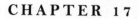

CHAPTER 17

Tutti Fresh Yogurt is heaven on earth.

I stare in awe at the massive buffet of toppings: fresh fruit, cookie dough, Oreos, sprinkles in every color imaginable. My one-size-fits-all paper cup is already filled to the brim with cookies-and-cream frozen yogurt, but now it's bound for overflow.

My forearm is practically sore from scooping by the time I reach the end, and I glance up to see Molly has added only one small scoop of *Rice Krispies* on top of her strawberry yogurt, like an actual psychopath.

"Of everything here, you get *that?*" I shake my head. "No wonder you don't have a girlfriend."

She rolls her eyes and jabs me with her elbow, giving me a *Really, Alex?* look that I've become all too familiar with over the past two weeks.

Only this time, there's a trace of a smile underneath it all.

We head over to the cash register and put our cups on the scale, mine probably quintupling the total. I pull out a stack of dollar bills I got from the tip jar this past weekend, but Molly holds up her hand.

"I said it's on me," she says, swiping her credit card before I can stop her.

I feel slightly guilty considering my frozen yogurt cup is eighteen times the size of hers, so I put a couple of ones in the tip jar for the uninterested teenager working behind the counter. He grunts a thanks, his eyes laser-focused on a YouTube video playing on his phone.

"Didn't pin you for a stripper," Molly says as we grab our fluorescent-pink spoons and find seats by the wall of windows that capture a breathtaking view of a Rite Aid, a Qdoba, and an overflowing trash can.

I laugh. "You caught me. I was thinking of throwing a dance routine together for my final project in bio." I point the spoon at her. "You're welcome to work lights. End of the semester? Ass-crack of dawn on a Monday? Any availability?"

"I'll see if I can pencil you in," Molly says as I dig into my top layer of whipped cream and rainbow sprinkles, unearthing the sea of cookie dough and cheesecake bites.

I jab at one of the blobs of cookie dough. "They're actually from—"

"Oh wait, that food truck job! You got it?" Her brown eyes light up, something about her excitement and the fact she remembered making my insides feel warm. I haven't been able to talk to anyone about it, with Natalie being upset at me this past week and my mom being . . . my mom. It feels good to have someone legitimately interested.

Besides, even if I could tell Natalie about it, she'd probably think it was kind of lame. She was always saying that about my job at Tilted Rabbit, telling me she wished I didn't work behind the counter and did something on the stage instead of watching from the crowd. I used to wonder sometimes if maybe she was embarrassed that I cleaned up glasses and poured drinks instead of banging out a sick bass line, but I shake it off now, just like I always have.

She said she loves me.

"Yeah! My boss, Jim, is . . . a little rough around the edges," I say as I picture him ripping the food truck across three lanes of traffic, middle finger hanging out the window while I bounce around in the jump seat every other evening. "But I think it'll be good. Pays in cash. And my hours are mostly on the weekends and at night, so it won't fuck with school. *Plus*, I get a cheesesteak or a burger every shift."

"Is the food good?" she asks, crunching on her Rice Krispies.

"Yeah! His cheesesteaks actually do Philly justice, which is saying something."

"Fresh-cut fries?" she asks, which I've learned is more of a Pittsburgh thing than a Philly one.

181

I nod, quoting Jim. "Only way to do it."

"Good," she says with a satisfied nod, but then her dark eyebrows furrow as she points at my cup. "What's that?"

I glance down to see a strawberry boba has surfaced from under the sea of rainbow sprinkles.

"This?" I scoop it up. "Just some boba."

"I don't know what that is."

"Like in bubble tea?" I laugh. "I nearly choke on them every time I get it, to be honest with you."

She stares at me, no glimmer of recognition in her eyes.

Oh dear God.

"You've never had bubble tea?"

"I mean, what am I missing out on if you almost *choke* on it?" she says, her cheeks turning red with embarrassment.

"Because it's part of the *experience*, Molly!"

I use my plastic spoon to flick the strawberry boba at her, and she swats it away like Serena Williams, the tiny pink ball soaring through the air and landing smack on the back of someone's shoe, the owner none the wiser. We dissolve into laughter, and I practically choke even though my mouth is boba-free.

I try to catch my breath as my phone lights up on the table, a—holy shit.

A *text* coming in from Natalie.

I drop my spoon and scoop the phone up to see: call me tomorrow ♥ I miss u

"Hell yes. The freeze is over!" That's what I call *progress*.

"The freeze?" Molly asks.

"Yeah, just . . . Natalie," I say as I tap a miss u 2 back to her. "My girlfriend," I add, because that's what she *will be* again at the end of this. "She was mad at me because I didn't reply to a Snapchat a few nights ago."

"Why didn't you?"

I scrape at the bottom of my frozen yogurt cup. "It was an accident. I fell asleep before I hit send. My first food truck shift really took it out of me."

Molly stops eating, her head snapping up to look at me. "I can't imagine being mad at someone for falling asleep."

Right? It feels kind of nice to have someone think I'm not the bad guy. Then again, if Molly knew the whole story, she probably wouldn't say that. I haven't given Natalie a lot of reason to trust me.

The last night in Philly was only the tipping point for *months* of me being a pretty terrible girlfriend. Natalie was right. She knew the truth about my mom and supported me through it when no one else ever would, and I repaid her by being just plain difficult to be with.

"Well, we didn't leave things on the best terms. And she's got a lot going on right now," I say, gesturing down to my Cereal Killers T-shirt. "She's actually in this band. They're on tour right now. They have a concert here in Pittsburgh at the end of the month."

I avert my eyes at the mention of my deadline, since I don't want to freak her out. Because even though I obviously want to show Natalie I've changed, *this* is starting to feel like something different now. Like I actually am doing this as much for Molly as I am for me.

I think she's even starting to trust me too. Despite getting tackled in the process.

"The end of *this* month?" Molly asks, and I look up to see her narrowing her eyes suspiciously at me. "There's something you're not telling me."

I flash her a sheepish grin from across the table. "I mean, it wouldn't hurt to have you kind of . . . *with* Cora by then. You know, to show I actually helped you."

Her eyes widen. "Alex. That is, like, *five seconds* away."

I wait for her to start spiraling, but I'm surprised to see her brow furrow again instead, a look of determination painted across her face. "Well, I've already got her number, right? It's like you said at the coffee shop. If I can just put in the work and complete all the assignments, I'll be golden for the final."

I give her a nod of approval. "Who are you and what have you done with Molly Parker?"

Molly snorts. "Maybe you're not the only one who's been underestimated."

She's got a point.

"Did you use the steps to get Natalie? The ones that I'm using for Cora?"

I lean back in my chair, thinking. "Yeah, I definitely used a version of them." The corner of my mouth ticks up. "Although, I got her number that first day."

Molly glares at me.

I lean forward on my elbows. "It felt pretty amazing, though, right? To get Cora Myers's phone number?"

Her face breaks out into a huge grin, dirt still smudged on her cheek, grass stains coating her shirt. "I would've gotten tackled a million times by that girl if it meant I got her number at the end of it."

I can't help but smile at that.

"You're a trooper, Parker. I mean, you got flattened like a damn pancake out there, but you played it so tough. How could Cora *not* fall for you?"

"Here's hoping. For both our sakes." Molly laughs, wincing as she reaches up to grip her battered ribs. "I'm gonna be feeling *that* for the next week."

I nod toward the door as a loud group of people make their way inside. "Want me to walk you back to your place?" I offer. "Gotta make sure your fragile body won't crumble to dust."

She laughs and nods.

We scoot our chairs out and leave Tutti Fresh Yogurt, tossing our empty cups into a trash can along the way. Outside, the sky has slowly darkened, and the streetlights flick on above our heads.

"So, are you going to tell me what the next step is?" Molly

185

asks as we walk side by side. I look over, taking in her jean shorts and grass-stained T-shirt, which I've seen her wear, like . . . five times in the past two weeks.

Which is why I've decided step two is "dress to impress." I think if Molly found some clothes she could feel confident in, she would not only catch Cora's eye, but she would be empowered to actually *do something* when she did.

"We've got to do something else first," I say.

There really isn't any reason to keep her in the dark, but . . . I just like to watch her squirm. She's so used to everything being planned out, so used to knowing everything. I feel like surprising her is a *good* thing.

It's why I planned tonight the way I did. She had no time to overthink it. No time to get nervous.

She just . . . did it.

I tap her forearm, where Cora's phone number is. "You've got to actually text her."

Molly's eyes widen as she looks down at the number in horror.

"Later, though. It's too soon now. You don't want to seem too eager."

We head down Forbes, slowing to a stop at a stoplight, but Molly is still biting her lip with worry. "So, would you rather get tackled five times or fail bio?" I ask, completely out of the blue, trying my best to distract her.

She gives me a quizzical look, but it works.

"Get tackled," Molly says with absolutely *no* hesitation. "If I had to retake bio, it would *completely* wreck my four-year plan for graduation."

Of course. She probably has all eight semesters of classes planned and penciled into her planner already.

"Would you rather only eat at Market for the rest of your life or only eat off that food truck you work for?" she asks me.

"Market, for sure. Can't beat the variety." I look both ways. "Don't tell my boss that, though."

The light changes, and we head across the intersection. "What's your favorite song?" I ask.

We keep this game of questions going the whole way back to her dorm room.

I find out her favorite movie is *Pride and Prejudice* (the 2005 version, which I *strongly* disagree with). Her favorite food is her mom's Bolognese. And . . . that she would rather die by shark attack than poop her pants in front of Cora.

"You're telling me you would rather poop your pants in front of Natalie?"

"Of course!" I say, spinning my ring of keys around on my finger. "I don't want to *die*."

"I feel like I'd probably die no matter which option I chose. Either by shark or sheer embarrassment." Her eyes widen, images flashing before her eyes. "Although, I almost die by sheer embarrassment just about every day of my life."

We end up squaring the block around the quad a few times

when it becomes clear neither of us wants to stop riding the high of her victory tonight. It's also . . . kind of fun. Seeing what we have in common after two weeks of butting heads. Seeing what we probably will always butt heads on.

"Top three hottest celebrities. Go."

"Easy. Keira Knightley."

Great choice.

"Cara Delevingne—"

"You know, some people might say that *I* resemble Cara Delevingne," I say, cutting her off.

Molly lets out a loud laugh and gives me a once-over. "Well, then, they would be lying." She taps her third and final finger, a dreamy expression on her face while I pretend to be wounded. "Oh, and Dominique Provost-Chalkley. Dom's probably number one."

"Who is that?"

"From *Wynonna Earp*? You know, that TV show on Syfy that blew up a few years back. Killing demons with a magic gun. Tiny bartender falls for swoony ginger cop?"

I shake my head, none of that ringing any bells.

Molly skids to a stop and gives me a look of absolute horror. "You've *never* heard of *Wynonna Earp*? And you're . . . a lesbian?"

I shrug. "I'm way more into, like . . . *Killing Eve*, I guess."

Molly rolls her eyes. "Of course you like the show with the hot psychopath assassin."

"You say that like it's a bad thing," I say as we reach her dorm for a third time, our laughter giving way to silence.

"I'd watch an episode," I say with a shrug. "If you want to hang out for a bit longer."

I hesitate after I say it.

This is cool . . . right? I mean, Natalie couldn't be mad at this. I'm not doing anything wrong. It's just friends hanging out. This is what she wanted.

Molly's words from earlier come back to me, pushing me forward. *I can't imagine being mad at someone for falling asleep.*

Molly furrows her eyebrows at me. "Like now?" she asks, checking the time on her phone: *9:42.* "You don't have to."

You don't have to? Does she think I'm just being polite or something?

"Is it past your bedtime?" I ask, the corner of my mouth ticking up.

"No." She laughs. "No, it's just . . . I don't know." She pauses but doesn't break our eye contact. "It's been a while since I've had someone to hang out with like . . ." She motions back and forth between us. "Well, like this."

That breaks my heart a little, but . . . I get it.

It's been a while since I just hung out with someone like this. Someone I wasn't trying to date or flirt with or keep comfortably at arm's length. Someone that just wanted to hang out with *me.*

"Yeah. Me too," I say.

I guess we're more alike than I thought. I wonder how Molly ended up here. Two different roads, but somehow, the same destination.

She shrugs and smiles up at me, the warmth radiating from it enough to make me smile right back at her. "Okay, let's do it."

CHAPTER 18

MOLLY

Last night Alex and I got so caught up in watching the pilot of *Wynonna Earp* (which she loved) that it wasn't until I walked her out to her bike that I realized we had forgotten to send a first text to Cora. By that point it was after midnight and Alex decided it would be best to hold off.

The following morning I slide up onto Noah's kitchen counter, watching him put together all the ingredients for palachinkas. My mouth is already watering as I picture the stack of thin Croatian pancakes that Grandma used to make for us every Sunday.

"So, what made you want to do this today?" I ask him.

He stops what he's doing long enough to let out a big sigh. "Mom asked me to check on you."

"Of course she did." I let out a huff of air in reply. On one hand I get it, given my history, but on the other it's like she has absolutely no faith in me. And I just told her I was busy when she texted last night! I don't need pity invites. At least, not anymore.

"But I wanted to hang out anyway." He shrugs, getting back to the task at hand.

Whether it was through his own volition or not, when he texted this morning to invite me over, it was *impossible* to turn down. Alex and I already had plans to work on what she called step 1B, which, to be honest, sounds a little bit made up, but I sent her Noah's address and told her to meet me here instead of my dorm. She sent me five replies asking where exactly I was sending her, but I didn't answer a single one. It was kind of nice to watch *her* flounder around in the dark for once.

I wasn't worried at all about this at first, but the more time I sit here and think about it, the more I start to panic. I've never actually had a friend to introduce to my brother. I just hope the two of them get along.

"Impressive," I say, forcing myself out of my head as I watch Noah crack an egg one-handed into the big metal mixing bowl beside me.

"The ladies love it," he says, cracking two more eggs into the bowl at the same time without breaking eye contact with me. I laugh and roll my eyes as he starts mixing everything together with a fork. I guess I should've brought him Mom's whisk. "So who's this girl you invited over?" he asks.

"Just a friend I met at that party," I reply.

"See? What did I tell you? Means to an end." Just then a

loud sound outside pulls our attention to the front window.

I hop off the counter and follow Noah through the small house. He opens the front door to find Alex loudly wrangling a fluorescent-orange bicycle up onto the front porch in obvious frustration. Before I can even say anything, Noah hops down the porch steps to take the bike from her.

"Thanks," she says, looking up at him. "Oh, dude, were you at Pitchfork this summer?" she asks, pointing at his beige T-shirt.

"Yeah, I go every year with my high school friends," he says as he lifts the bike onto the porch with ease and rests it against the metal railing. "You?"

"It was my first music festival. I loved it! Saturday was unbelievable. I mean . . ."

"Bed Revival!?" Noah asks, lighting up.

"Yes! Holy shit. They killed it." My shoulders relax a little, seeing how well they're getting along.

"Hi," I say, making my presence known as I step out onto the porch. "New bike?"

"Marketplace." Alex shrugs, glancing between me and her bike. "Better than the bus."

"I'm pretty sure rolling down the street would be better than taking Port Authority," I say, and she laughs, nodding in agreement.

"Alex, this is my brother, Noah." I motion between them. "Noah, Alex." They quickly shake hands, and Noah excuses himself to finish getting things ready in the kitchen.

"Why didn't you answer me!?" she shouts from the bottom step. "We're supposed to be doing step one-B today. Are you trying to chicken out?"

"No, but that's not really a location-specific activity. We can just do it from here, because right now we're gonna make some palachinkas."

"Pala-who?" she asks, twisting her face in confusion as she looks up at me.

"Palachinkas." I laugh. "They're like . . . crepes but better." I take a step toward the door, but she doesn't budge.

"I have a shift at noon at Hitchhiker Brewing," she says.

"We'll be done by then. I promise."

"But—"

"Alex." I stop her so that we're not out here arguing all day. "Palachinkas demand you go with the flow, so let's do it."

"*Molly Parker* is telling *me* to go with the flow?" she asks, a smile stretching across her face as she walks up another two steps so we're at eye level. "These pinkachalas must be *something.*"

"They are. Plus, this is, like, two of your favorite things." I move backward toward the door as she stops to give me a confused look. "Stuffing your face and hanging out with me."

She rolls her eyes but follows me inside anyway.

"So, did you come up with a text to send her?" she asks as we get into the kitchen.

"*Ooooh*. A text to send to whom?" Noah asks, turning to face us with his arm around the big mixing bowl.

"Thanks, Alex." I give her a deadpan look, and she shrugs innocently. "Cora," I reply, and Noah's eyebrows shoot up. "And yes. I was thinking I'd just say, 'Hey, it's Molly!'"

"Molly!" Alex scolds, horrified with me. "Give me your phone." She holds out her hand.

"What are you going to say?" I ask, skeptical.

"Oh, just give it to her, Molly," Noah says, still mixing away.

"Don't you trust me by now?" Alex asks, wiggling the fingers of her outstretched hand.

It's obvious why I'd be a little apprehensive to just *hand over* my phone. I'd be giving her full power to say whatever she wants to Cora. And I've heard the kind of stuff Alex says.

But . . . I've gotten to know her better, and she's not the person she appeared to be during our game of Never Have I Ever. Even though she said this was just a trade-off so she could prove herself worthy of Natalie, I think she really cares what happens between me and Cora. She knows how much this means to me, and I'm pretty sure she wouldn't screw me over.

I dig my phone out of my back pocket and set it in her hand. Instantly, her thumbs are flying across the keyboard, making me even more nervous than before. And then, on top of all that, *Noah* steps across the small kitchen to stand beside her.

"What's that mean?" he asks, reading the text over Alex's shoulder.

"Inside joke," she replies.

"Molly, you've got inside jokes with her already?" he asks.

"Uh . . . no?" I reply, trying to get a peek at the screen, but Alex turns so only the two of them can see. *What the heck is she typing?*

"No, no," Noah says, dropping his mixing fork to point at my phone. "Add that one."

"Let me see," I plead, watching them both toy with my love life.

"Aaand . . . sent. See?" Alex turns the phone to me.

Well, I made it through the night, Doc 😌

"Alex! Winky face?" I ask, grabbing my phone back. I can feel the familiar panic creep back up in me. Of course she couldn't show it to me *before* she pressed send. "That's *way* too flirty!"

"Don't look at me. That was all your brother," Alex replies. Maybe it's not too late to play it off like it's not even me texting her. I inspect the message more closely.

"Wait. How did you even know about the 'Doc' joke?" I ask.

"I was, like, fifteen feet away. I could hear every word you guys were saying," she replies, plopping down onto one of the dining chairs. "Just relax. It's a good text."

Relax? I'm Molly. I don't . . . *relax*. I don't text winky face

196

emojis. I sit down in the chair across from her, staring at my phone as I await a reply. Maybe I should've just texted Cora "hi," like I had originally planned before Alex got here. Why couldn't I just do this one thing by myself?

"Hey," Noah says, and I look up long enough to see him scrolling through his phone. "I gotta do something for work real quick. The batter's ready. You guys get started." He sets the bowl on the counter and disappears upstairs to his office, set up in the second bedroom.

"So what do we do?" Alex asks, but I'm already staring at my phone again, my text still unread. "Molly, quit obsessing over it. Don't stress so much about what you text and how you word it and what she's going to reply. It's like . . . real-life con-versations. You just have to pinkachala it, *go with the flow*," she quotes my words back to me. "Come on. Put the phone down. You dragged me here for these things, so . . ." I look up to find her looking down at the batter.

"Right. Sorry." I let out a big sigh, leaving my phone behind as I get up to turn the burner on and find a spatula.

I show her how to make one, pouring some batter onto the hot pan and spreading it out evenly. I look up at Alex, standing super close to me as she takes it all in. I use a spatula to carefully flip it over, then let it fry for another two seconds before dumping it onto the plate.

"Cool," she says, inspecting it.

At first, the text is all I can think about. But with each

palachinka, I find myself glancing back at my phone a little less.

"Hey!" I yell just as I finish another. I slap the back of Alex's hand with the spatula as she tries to steal one off the plate, *again*. "Just *wait*. You need the full experience." She sighs dramatically, walking a circle around the kitchen. "Here." I set the spatula on the counter and step back. "You make some."

She just about shoves me into the wall as she excitedly takes my spot, clearly having been waiting for me to offer. I watch her pour a scoop of batter and then try to add a second one.

"That's too much," I tell her, grabbing ahold of her wrist.

"I want to make a *big* one," she says. She's so excited I have to let go. She looks down at her masterpiece, her eyes as wide as dinner plates. She doesn't even have to tilt the pan to spread all the batter.

"You should see my grandma make these," I tell her, leaning on the counter as she picks up the spatula. "She used to make them at her house on Sundays. I always loved how big of a batch her recipe made. It didn't matter if the whole neighborhood showed up, everyone always left full. She doesn't even need the spatula. She can flip them from the pan like a pro."

"Like this?" Alex asks, grabbing the pan and stepping back into the center of the kitchen.

"*Nooo!*" I try to stop her, but it's too late. I watch with horror as she jerks the pan, sending her ginormous palachinka flipping through the air between us. "Catch it!" I yell, but I can tell by the wild laugh coming out of her that that is very much not going to happen.

Splat.

It smacks onto the floor, spreading the raw batter across the tile.

I give her a blank look from down on my knees, where I somehow ended up in an effort to . . . I have no idea. She throws me a guilty smile, her pan still frozen in—

Ding-ding.

The entire thing is instantly forgotten as I lunge for my phone on the table.

Please don't let it be Mom. Please don't let it be Mom.

"She replied!" I announce, sitting back against the fridge, taking a deep breath as I open Cora's text.

Good sign. No internal bleeding. I prescribe lots of ice cream and movies.

I hold in my breath, just trying to process. She's playing along with my little joke. She's being funny, and *cute*! My lungs are screams, so I force myself to breathe in and out.

"Oh my God, what do I say?" I ask, showing my phone to Alex as she steps around the mess, turning the stove off along the way.

"Say, 'Got it. Any recommendations?'" she says, sliding down the fridge beside me. I send the text, and this time Cora replies right away.

Maybe binge a Netflix original. Anything goes good with mint chip 😉

"A winky face! She sent me a winky face!" I yell, even though Alex is reading the text over my shoulder.

"Just heart it," Alex replies.

"*What?*" I ask, looking at her in confusion. "All of that and I'm not even supposed to reply? She's going to think I hate her!"

"Trust me, Molly. You gotta leave her wanting more. Girls like the chase," she tells me, but I don't think that's true in all cases. *I* certainly don't like it. "Give her some space. Meanwhile, we need to move on to—"

"*What* did you guys do?" Noah asks, standing in the doorway of the kitchen, looking between us and the giant palachinka splattered on his floor.

"Molly tried to show off," Alex says, and I shake my head at Noah.

He tiptoes over to the stack of palachinkas and puts a few on a plate. "Well, I'm getting started while you show-offs clean it up." We both watch as he spreads a thin layer of strawberry jelly on each one before rolling them up tightly.

"That's why they're supposed to be thin, genius," I whisper as we both hop up off the floor to clean up *her* mess.

I look down at my phone, press my thumb down on Cora's message, and slide it over the heart. But it doesn't feel right. It doesn't feel like me. I slide my thumb all the way off the screen as Alex wipes some of the batter off the floor and drops the paper towel into the trash can.

Movies, ice cream, I mean that's pretty much how I got through high school. This is common ground. After a few seconds I type something up I'm actually happy with. I read it seven or eight times just to make sure, but it's so much easier than I thought it would be. There's no pause, no time limit. I can just think and be myself like everyone's always telling me to be.

I think I can do that. Sounds like an ideal Saturday.

Send.

CHAPTER 19

ALEX

I zip down the winding hills of Lawrenceville and along Butler Street, then head across the bridge into Sharpsburg as my phone chirps out directions to Hitchhiker Brewing from my back pocket.

I am *stuffed.*

I ate a *ton* of palachinkas. Molly was right. Once you slathered them with her mom's homemade strawberry jelly, it was game over. Sugary and delicious, with the warm, thin pastry tasting almost sweet. Like crepes but . . . better.

I recognize Hitchhiker Brewing's tall smokestack from my Google searches, a holdover from its former factory days. I bank left and slow to a stop just outside before hopping off my bike, my phone's GPS calling out a "You have arrived!"

Jim still isn't here. Which makes sense. Molly practically pushed me out the door so I wouldn't be late, and I took those Lawrenceville hills pretty fast, thinking about calling

Natalie the whole way here. My eyes are still stinging from the wind.

I sit down on the curb and, with some time to spare, press the call button just under her name. Since Nat sleeps late, I couldn't call this morning, and I'll be busy with work until late tonight, so now is the *perfect* time.

Plus, something about the palachinkas reminded me of our diner pancakes, and I spent most of the bike ride *extra* excited to hear her voice.

I hold my breath as it rings. Once. Twice.

"Alex?" she says as she picks up. I jump to my feet at the sound of her voice, but . . . it doesn't sound as excited as I was hoping for. I nervously pace along the cracked sidewalk that runs alongside the parking lot. There are muffled voices in the background, the sound of a bass thumping out a few notes.

"Hey, babe! How's it going?"

"Why are you calling me now?" she asks, and I frown in confusion, pulling the phone away from my ear to stare at the screen for a second before putting it back up.

"You *told* me to call you."

Yesterday? At frozen yogurt? There was a heart emoji and everything.

"Yeah," she says. "But I didn't mean *now*. I have a gig tonight. I have to get ready."

So much for the perfect time to call.

"I know. In Kansas City." I do the math in my head. "Doesn't it not start for, like . . . six more hours?"

There's no way in hell she has to "get ready" for six hours. Not when I know for a fact she doesn't help carry any of the equipment.

Natalie lets out a long sigh. "Things are different on the road, Alex. You wouldn't understand." The muffled voices in the background fade as she moves somewhere quieter. "But I guess we can talk now since it works for you."

"If you can't, it's—"

"No, no. Go ahead," she says. "What's up with you?"

"I got a job working on a food truck. It's been pretty good so far. Some solid tips. All cash. I'm just waiting for my shift to start." I kick at a small rock on the ground, watching it bounce its way down the street.

"Oh. Cool."

She doesn't ask any follow-up questions, and the silence that follows is deafening. So I ask her one instead. "How's the tour going?"

"It's been *so* great. People actually know our music! They sing along and everything. It's been super wild."

"That sounds *awesome*. I can't wait for your Pittsburgh date," I say, holding my breath.

"Yeah, me neither," Natalie says, and her words bring a smile to my face, especially after such a precarious start.

"Twenty more days."

"Is that it? Wow." She's silent for a second. "So, you got a new girlfriend, or . . . ?"

I frown as a slight pang of queasiness grips my stomach, and not because of the mountain of palachinkas taking up space in there.

I haven't told her about Molly and what we're doing just yet, and her making a comment like that leaves me to believe this is . . . absolutely not the time to do so, even though this is my first real chance since I left Philly. I just don't want her misunderstanding and getting angry with me over nothing.

Especially not when I just got off silent treatment.

"Too busy thinking about you," I say, watching as a black food truck whips around the corner, the back tires bumping violently over the curb. I jump out of the way before Jim has a chance to flatten me, the truck hissing to a stop outside the brewery.

"Mm-hmm," Natalie says, clearly skeptical.

"You'll see when you get here," I say, watching as Jim busts out the back door. He lights up his preshift cigarette while the fryer heats up to temperature.

"I hope so," she says, before pulling the phone away from her ear to call out *"Coming!"* to someone waiting in the distance. "I've got to go. We want to rehearse 'Sleepy Girl' a few times, since Ethan messed up that sick bass line in the bridge two nights ago."

"I love that song."

"Of course you do," she says, and I can hear the smile in her voice. "I mean, I wrote it *for* you."

I can hear her name being called, and she lets out a frustrated sigh, her voice muffled as she yells out, "I need literally, like, *two more seconds*, Paul!"

"Break a leg tonight, okay?" I say when she comes back on, and she laughs, the vibe suddenly so different than it is when we're texting. So . . . *right*.

Sometimes it feels like every day is a different Natalie. Sometimes I wish it were just *this* Natalie.

"If Ethan fucks it up tonight, *someone's* leg is going to be broken, that's for sure."

I smile, the familiar flow from before our fight two weeks ago finally finding its way back.

"I'll call you later, okay? Maybe tomorrow?"

"That sounds good," I say, hoping she does. We say our goodbyes, and I head over to where Jim is lounging against the back of the truck.

"That your bike?" he asks, pointing to my fluorescent-orange Facebook Marketplace find, locked up on the side of the building.

I nod and Jim snorts, even though he was the person who suggested getting one after I found out it would take me an hour and a half on a Port Authority bus to get to the lunch shift we're working this week. Biking there will take fifteen minutes flat. Truly life-changing.

"It's ugly as fuck," he says, snuffing out his cigarette before swinging open the truck door and hopping on.

I roll my eyes and follow after him to set everything up, a comfortable silence falling over us as our usual routine begins. Jim handles the prep cooler while I put out the menu, get the cash register ready, and open the window when it's go time.

Almost instantly, the customers stroll out from inside, and our steady rhythm kicks in. My mind shuts off as I take orders and hand out the finished product (with just one napkin!) again and again. It's easy to keep a smile plastered on my face after that phone call with Natalie, even though . . . the queasiness still lingers when I think of how things are going on the Molly front.

It took Molly *two weeks* to get Cora's number.

And Natalie is going to be here in only three weeks.

I know this is a Molly-centric plan, but I don't have that kind of time. I can't fuck around and make palachinkas and eat frozen yogurt when Natalie is coming in just twenty days. Natalie needs to see that I can really connect with and help people. That I can have friends who are *just friends*. That people can open up to me about their feelings and I won't just run off into the night.

She's not going to believe me if I just say I've been hanging out with some girl to help her get a girlfriend. That girl needs to either *have the girlfriend* or be pretty damn close.

When the lull sets in, I pull out my phone and fire off a text to Molly:

We're doing Step 2. Tomorrow. I'll be there by 10:30.

I need proof. And I need it *fast.*

Molly isn't the only one trying to get the girl.

Here's hoping I can keep mine.

CHAPTER 20

MOLLY

"Okay. Step two: dress to impress. Now that you got her number, you've gotta get all of"—she motions vaguely at my clothes—"*that* together."

"Alex, shouldn't this step have come before step one? I mean, shouldn't I have been dressing better *before* I got her number? So I could make a good impression right from the start?" I ask, following my hunch that she's just making stuff up as she goes here. Not that I can really complain too much. I mean . . . it's working. Isn't it?

"Okay, first of all . . . I didn't know how bad the wardrobe situation was until I saw you wear the same plain T-shirt in three different colors." *That's a fair point.* "And second, I wanted you to get her number just as you are. If she gave it to you dressed like that, just think about the possibilities when we get you put together a little better." She pauses, flinching at herself. "No offense."

"I think you're being a little dramatic. It's not *so* bad," I say.

"Molly—and I'm saying this as a friend—I'm truly terrified to open that closet door. . . ." She looks me up and down.

"Fine," I reply with a huff. We might as well get this over with. She steps past me to stand in front of it.

"You have Cora's number now. We *have* to get this nailed down, because step three is coming and you are *not* ready," she tells me. I don't even bother asking what step three is, because I know she won't tell me.

Also, I don't *just* have Cora's number. I've been using it. After I replied to her at Noah's, when Alex told me not to, we talked on and off for the rest of the day. I decide not to say anything to Alex, because, to be honest, I'm a little scared to tell her that I went rogue. Plus, I've got enough on my plate today with step two.

"Let's see what we're working with." She pulls open the door to my closet. "Organized," she says more to herself than to me, then immediately starts tearing through it like a category 5 hurricane.

"Molly!" she yells, feigning a posh English accent. "How many sweatpants does one girl need!?" She whirls around and holds a stack of what I call my "weekend lounge pants" out to me but drops them straight onto the floor with the rest of my clothes before I can grab them. Her hands immediately grab for more hangers, but when I don't laugh, she peeks over her shoulder at me, dropping the crappy accent. "That was Tan from *Queer Eye*."

"Yeah, I don't live under a rock." I scoot to the edge of my bed, looking at all the destruction she's caused in the few minutes she's been in my dorm room. "But do you *have* to throw everything on the floor?" I ask. My skin is prickling just looking at the chaos.

But as I watch her, I start to realize maybe this isn't a bad thing after all. It just means that I'll *have* to clean up later. And maybe while I'm at it, I'll just do a full-on room reorganization. Cora would probably laugh if I told her that. Last night she texted me that Abby has been leaving her bowls of unfinished oatmeal on their coffee table every morning and it's been driving her nuts. Yet *another* thing we have in common.

Alex holds up blouse after blouse, criticizing each one before tossing it behind her.

"Is this from QVC?" she says, pulling out a purple flowy tank top with green jewels sewn into the neckline that I'm pretty sure I wore to my eighth-grade graduation. And never since.

"Did this come with matching Bermuda shorts?" This time it's a pink-and-black plaid button-down that I got for Christmas in high school.

"No?" I reply, embarrassed, but the second the word leaves my mouth, she's already found them. She gives me a judgmental look and drops them onto the floor with everything else before digging right back in.

White pullover. Red paisley split-neck. Striped cardigan.

"Girl. What is all this shit? I've never even seen you wear any of it." She looks down at my simple olive-green T-shirt and skinny blue jeans.

"Well, you've only known me for a couple of weeks, so . . ." I shrug.

"You're right. So why is it that I've seen you in that shirt four times already?" she asks.

I sigh, looking down at my shirt, one of the few articles of clothing I actually feel comfortable in. I reach down to pick up a lavender sweater off the floor that I haven't touched for an entire year. "I guess I don't wear most of this. I'm just not very good at finding stuff I like," I admit.

"Who do you go shopping with?" She comes over to me wearing a very serious face, then places her hands on my shoulders and looks me dead in the eye. "Just tell me who did this to you."

Before I can answer, there's a rhythmic knock that pulls our attention to my door. As soon as I push down on the handle, it swings wide open and bounces off my bedpost.

"Hi, baby!" My mom starts toward me but stops short when she realizes there's someone else here with us. "Oh! I'm sorry. I didn't mean to . . ." She motions her hands around in the air, waiting for one of us to save her, but neither of us does. "You must be Cora."

Alex's eyes get big as she grins back at her. "Oh my God. You know about Cora!?"

I squeeze my eyes shut and shake my head. "No, Mom." I bury my face in my hands. My mom and Alex and me. All in the same room. Talking about Cora.

This is my worst nightmare.

"I'm Alex, Molly's love guru." She shakes my mom's hand, and the two of them start giggling like best friends sharing an inside joke.

"No, she's not. She's . . . she's just Alex." I shake my head, because actually, she's not wrong. I mean, what else is she to me?

"Mom, what are you doing here? How did you even get past the security guard?" I ask, stepping forward to give her a hug. I try my best not to flinch, but somehow my ribs are twice as sore as they were yesterday.

"I told you I was going to come down for lunch. The guard just let me in." She shrugs and then releases me from her hug.

"Alex, do you want to join us?" she asks before I even say I want to go with her.

Alex's eyes flick over to my closet and then to my mom, who's wearing a bright yellow neoprene skort and a blue paisley tank top.

She looks at me with a knowing smile.

"Actually, Molly was just telling me she was looking into getting some new clothes. Do you guys have a mall around here?"

"Ooooh!" My mom squeals, doing a little dance. "Let's go to Ross Park and make a whole day of it!" The room spins around me.

"Maybe we should just go for lunch, Mom. I have a ton of clothes," I say, not wanting to offend the person who bought most of them for me and also trying my best to keep these two worlds separate. Either she's going to say something embarrassing about me that I'll never hear the end of from Alex, or she's going to be straight-up jealous that I have someone else to hang out with. She just *had* to come down here right when I was finally getting some traction.

"Oh, *come on*," my mom says, winking at Alex. "Let's have a girls' day. It'll be good for you to get out of this dorm for a day," she adds, completely unaware of how little time I've spent here this semester. It sets my teeth on edge.

"Yeah, Molly, get out of your dorm for a day," Alex repeats, somehow managing to get under my skin even more than my mom.

"Also, your room is a *wreck*," my mom says, leaning around me to get the full view.

"I told you to clean it up, Molly," Alex tells me. "You should really take better care of your stuff."

I close my eyes, take a deep breath and let it out, knowing I've already lost the battle.

We're going whether I want to or not.

• • •

As we walk through the second floor of the bustling mall, I turn to follow my mom into Talbots, but a hand catches my arm and tugs me back.

"What the *hell* are you doing?" Alex hisses, her green eyes wide.

"Shopping?"

"And when is your AARP card coming?" she asks, taking a breath to gather herself. "You are endlessly frustrating." Then she turns her attention to my mom. "Mrs. Parker? Is it cool if I steal Molly away for a bit? I need her fashion expertise on a few shirts I've had my eye on."

"Go. Go. Go. Have fun." She gives me a genuine smile. "But, Molly, come here for a sec," she says, and I do, while Alex drifts over to the railing.

"What's up?" I ask.

"I like that Alex," she says, pulling me in closer to make sure no one else can hear. "Are you sure she's not the one you like? Maybe go buy her a pretzel or something." I cringe immediately.

"Absolutely not. Oh my God, Mom, please." I laugh at the thought of that. "I'd rather poop my pants in front of Dominique Provost-Chalkley, fail bio, *and* get eaten by a shark."

"What?" she asks, confused.

"Never mind. I'll text you later to meet up," I say as I leave her with the all-too-familiar rows of cardigans and button-ups at Talbots.

"Okay, so we're looking for date clothes," Alex says.

"Got it. Date clothes," I reply, like I know what that entails.

Alex leads me around the mall and into stores I've been to only a couple of times. We manage to walk into and out of Forever 21 *and* PacSun without me even picking anything up.

"Molly, are you even *looking*?" she asks with a sigh as we step back out into the mall.

"None of this feels like me," I tell her, frustrated. "The shirts are too small. The pants are too tight."

"Not *everything* in the store is like that, though. You have to hunt through the racks. Come on." She looks across to the other side of the mall and pulls me into Urban Outfitters. "Point out three things you like."

I look around at the trendy plywood shelves, the Calvin Klein thongs spread out on the table right in front of us. My face naturally twists into a cringe as I give her a look.

"Okay, fine. Three things you don't *hate*," she says.

I can do this.

It takes me two trips around the store, but finally, I manage to point out three things. A standard pair of skinny jeans not unlike the ones I have on, a red T-shirt with a heart embroidered onto the chest, and a plain white tank top.

"This stuff is too much like the stuff you already have," Alex says.

"Well, I can't pull off these kinds of clothes, Alex." It's the truth. I don't exactly have the body to rock a crop top or one of those skintight onesies that I will never understand.

"People don't see you the way you see yourself, Molly." She takes a frustrated breath but doesn't elaborate. "Pick out three things you like but think you can't pull off. You're going to try them on," she says, hanging my selections back on a rack where they don't belong.

So I do, and Alex follows me back toward the dressing room as I reluctantly try them on.

"Try these, too," she says from the other side of the stall door as a pair of light-washed, high-waisted Levi's come flying over the top. "They're not as tight as most of the other jeans, but they're still going to make your ass look good."

"Alex!"

"Just try them on. I think you'll like them," she adds.

"Fine."

A couple of minutes later I step out of the dressing room to show her. I didn't have the courage to try on the three shirts I pulled, but I did tuck the one I'm wearing into the jeans.

"What do you think?" I ask, turning toward myself in the mirror. There's almost a surprised look on my reflection's face as I run my eyes up and down my own body. I look like I didn't know I could look, but I still feel like myself. I didn't know pants could *fit* me like this. I actually have, like . . . a waist, and, well, Alex was kind of right. I turn to the side, breaking out into a smile as I check out my own butt.

"They look *good*, Parker," Alex confirms.

"They *feel* good," I reply, doing a couple of air squats. "A lot of movement in these babies."

"Just go change so we can check out, Parker." Alex laughs. "We've still got some ground to cover."

But something about finally finding a new pair of jeans that I like unleashes a shopping beast within me that I didn't know was there. I want to find clothes that I actually feel like *me* in, clothes that maybe make me want to check out my own butt in the mirror once in a while. That might make someone else want to check me out too for once, instead of just blending in.

By the time we make it to the H&M dressing rooms, I've got a whole pile of clothes and Alex has a few things to try on too.

She starts to follow me into the same dressing room.

"What are you doing?" I ask, motioning to the twenty empty stalls.

"It'll take forever for you to come out and show me every-thing," she says, locking the door behind us.

My face goes red. Getting undressed in front of people isn't really something I'm used to. I've never played sports, and I managed to successfully dodge PE all four years of high school by volunteering in the main office.

Not that getting undressed in front of Alex should be a big deal. I mean . . . it's Alex.

As we peel off our shirts, we face away from each other and I make sure I'm angled away from the mirror, too.

"Try the crop top with those jeans you just got. I know you're not sure about it, but you really won't even notice because the jeans come up so high," she says as we each pull on a different article of clothing and turn to face each other to decide yay or nay. After two nays, I try the combo she suggested, and I hate to admit it, but . . . she's kind of right, *again*.

I slide my hands onto my lower back and turn a couple of different ways to check myself out in the mirror. Alex laughs, and I quickly drop my hands to my sides.

"That's what you should feel like when you talk to Cora. That's what you should feel like on a date," she says, making me smile. "Confident."

About halfway through the pile, I actually end up with more than a few shirts hanging on my "buy" hook.

"I'm getting pretty hungry," Alex says as I take off a black tank top I was sure I'd like. Too plain. Too boring.

"Wow, Alex Blackwood is hungry? Who would've thought," I reply.

"Shut up." She laughs. "Anyway, as I was saying, I saw this sick Korean place at the food court," she says.

"Oh," I say, feeling my anxiety curl around me as I picture my mom anywhere *near* that place. "You remember when I told you I've never tried bubble tea? Well, I haven't really had *any* Asian food, to be honest." I cringe, waiting for her to ask why. I mean, what half Korean hasn't *tried* Korean food? But she doesn't even think twice.

"Oh man. We *definitely* need to check it out, then."

I take a deep breath, preparing myself to tell her why we maybe shouldn't. It's not something I ever share with anyone, but I don't see any other way out of this.

"My mom is kinda . . ."

As I turn to face Alex, I realize I still don't have a shirt on. And neither does she.

"Oh shit, Molly." Her hand reaches out, landing on the purple bruise that has managed to spread the length of my torso over the last couple of days. I suck in a gasp even though her touch is as light as a feather, something about it startling me. "Sorry," she says, pulling her hand back. "I didn't know it was that bad. You should've said some—"

Her voice trails off as I look down at her push-up bra, her chest rising and falling in rhythm with my breaths. Down farther, my eyes trace the soft outline of her abs, her blue underwear peeking out from unbuttoned pants.

I force my eyes back up to hers, but she's not looking at my face.

She's looking down at me, too. My skin flushes as her eyes scan over my stomach, across my white bra, and then up to my face.

I stand there, feeling frozen under her gaze, until a woman knocks on the stall door, breaking me out of my trance and sending my heart through my skin.

"Can I help you two with anything?" she asks, and I

quickly turn away from Alex and yank my green T-shirt on over my head.

"Umm. I'm gonna . . ." I grab the things off my "buy" hook, leaving the plain black tank behind as I squeeze past Alex as fast as I can. "I'll wait outside," I say, already halfway out of the dressing room, blowing right past the employee.

I plop down on a wooden block at the feet of a mannequin, sending a quick text to my mom to meet me here.

I press my hand against my warm chest, my heart still hammering away.

That was . . . uncomfortable.

God, I hope things aren't weird between us when she comes out.

No, they won't be.

We were just trying on clothes. That's all. There's nothing weird about it. This is just me overthinking as usual.

"Hey, there you are," my mom says, coming around the corner, and I jump. "Where's Alex?" Right on cue, Alex emerges, and I'm actually thankful that it isn't just the two of us.

My mom follows my eyes toward where Alex is inspecting two of the shirts she tried on like she's still deciding. She flips the tags over, then leaves them both on the return hook even though I *know* she liked them. We watch her look around the store for a second before she spots us.

"Molly, you getting that stuff?" she asks, like everything is totally normal.

I nod, focusing my vision just to the left of her face.

"Cool." She smiles in approval.

"Molly, I'll get that stuff for you," my mom says.

"No, you don't have to, Mom," I reply, even though we both already know how this is going to end.

"Give it here. I'll meet you two outside and then we can grab lunch," she says, taking the haul out of my hands. Alex and I float out into the mall, looking over the railing at the shoppers below.

"Why didn't you buy your stuff?" I ask.

"I don't need it," she says with a shrug. "And I've got rent coming up at the end of the month."

"Oh" is all I can manage to reply. I think this is the first time I've ever been tongue-tied around her. But she's not being weird about what happened, so maybe the dressing room was just me being awkward as usual.

"Here," my mom says from behind us. She's holding out two H&M bags—one to me and also one to Alex, who cocks her head at her in reply. "Here. Take it," my mom encourages, and Alex complies. She looks extremely confused until she reaches in and pulls out the shirts that she left on the hook.

"Oh." She shakes her head at the bag, and when she looks up, I swear her eyes might be coated in tears. "This is . . . No, I can't . . ." She struggles for the right words.

"I worked the night shift to put myself through pharmacy school in the daytime. I remember what it's like," my

222

mom says with a small smile. "Come on." She pats Alex on the shoulder. "Let's eat."

"Thank you, Mrs. Parker," Alex says, more earnestly than I've ever heard her say anything. She sends me a look like she can't believe my mom bought her a couple of shirts.

It's a look that makes me think maybe I've been all wrong about her from the beginning.

And I'm a bit ashamed to realize how little I've actually thought about Alex's life outside of just being my love guru.

Maybe she's not the girl that gets everything so easily.

Maybe she's so good at helping me show myself to the world because she's put up a front of her own.

CHAPTER 21

ALEX

The food court is *packed.* The sound of screaming toddlers and gossiping high school freshmen could probably break the sound barrier. I grab every sample available as we make our way around, peering at the different options, my eyes widening when I see *exactly* what I'm looking for.

Bulgogi Boyz. Squeezed in between a Subway and a burger place.

There's a group of twentysomething guys absolutely *crushing* it on the grill and prep line, meat and veggies flying everywhere through a cloud of steam and smoke. It reminds me of the food truck, only way less greasy, way more organized, and with elbow room to spare.

"Oh, *heck* yes. It's here," I say, my mouth full of chicken teriyaki and mini-cheesesteak bites. I grab Molly's arm, leading her through the crowd to the Korean place, Beth trailing just behind us. "Natalie introduced me to Bulgogi Boyz this summer. There was one down the block from Tilted Rabbit, where I worked. She got takeout from there *all* the time, and I've been craving it like crazy since I left."

Molly hesitates as we get into line, biting her lip as she shoots a glance back at her mom. Her unfinished words from the dressing room come back to me as I pop one of the sample toothpicks in my mouth and follow her gaze to see Mrs. Parker's arms are crossed, her face scrunched up as she watches someone carry off a red tray of rice and delicious, steaming beef.

I don't really understand what's happening, but I can tell something's off.

"We can totally get something else," I say, reaching out to tap Molly's arm. "That mini-cheesesteak bite was *delicious*."

Molly's eyes flick back to my face, and she shakes her head. "No, no. It's cool." She shrugs, and she looks . . . almost defiant, her arms crossing over her chest. "I want to try it."

When we get to the front, the older man working the counter gives us a big smile, taking our orders before calling them back to the younger guys on the grill.

Then he looks past us at Molly's mom. "What can I get for you?" he asks.

She doesn't say anything, his voice likely getting drowned out by the bustling food court of people.

And then . . .

He repeats the question in Korean, thinking *that* may be the problem.

I watch Molly wince as Beth gives him a look of contempt. "I don't speak"—she waves her hand around—"your language."

Oh shit.

A couple of people waiting for their food turn to look in our direction.

Beth hoists up her bags, nodding to the burger place next door. "I'm craving a burger. Can you guys grab a table?"

Molly nods, turning back to the man behind the counter, who looks more confused than anything else. When Beth is out of earshot, she gives a hurried apology. "Sorry about . . . that. She just . . . I . . ." Her cheeks are bright red, and I watch as she fumbles with her wallet, trying to get her money out from the small inner pocket. The entire thing falls onto the floor, which I'm pretty sure she's hoping will open up and swallow her at this point.

"I got it." I hold out a twenty to the man before reaching down to scoop up the wallet and hand it back to her.

I put the three dollars of change into the tip jar and grab Molly's hand, pulling her away to wait for our number to be called.

"You good?" I ask her, studying her red cheeks, her slightly glassy brown eyes.

She nods, but as we pick up our food and find a table, it's pretty clear she's not. She's quiet when her mom comes over with a red tray, piled high with fries and a burger.

"I am *starving*," Beth says as she pushes an overflowing container of fries to the edge of her tray. "Help yourselves, ladies!" She sips on her fountain drink before digging in, acting like absolutely nothing happened.

Molly doesn't even look up from her food.

I grab a fry and pop it in my mouth, trying to stave off any awkwardness. "You know, the food truck I work on has some *great* fries," I say. "Fresh-cut." I hope this will get a smile out of Molly, but it doesn't.

"I *love* fresh-cut fries," Beth says. "Oh my gosh. I'll have to come down sometime and get some food! Right, Molly? That would be so fun!"

Molly nods, but she doesn't say anything.

Beth fake-whispers, "Look who's being shy all of a sudden."

I give her a thin-lipped smile before changing the subject to ask her about being a pharmacist. Thankfully, she goes off on a tangent for the rest of the meal, telling me all the ins and outs of the small local pharmacy she works at. The gossip with Brittney and Dylan, two of the techs that work there, nursing crushes on each other. How she knows *all* the men in her town with Viagra prescriptions. How there was a break-in a few years back and they never found the perpetrator.

Molly stays quiet, though. The only thing she says is a mumbled "This is *really* good" when her mom gets up to throw out her trash.

Finally, as the sun begins to set, she drives us back to campus, giving us a cheery goodbye and waiting until we get inside before heading on down the road.

"You want to come up?" Molly asks, and I nod. When we get to her single, Molly grabs a fork and hops onto her bed, cracking open her Bulgogi Boyz leftovers.

She closes her eyes as she chews, the reaction she muted at the food court finally breaking through. "I honestly could eat this every day. No joke."

"You want the rest of mine?" I offer, hopping up next to her.

Her eyes fly open with excitement. "Really?"

I nod and pass over my Styrofoam container. "Really, really."

She loads the contents on top of hers, shaking her head. "I *knew* she was going to act like that. She *always* does." She lets out a long sigh. "I just wasn't sure if she'd screw her face up at the food, or make some comment about how disgusting it is, but . . . that was definitely worse."

I'm silent, waiting for her to continue. Or to stop. I'm not going to push her to talk about something when she doesn't want to. Especially because I get what it's like when it's hard to talk about your mom.

"She's got a pretty twisted view of her heritage." Molly prods at the bulgogi with her fork. "She was adopted from South Korea and grew up in a white family in this total craphole of a town, and people were just really shitty to her. . . ." Her voice trails off, and she cringes. "And part of me gets it. When you grow up getting called racial slurs and being pushed into thornbushes in elementary school, or shot with a BB gun on your walk home from the grocery store, I can see why you'd start hating that part of yourself and everything else associated with it."

"Has that kind of stuff happened to you, too?" I ask, my insides hurting at the thought until Molly shakes her head.

"*Nothing* as bad as that, but . . . I can see that the way I look has set me apart my entire life, and sometimes that makes me not want to embrace that part of myself either." She shrugs. "Even something as simple as this." She holds a forkful of bulgogi up. "I know it's just food, but there's a part of me that doesn't *want* to like it. Like if I do, I'm inviting people to see that I *am* Korean, which still feels like a bad thing sometimes. I don't *want* to feel ashamed of that part of me, but it's a hard thing to shake after it's been ingrained in me my whole life," she says, popping the bulgogi into her mouth. "I know that sounds stupid."

"It's not stupid," I reply, looking her right in the eye so she knows I mean it.

"I think that's how my mom feels but, like, tenfold." She lets out a big, audible sigh. "Still, I can't believe she did that today. That was so mortifying."

I shake my head. "No worries. I've had my fair share of

229

mom-induced embarrassment." I laugh and swing my legs back and forth under me. "My mom has gotten thrown out of quite a few Applebee's for blacking out on their Dollarita Dollar Strawberry Margaritas."

I stop chuckling when I see Molly isn't laughing. Her face is serious, her eyes studying mine.

It takes me a second to realize what I just said. What I just *told* her.

"That must have been really hard. What . . . what did you do?"

I clear my throat and stop swinging my legs, digging my fingers into her patterned comforter, the room suddenly feeling warm. "Uh, just took her home to pass out in bed. Nothing out of the ordinary."

Molly narrows her eyes at that. "Has she always drunk a lot?"

I scratch my chin. "It got way worse after my dad left, but, hey, at least the fighting stopped."

I plaster a smirk onto my face, but it doesn't hold up for more than a few seconds. It's too heavy. Too fake. I hate fake.

I suddenly feel like a gaping wound, bleeding out onto the carpet and the comforter and the bed, this hidden part of me suddenly impossible to hide.

I hate this feeling. I hate feeling weak. I hate feeling vulnerable. I can't even *look* at her because the thought of seeing all of that in her eyes, seeing *pity*, makes my skin prickle.

It's why I hide things and keep secrets, leaving Natalie grasping at straws. Like I've done for our whole relationship. I don't want to be an open book. I *can't* be. Because I'm rotten just beneath the surface, and deep down I'm scared she knows that.

Sometimes I think you really might end up just like your mom.

Molly reaches for my hand, her fingers barely grazing mine, but I abruptly pull away, making a show of checking my phone.

"I totally forgot to do some homework . . . for . . . class tomorrow morning," I mumble, staring at the cracks in my screen, the white numbers, the blurry wallpaper photo. Anywhere but at Molly, her hand now resting on the comforter in the space in between us.

I hop off the bed and grab the small bag of shirts, stuffing my feet into my Converse. "Uh, *speaking* of class tomorrow. Be sure to wear some of your new clothes, okay? Put step two into action and we'll be well on our way to step three!" I call over my shoulder.

She barely has time to wave before the door slams behind me. I take the steps down instead of the elevator, my footsteps echoing noisily in the stairwell. I grab my bike from the bike stand, wrangling it off the curb before I hop on. Soon my legs are burning as I fly down the street and up the steep hill that will take me around Schenley Park and back to my apartment.

It's the long way, but I need a minute to breathe.

I whiz past storefronts and Phipps Conservatory, past street signs and parked cars, the colors blurring all around me. As I look out at Oakland's skyline, the Cathedral of Learning looming in the distance, the reality of what just happened fully dawns on me.

I've never just . . . *told* anyone that.

Not even Natalie. She found out through an accidental discovery.

It feels like such a betrayal, to share this secret with someone else. To open up so easily to *Molly* instead of her.

I can't help but feel a swell of guilt at that.

What the fuck, Alex?

I bank a right turn and then a left, slowing to a stop outside my apartment, my chest heaving as I put my hands on my hips and squint at that hideous red door.

She said she'd call today, but she hasn't yet. Maybe *I* should call *her*. Talk to her. The same way I opened up to Molly tonight.

I hop off my bike and lock it up, then take the steps by twos as I pull my phone out of my pocket and tap the call button under Natalie's name.

I feel . . . desperate. Like I need to fix something even though I didn't break anything.

I hold the phone up to my ear as I unlock the front door, then close it with my heel as I flick on the lights.

It rings once. Twice. *Five* times.

I collapse on my bed, resigned to leave a voicemail, when I hear the speaker crackle to life.

"Hey, Alex."

"Natalie! Hey. Hi. How are you?" I sit up and start pacing around the room, back and forth, over and over again. "How was Kansas City last night?"

"Good." I hear her munching on something. "Just stopped to grab some dinner before we drive the rest of the way to Des Moines."

"Cool! Cool. That's great." I spin around on my heel, completing another lap.

"What's up?"

"Nothing, I just . . . You said you were going to call me today, so . . ."

"Okay, well, *you* called *me*. What's up?" More chewing. The sound of ice rattling around at the bottom of a soda cup.

"I just . . ."

Say something, Alex. You just told Molly your entire freaking life story.

"I wanted to talk. *Really* talk. About us. About where your head is at. I know we said we'd wait until you came to Pittsburgh, but I feel like things have been a little off lately, and I just want to tell you all the things I didn't say that night back in Philly. How I feel about you. How I—"

The chewing stops as Natalie cuts me off midsentence. "Why are you telling me this now?" she asks suspiciously.

233

"Because I miss you. Because I didn't say this back in—"

"It's too late for that, Alex," she says, sighing loudly. "I gave you a chance that night and you didn't take it. I've given you *so many* chances, for so long. We're not going to do this right now just because it's on your timetable, okay?"

"Right. Okay. Sorry. I just—"

"I'll see you in Pittsburgh, Alex," she says, and the line goes dead.

I pull the phone away from my ear, but my home screen stares back at me, the call ended.

Great. Just fucking great.

I chuck my phone onto my bed and let out a long sigh, hoping that in nineteen days, when Natalie arrives in Pittsburgh, I'll be able to make her see how different I am now.

I *have* to make her see.

I'm about to head into the bathroom to take my makeup off when my phone lights up, vibrating noisily against my patterned bedspread. I swoop across the room and scoop it up, hoping to see Natalie's name on the screen, but it's . . . a *FaceTime.* From my mom.

This is a first.

I tap the green button to accept, and my mom's blue eyes and shoulder-length hair appear on the screen.

"Hey, Mom. Now isn't exactly the best—"

I can see her eyes are glassy, her head swaying in and out of the frame. Just fucking perfect.

"Alex, listen . . . ," she slurs, cutting me off. "I just need some mon—"

"No," I say, still raw after my fight with Natalie and having nothing left to give. "Not now. I just . . ." I shake my head. "I just can't right now."

"But I've been texting you! Every day."

I clench my jaw and look away from the screen, trying not to cry, thinking of Molly's mom just showing up for lunch because she missed her. "That's not enough. You're *supposed* to do that. You're supposed to want to talk to me. You're supposed to want to ask me how I'm doing. You're supposed to *care* about how I'm doing, instead of it *always* being the other way around."

"*Of course* I care about how you're doing. I just—"

"Not unless you want something," I say.

And, for the first time in my life, I hang up on her, the tears starting to fall the second the screen goes black.

CHAPTER 22

MOLLY

I reach up and tug my hood down over my forehead, trying desperately to block out the rain. Alex wasn't too happy when I showed up to bio this morning in my regular old clothes, but I *couldn't* break out my new wardrobe today. The weather is way too crappy. Everything would've just gotten soaked . . . or at least that's what I told myself. In reality, I *may* have chickened out.

As I swipe into my building, I pull the hood of my rain jacket down and slip into the elevator. Just as the doors are about to close, a girl comes through the front door absolutely *drenched* from head to toe. Normally, I would step deeper into the elevator and pretend not to see her to avoid an interaction, but I reflexively stick my arm out, and the doors pop open again.

"Thanks," she says as she hurries in, shuffling over to the other side with the buttons.

"No problem," I reply, recognizing the girl who lives a

couple of doors down from me, a Pitt soccer player according to her backpack, which is also soaked. She presses 5, and I wait for her to ask what floor I'm on, knowing she most likely doesn't recognize me. But instead, she drops her arm back to her side and gives me a friendly smile.

"You're in the single just down from me, right?" she asks, and I look over at her, slightly shocked, but I remind myself to take a breath and not overthink.

"Yeah. I'm Molly," I say, extending my hand to her.

"Jordan." She shakes it. "I like your raincoat. People warned me about the weather, but I still didn't come prepared." She wipes her hand down her bare arms, water dripping off onto the floor.

"Where are you from?" I ask as the elevator carries us up.

"Small town south of LA. You?"

"Yinzer, born and raised." I point over my shoulder. "If *this* bothers you, I worry for your mental health through your first Pittsburgh winter," I say, instantly tensing up as I realize the joke might not land right with her. But, to my surprise, she actually *laughs* in reply, and I feel a surge of confidence for this small win.

"Oh God, don't remind me," she pleads. "I don't even want to *think* about it yet." The elevator doors open, and we walk side by side toward our rooms. "Hey, my roommate, Kendall, and I are trying to get a game night going on Thursdays. Would you be interested?"

"What kind of games?" I ask, having flashbacks to the

party and that horrible game of Never Have I Ever. That night feels like so long ago now, but it still stings.

"Monopoly, Cards Against Humanity, maybe even Ping-Pong in the common room, whatever." She shrugs. "Kendall's a little game obsessed. They have, like, thirty board games in our room right now." *Ping-Pong.* One of my great loves. Immediately I think of the table in our basement, where Noah and I used to battle it out for chores. It was the one thing I was actually able to compete with him at.

"Yeah, I'd totally be up for that." I try not to show how dorkily excited I am. That's . . . exactly my jam. "Is it cool if I bring someone?" Maybe I'll end up inviting Cora or something.

"For sure. We could use some more people. Common room, Thursday at eight?"

"See you there," I reply as I stop in front of my door and she continues down the hall.

I close the door behind me and lean back against it.

That was odd.

It all felt so . . . so *normal.*

Like I wasn't quiet Molly, who only thinks about school and doesn't talk to anyone.

I was just . . . Molly.

Now that I think about it, maybe that reputation was more my fault than anyone else's. Today I let Jordan in. Sure, on a very small scale, but I did it. I caught the elevator doors for her. I physically extended my hand out to her to introduce myself instead of shrinking into the corner.

Maybe this plan of Alex's is helping me in more ways than one. Because yeah, while I know I'm destined to be with Cora, this year has also been about making a real friend, too.

I've never had someone like Alex to listen and hang out and tell me the things that she must not share very often. I mean yeah, she gets under my skin just like my mom does, but . . . any best friend knows how to do that.

Any *best friend*.

Huh . . .

I can't put my finger on when exactly it happened, but I think it might be the truth.

I just wish she hadn't run off last night.

It makes me think maybe this whole thing isn't *just* about helping me break out of my shell anymore. Maybe it's actually about both of us. Because I think in some small way, I'm helping her, too, and she finds it just as scary as I did.

My phone vibrates in my pocket, and I pull it out to find a text from Cora.

Abby and I are hitting up the library tonight if you and Alex want to join 📚

Cool, when? We'll meet you there!

6. Main floor. I'll be the one next to the girl complaining a lot 😊

I reply with a 😂. Abby spent most of biology class today groaning about how she doesn't understand any of it, even though we're still in the basic introduction to the class.

Library with Cora and Abby tonight at 6!!! I text Alex.

YOU asked her!? 🙄 Slow DOWN, you're jumping ahead in the plan! JKJK

I laugh, but as I'm typing up a reply, a text comes in from my mom. I quickly swipe it out of sight to finish my text to Alex.

Lol no, Cora texted ME!

Even better. Wow I am GOOD. Meet you there.

One second later . . .

AND MOLLY YOU BETTER WEAR THE NEW CLOTHES IDC IF ITS BLIZZARDING

I smile to myself as I toss my phone onto the bed and slip out of my raincoat. I still haven't found the time to clean up, so I have to step around all the clothes that are strewn about my room from Alex's *Queer Eye* closet cleanout.

I run my hand across my new jeans, draped over the back of my desk chair, then look over at my new shirts, hanging up in my near-empty closet.

I feel a lot less nervous about wearing my new clothes in front of Cora after my successful interaction with Jordan. I try to remember how I felt looking at myself in the mirror at the mall. These clothes are only going to add to my confidence tonight, and I'll take all I can get.

CHAPTER 23

ALEX

I duck inside the library, completely soaked from head to toe. Nothing like biking down a hill in a torrential downpour to make you feel alive.

As I'm drying my squeaking shoes off on the entryway rug, a hand wraps around my arm, pulling me into a small alcove just next to the front doors.

"Ew," Molly says, rubbing her hand against her new Levi's jeans. "You're wet."

I roll my eyes, then pretend to squeegee the edge of my shirt onto her. She jumps out of the way, glaring at me. "Yeah, well, I would've waited out the storm in the chem building if it weren't for *someone* texting me every ten seconds asking when I was getting here."

I crane my neck, looking past her into the main room, my eyes landing on a rectangular table by the café where Abby and Cora are already sitting, books open in front of them.

"Did you go over yet, or have you just been creepily standing by the front door this whole time?"

"Creepily standing by the front door," Molly replies, hoisting up the straps on her enormous backpack.

I give her a once-over. Not only does she clearly own an umbrella, but she looks pretty good. She's got her new jeans on and a cute graphic T-shirt we picked up from H&M, her dark-brown hair in a messy bun to protect it from the rain.

I nod, slightly impressed. It's a definite improvement from her usual four outfits. "I like your jeans!"

Molly's cheeks redden slightly. "Thanks." She glances down at her clothes. "Took me, like, an hour to decide on an outfit. Wanted to save the best stuff for a real date."

"Nice. I like that kind of thinking. Now . . ." I grab *her* arm this time, spinning her around to face the main floor of the library. "Let's see what Cora thinks."

We head over to the table, and Cora and Abby look up as we arrive.

"Hey!" Cora says, scooching her books closer to make room for us. Abby follows suit, hoisting her enormous engineering textbook out of the way, a sea of brightly colored highlighters sitting in front of her.

"Hey," Molly responds as she . . . plunks down in the chair farthest from Cora.

"Cute shirt!" Abby says, and Cora nods in agreement, which . . . is better than nothing.

"Hey, Molly," I say, tapping her chair leg with my foot. "Don't you need to use the outlet?" I nod to the open seat *directly across* from Cora, hoping she gets the hint.

Thankfully, she does.

"Oh! Right. Yeah," Molly says, her eyes wide with nerves as she switches seats.

Pull it together, kid. The whole team is counting on you.

"You do the reading for Jon's class?" Cora asks, holding up a copy of *1984.*

Molly and I nod, and I give her a look that screams, *Say something.*

"Yeah, uh, thought we left that in high school, but I guess not."

Good, finally some progress. The joke hits and Cora laughs, shaking her head. "Tell me about it. Once was *more* than enough."

On this particular book, I actually agree with her.

The small talk gives way to studying, and I spend the next hour trying to be interested in ionic and covalent bonds, while Molly not-so-casually glances across the table at Cora a hundred and one times, her pen tapping noisily against her notebook.

I lean back and stretch, my damp clothes squeaking on the chair under me as I eye the bookshelves at the front of the library.

I'm already through the chunky fantasy I got the second

week of classes, and I've been itching to grab a couple of books after my fight with Natalie. And with my mom. Especially since I haven't heard from either of them since last night.

My fingers tap on the table in front of me as I glance down at my phone. No new messages.

Feeling guilty over what I said last night, I sent my mom fifty dollars this morning, and she sent it back instantly, without a word of explanation. I tried calling her and she wouldn't pick up. Tried texting her . . . no reply.

I know it shouldn't make me nervous. I mean, her bills are on autopay, and I have groceries delivered, and Tonya's swinging by to check in on her, but I haven't been able to stop . . .

I scoot my chair back and stand, everyone's heads turning to look up at my sudden movement.

Relax, Alex. Play it cool.

"I'm gonna take a lap. Can't learn any more about atomic bonds with the temptation of a new read just inches away, am I right?" I say, stretching casually before pushing my chair in and heading across the main floor to disappear into the stacks. Molly's eyes widen at my words, but I give her shoulder a reassuring squeeze as I pass.

On my way, I catch sight of Heather, my roommate, waiting in a line at the café. I nod hello, and she miraculously gives me a small wave back.

Talk about progress!

Jackson hasn't been around as much, so I've been wondering if that's been the cause for the slight uptick in niceties. She even said thank you to me the other night for taking out the trash.

I should probably start making our friendship bracelets now.

I head to the young adult fiction section, where I grab a *Romeo and Juliet* retelling and a fantasy book I've seen plastered all over BookTok, before scooping up a couple of old favorites: *Cyrano de Bergerac, Little Women,* and *Pride and Prejudice.* That last one has been stuck in my head since my questions game with Molly last week. I know I won't have time to read all of them in two weeks, but just having them makes me feel more grounded, and with everything going on with Natalie and my mom, I definitely need that.

When I get back to the table, Cora is *belly laughing* at something Molly said, and Molly is grinning from ear to ear like she just won an Oscar.

"Jeez," she says, prodding my stack of books as I set them down on the table. "Why exactly are you premed when all you do is read?"

I slap her prodding finger away. "I don't know, job security? A $208,000 starting salary?"

Molly rolls her eyes. "Do you even like this stuff?" she asks, holding up my chem textbook, her arm giving way from the weight.

"Not particularly," I say as I grab it back from her. I point to Cora's copy of *1984*. "But you don't like *that* stuff, so . . ."

"Yeah, but you *love* this stuff. Probably more than either of us," Molly says as she pulls *Pride and Prejudice* from my stack. Cora nods in agreement from across the table. "Can you say that about anything in premed?"

I raise my eyebrows at her. "Did you not hear me say 'a $208,000 starting salary'?"

"Oh, come on," Cora says. "Money's not as important as doing what you love."

I roll my eyes so hard they practically pop out of my skull. "Do either of you even *know* what you're going to do to pay the bills with a degree in English?"

Molly shrugs. "Well, no. Not yet, but—"

"That doesn't matter right now." Cora speaks over her, jumping to her defense.

Seriously? I open my mouth to say something, but Molly swoops in, trying to smooth things over.

"I think they can both be important. Money, doing what you love," she says, glancing between me and Cora, her eyes landing and staying on mine. "Agree to disagree, I guess."

She gives me an apologetic smile and plunks the book back down on top of the pile. I snort and scoop it up, opening to the first page, glad for once that the conversation is over.

But . . . the words blur in front of me as I keep thinking about it. While I'm not sure I really want to spend the next decade in school for something I don't even like, I don't exactly have the luxury of worrying about what I *do* like. I don't have the privilege to just *do what I love*. Not with things the way they are. Not when I have to support my mom.

I glance over at my phone, resisting the urge to send *another* text her way.

"Well, I'm going to get something from the café," Molly says, scooching her chair back.

"I'll come with you!" Cora says. Molly's eyes form a near-perfect imitation of a deer caught in the headlights. But she pulls herself together quickly.

I swallow my annoyance and shoot her a thumbs-up when Cora ducks down to grab her wallet out of her bright yellow backpack.

"You guys want anything?" Cora asks.

"Chocolate chip cookie," Abby says, handing Cora her dining card to scan.

I shake my head, watching them walk off. Molly's hands are nervously shoved into the pockets of her jeans as Cora talks about the biscotti she got here the other day that Molly just *has* to try.

I smile to myself, a wave of relief washing over me. How about that, Natalie? Talk about progress!

It's a weird feeling, though. Especially after the less-than-ideal phone call the other day. Like . . . this might not prove anything to her anymore, but even if it doesn't, I just . . .

I genuinely want Molly to succeed. Because I care about her. Because she's my friend. No matter what Natalie thinks.

I shake my head and look back down at my book.

Let step three commence.

CHAPTER 24

MOLLY

I place my hands firmly on either side of her shoulders, looking her square in the eye. A bead of sweat rolls down my forehead as the voices around us grow more and more muffled, until it's just me . . . and her.

"Blackwood, I need you to focus. Do you hear me?" I say, more seriously than I've said anything before. She nods, firm, like she understands the gravity of the situation.

"Are you two going to make out or are we going to play?" Kendall asks, pulling us out of our huddle and back into the Holland Hall common room. They have a challenging smirk smeared across their face as they bounce the ball off the worn Ping-Pong table.

"Just serve the ball," I say, doing my best to swallow a laugh and keep a straight face for the sake of the competition. Alex looks at me and then across the table to Jordan and Kendall, our opponents.

"I have *never* seen her like this," Alex says through an amused chuckle.

"Twenty, eighteen. Game point," Jordan announces as Kendall serves the ball, and just like that we're in it. All four of us are laser-focused as we volley back and forth.

I was pretty nervous to come to the first game night by myself, but even though I know Alex is on a deadline, I'm not at that point with Cora yet, so naturally, I asked Alex to join me. The nerves wore off surprisingly quickly, though. Something about getting my blood pumping playing a game that I *love* really set me at ease and helped me to just be myself.

Alex is holding up her side of the table pretty well, considering how little she's played, but Kendall is *good.* If we're going to beat them, I need to pull out a few tricks that Noah taught me over summer breaks when he was home from college.

As the ball comes flying off Jordan's paddle and over to me, I attempt a return with backspin, but it falls a little flat . . . right into Kendall's corner.

"You trying for this, Molly?" they ask, sliding the paddle at a perfect angle, along the bottom of the ball. It sails over the net to Alex, who is not at all ready for the abrupt backspin. She swings her paddle right through empty air, and the ball goes bouncing onto the floor.

Game over.

"Dang!" I yell, before a smile spreads across my face. "Good game, good game."

"Sorry, Parker," Alex says.

"We'll get 'em next time," I reply, loud enough for our opponents to hear.

"Like hell you will," Jordan says with a laugh as the two girls who live across the hall from me take our paddles to play the winners.

Alex and I head over to the "potluck table," which is just a bunch of incredibly low-quality snacks spread out across a pool table that's so old, the green felt is practically gray. We were all asked to bring something. I managed to cut up a block of cheddar cheese and put it with some crackers on a paper plate, and Alex brought two bags of chips from, wait for it . . . 7-Eleven.

"Oh my God, who did this?" I ask, directing Alex's attention to an open tube of raw cookie dough, a plastic knife stuck into the top.

"I don't know, but I think I might marry them," she replies as I twist my face up in disgust, watching her cut off a slab from the end and pop the whole thing into her mouth.

"That is *so* gross." I reach for a couple of 7-Eleven chips.

"Hey." Alex pauses to move the mass of cookie dough into her cheek so she can talk. "You're, like . . . *really* good. I thought you told me you weren't a 'sporty lesbian.'" She says the last bit with air quotes.

"Ping-Pong isn't a sport. It's an art form," I say.

Alex shoves me playfully in response. "You're ridiculous."

A text buzzes in, and I pull out my phone to find a whole chain of texts from my mom that I must've missed during the heat of the game.

The first is a picture of Leonard, chasing a flock of geese into a pond at the park.

I'm taking a walk with your dad.

I was thinking about coming down tomorrow?

Maybe lunch with your brother?

How's Alex? Did you wear any of your new clothes yet?

Are you busy?

Molly?

Do you want to do lunch?

. . . I'll take that as a no?

"Oh my God, my mom is like . . ." My voice trails off as I tuck my phone into my pocket and rub my face in frustration.

"What?" Alex asks, smearing cookie dough on top of one of the crackers I brought.

"She's just being, like . . . *a lot*. I told her that I needed some space, but . . . it seemed to only work for about a week."

"Maybe you should just call her? When's the last time you talked to her?" she asks.

"That's not the point. I mean, I'm in college now. She can't just come crashing into my dorm room unannounced and whisk me away for a *girls' day* whenever she wants."

"Molly, I think she just wants to be a part of your life," Alex says. "I mean, I would kinda kill for a mom that actually . . . cares."

"Oh. Sorry. I . . ." I want to be sympathetic, but I don't want her to run away again, like she did the other night. I decide that the best thing to do is to explain myself. "I just . . . for a long time my mom was my best friend. My only friend. But now . . . I need some freaking space from her. I'm trying to gain a little independence." I take a deep breath. "I mean, it's working. *This* is working. I'm like a different person from the one who moved here at the beginning of the semester."

"Yeah." She huffs out a laugh, thinking of some embarrassing memory of me, I'm sure. "You've come a long way, but we still have three more steps, and—"

"Alex, Molly, you two ready for a rematch?" Jordan asks.

"We'll go easy on you this time," Kendall adds. I shake my head with a laugh as I try to push my mom out of my mind.

We step up to the table, but just as they're about to serve, my phone buzzes in my pocket a couple of times.

"Hang on." I slip it out, thinking it might be Cora, but it's *still* my mom, and this time she's trying to call me. I flip the phone for Alex to see, letting my shoulders drop.

"Maybe just answer it?" she says with a cringe, knowing that I don't want to.

"Be right back," I say to Kendall and Jordan before stepping out into the hall. I swipe right and my mom's grainy face comes into view.

"Hey, baby! Ooooh, what's that? Sounds like you're with your friends? *Friends*. I *love* that!" she says, and I glance behind me, realizing she can hear them on the other side of the double doors. I step down the hall to get away from it, then lean back against the wall.

"Mom, what's up?" I say, trying to not sound too irritated, but it's not easy right now.

"I was just calling to catch up. It's been a while."

"It's been, like, three days," I reply, another stab of frustration hitting me as I remember what happened that day at the food court.

"I know, I just——" she starts.

"Mom, I gotta go. I'm busy right now, okay?" I tap my foot against the floor over and over.

"Okay, I won't keep you from your friends. But don't forget to call me sometime when you're free."

"Sure," I reply shortly, before ending the call and slipping the phone back into my pocket.

Alex hands me my paddle as I step back into the room to join her at the table. I try to forget about it as we play, but there's a nagging feeling in the back of my head that I can't shake.

I just *know* at some point I need to have a *real* talk with my mom about this, about needing space from her. About that embarrassing scene at the food court and what that stuff does to me. But not right now. Right now, all I want to do is crush this game.

CHAPTER 25

ALEX

I can't believe I'm watching a rugby game. On a *Friday* *night.* I used to go out! I used to go to parties!

Who'd have thought my life would come to this?

I lock up my bike and jog across the street to where the field is. The crowd explodes in cheers as a girl in maroon and white gets pancaked like Molly did two weeks ago, the ball tumbling out of her grip.

"You're late," a familiar voice calls out, Molly Parker leaning against a huge oak tree, her arms crossed over her chest. "As usual."

"I brought snacks," I say, holding up a paper bag with the same kind of sugar cookie she bought that one time at the library before class. I don't add the fact that I ate three on the way here.

"Way to show your school pride," Molly prods, pushing off the tree to inspect my all-black outfit.

She's decked out in Pitt gear. Head-to-toe blue and gold. Her underwear probably even has "PITT" stamped across the butt.

"Well, they're playing a Philly team, so I have to be Switzer-land," I say, giving her a big grin as she slowly unwinds the scarf she's wearing. "Kissed too many Temple girls to betray their trust now."

She rolls her eyes and turns to face me, standing on her tippy-toes to wrap the scarf once, twice around my neck. "Well, you're here now, so start acting like it."

Our eyes lock as she tucks the corner in.

With her so close, I can't help but think of that moment in the changing room. The way Molly's eyes . . . I clear my throat, and we move apart.

It was *nothing*. People look at me like that *all* the time.

Besides, I'm not her type at *all*, just like she's *definitely* not mine.

"So, do you have *any* idea how a rugby game works?" I mumble to her as Abby waves us over from the metal bleachers.

"Oh yeah," she says as we climb up. "From my near-death experience after three minutes of play, I'm a certified expert."

I chuckle as we slide into our spots, nodding hello to Abby. "What'd we miss?"

"Not much," she says, like I didn't just see a human person turn into a real-life Flat Stanley on the way over. "No one's scored yet, which is better than losing."

I watch as the players on both teams pack closely together,

arms over waists, the ball rolled into the middle as Pitt gains dominance and pushes down the field with it. The people all around us go wild.

"Oh, what a scrum!" a guy on the bleachers calls, clapping loudly as our team manages to move the ball well over a few feet and gain possession.

A *what now*?

I raise my eyebrows at Molly and she shrugs, reaching into the paper bag I'm holding to break off a piece of cookie. Crumbs tumble onto her faded jeans as she freezes, her eyes widening when she catches sight of Cora, jogging down the field like a tiny, graceful gazelle, sending a small wave in our direction as she goes. She has on a mustard-yellow sweatband and an aggressive amount of eye black, smeared messily down her cheeks like she's heading into war.

Which is fair.

I'm not sure if I'm watching a sport or . . . a fight-to-the-death gladiator battle. Two girls are carted off by halftime, one with a concussion, the other with a broken nose. I wince and turn away at the sight of the blood dripping down her face, Molly giving me an amused look.

"Thought you were going to be a doctor?"

I glare at her, chucking the rolled-up paper bag in her direction as we slide off the bleachers to stretch our legs for a few minutes.

"I'm gonna run to the bathroom," Abby says, nodding toward a precarious trio of baby-blue porta-potties.

We watch her jog off, and I wait until she's a safe distance away to say, "So, we should probably talk about step—"

Molly smacks her hand over my mouth. "Nope. Not now."

I furrow my eyebrows, wrangling out of her grip. "What? Why not?"

"I know you're on a time crunch, but I'm not . . . ready. I mean, texting her is going so well, I don't want to ruin it."

I give her a look. "Molly. You're not going to *ruin it*. If anything—"

"I'm not ready, okay?" she says, cutting me off, her voice firm. I let out a long exhale, shaking my head. Time is running out, but more importantly . . .

"Listen, that's cool with me, but just know, she isn't going to wait forever. . . ." I nod behind her, and she spins around to see Cora on the bench, laughing at something one of her teammates is saying, her hand resting on their forearm. There's *definitely* some flirty energy behind it.

I turn Molly back around to face me before her gaping can become too obvious. "So, like, no rush. I don't want to push you into something you're not ready for. But don't wait too long and lose your chance, okay?"

She nods, biting her lip.

When the game starts up again, we slide back into the

bleachers, and I pull my phone out of my pocket and swipe into my text thread with my mom.

Hey. Hope your day is going well.

I tap send, adding another text to a sea of blue messages on the right side, the occasional one-word response appearing on the left. She's been increasingly erratic about texting since our fight almost two weeks ago.

Luckily, Tonya's been checking up on her, and she says nothing seems super out of the ordinary, but . . . I'm still worried. And even though I feel guilty, I'm also the tiniest bit annoyed. I shouldn't be sitting here worrying about my mom in the middle of a college rugby game.

The crowd begins to erupt in cheers, and I swing my head up to see a girl in blue and gold making a break for it, ball tucked under her arm. Even though I have no idea what's happening, I get all swept up in it too. Everyone jumps to their feet, the stands shaking with cheers as she makes her way down the field, a defender hot on her tail.

Fifteen yards.

Ten yards.

Five yards.

She makes it to the end zone, slamming the ball defiantly into the ground, her teammates swarming her as the crowd goes wild all around me. I rip Molly's scarf off and swing it over my head as Molly hops up onto her seat next to me. Abby starts a "Let's go, Panthers!" chant from her other side, and all of us join in.

Soon our cheering dies down as the game resumes, and everyone takes their seats. I watch as Cora jogs off the field, high-fiving her substitute as she goes.

There's an unexpected feeling in my chest as she gives Molly a small smile before taking the bench.

I rub the spot thoughtfully.

Probably shouldn't have eaten three cookies on my way here.

CHAPTER 26

MOLLY

Still floating from watching Cora kick some absolute ass on the rugby pitch yesterday, I follow the groups of students across the quad until I catch sight of what *used* to be Bigelow Boulevard but is now a mini street fair. I can already smell the food cooking as I walk through the grass, getting a peek of a woman dangling from two long ribbons of fabric attached to a pole fifteen feet above the ground right in front of the Cathedral. An oversize banner hangs from a metal frame, reading BIGELOW BASH, an event that Pitt puts on every year.

There's an ocean of sweaty students, all stuffed into picnic tables set up in the middle of the street. There are about thirty white tents on either side of them, giving out free samples and selling art. On the opposite end of the street, the food vendors are lined up along the wooden barriers blocking traffic from coming through.

My phone buzzes in my hand, and I raise it to find my

mom calling for the second time today. I talked to her for a couple of minutes this morning, but she started asking all kinds of questions about Cora and whether we had "linked up" yet. It's like she thinks that's the only reason I could be busy.

Then I tried to switch topics, to tell her about the food trucks on campus, but that didn't go so well either. After I mentioned Bulgogi Boyz would be here, I could practically hear her curling her lip up as she told me to be careful what I ordered, since "you never know what they put in that stuff."

What a fucked-up thing to say. Not that I haven't heard it from her before. My blood was practically boiling under my skin, so I ended the conversation pretty quickly. And I'm not about to go for round two, so I send her straight to voicemail.

I head toward the food vendors, where the crowd is much thinner. I'm not here for whatever is in the tents *or* to watch a woman twist herself around on a couple of ribbons. I'm just here to see . . .

That.

Alex hangs out the window of a black food truck at the back of the line, the generator growling loudly as it struggles to power everything. They're not very busy, only a couple of people waiting in line to order.

When she told me her food truck was working Bigelow Bash today, I *had* to see it for myself. Plus, she promised she could score me a free cheesesteak if I came at closing time.

I'm five minutes early, so I grab a seat off to the side on the curb to watch Alex work.

There's something about seeing her serve the public that makes me chuckle.

I mean, I wasn't expecting anything glamorous, but it looks like it's . . . actually pretty tough. From the sweat beading Alex's face, I'd say it's even hotter than it looks in there.

And then there's her boss, who looks a little rougher around the edges than she let on. I watch him hop down off the back of the truck, light up a cigarette, and basically shotgun his secondhand smoke right into the face of a customer who just picked up his food.

I look back at Alex, who has a very fake customer service smile plastered on, and grin. The customers probably don't know it's fake, but I do. I've gotten pretty good at reading her the last few weeks. I watch as she takes an upperclassman's order at the window, asking for his first name along with it. He reaches into the back pocket of his jeans and hands over some cash for the order.

"Well, you've got my name. You want my number, too, babe?" he asks, grabbing on to his oversize belt buckle like he's the campus sheriff.

I wait for her to flirt with him, to brush her long blond hair behind one ear and charm him into leaving a big tip. But instead, she drops the phony smile, giving him an almost despondent look that I've seen only once before.

It's the way she looked at me before rugby tryouts, when she talked about how people treat her like a "bimbo" because she looks the way she does. I've never given much thought to how people thinking you're hot could possibly be a negative, but . . . clearly it can suck around assholes like this. Or even not total assholes. *I* jumped to conclusions about her, which, after seeing this . . . makes me feel even crappier. I didn't treat her much better than Belt Buckle is.

I always accused people of not giving me a chance, but that's what I did to her.

"Come on," he presses. "I'll take you somewhere real nice."

Alex rolls her eyes as she digs his change out of the register. Normally I'm *sure* she'd defend herself just like she did with me, but maybe she doesn't want to make a scene in front of her boss.

Just as she's about to hand him the change, Jim steps up from behind her. He takes the guy's ten back out of the register and leans out the window.

"Why don't you take *yourself* somewhere real nice?" he says, throwing the bill out the window, making Belt Buckle chase it all the way down to the sidewalk.

"You're gonna regret that," Belt Buckle says, still struggling to pick up the bill. "I'm gonna trash your Facebook page with one-star reviews."

"Do we look like the type of truck to have a Facebook?" Jim asks, and I can say based on the peeling plywood menu and the pile of cigarette butts on the ground just outside the back door that they absolutely do not.

"Well, I'll—"

"Get lost, pal," Jim says, before turning back to the grill, the conversation over. Alex smiles, and Belt Buckle mutters a few cusswords under his breath, but he does what he's told and heads back toward the sea of students.

A few minutes later Alex jumps out the back door holding two sandwiches wrapped in foil and two old-fashioned grape sodas in glass bottles. I wave her down, and she jogs over to me, juggling everything in her hands. The moment she sits next to me on the curb, a wave of burger meat and fry grease hits me right in the olfactories.

"You smell," I say, scrunching my face up at her.

"You want a sandwich or not?" she asks, wiping the sweat off her brow. I smile, and she slaps the heavy tinfoil lump into my waiting hands with a thud.

"You two make quite the pair," I say, nodding in her boss's direction as he pulls the hand-painted menu board off the side of the truck.

"Me and Jim?" Alex laughs. "He's an interesting guy. A good one."

She sinks her teeth into her sandwich, the melted cheese stretching as she pulls away.

Just then my phone lights up, sitting between us on the curb.

Cora Myers: iMessage

"Umm. *Excuse me?*" Alex says in a sassy voice as she quickly scoops it up.

"Hey!" I swipe for it, but she leans away, blocking me with her sandwich arm, the melted cheese almost dripping onto my leg.

"Just shut up and let me look," she says, and I stop fighting. Instead, I unwrap my sandwich as I watch her scroll up through our lengthy text chain from this past week. Our texting frequency has really ramped up since our study session at the library. We're sort of just texting constantly, sometimes saying good night but never goodbye. I still feel like I'm playing a part, like I'm not *really* being myself around her even via text. But I'll get there.

"When were you going to tell me about this!?" she gasps.

"What? You *know* we've been texting," I reply.

"But, Molly, you didn't tell me she was texting you like *this*! You gotta keep me updated on this stuff!" She turns the phone to face me, revealing Cora's newest text.

Hey! Thanks for coming to cheer me on yesterday! ♥ 😊 What are you up to this weekend?

My entire body buzzes with excitement as I snatch the phone out of her hands, holding it right up to my face.

"She's never asked me something like *this* before," I say, looking over at Alex in disbelief.

"There are *a lot* of emojis in these texts. *And* she just sent a heart? She's *totally* into you. Like . . . for sure."

"But . . . ," I start as my self-doubts start to kick in. "Emojis don't always equate to that. I mean, you use a lot of them when you text me," I say, showing her our chain.

"Well, yeah." She pauses to take a swig of grape soda. "But that's different. I always text like that."

I squint at her suspiciously.

"Molly, I'm serious. I'm *positive* she likes you," she says. "She just texted you out of the blue to ask what you're doing this weekend! Why else would she do that?"

"Maybe she wants to study with us again," I reply in a mousey voice, and Alex sighs.

"She wants to hang out with *you*," she says. "Which is *perfect*, because step three is to ask her out!"

"ASK HER OUT!?" I practically yell, a group of students looking over at us. I take a second to swallow and gather myself, lowering my voice, mortified. "How is that the next step and not, like, step ten? That's like teaching me how to doggy-paddle and then dumping me off in the middle of the Pacific. I can't *ask her out*." I laugh a crazy-sounding laugh. "From getting a new shirt to asking Cora out on an *actual* date? What kind of crappy plan is this? How does that make any sense at all?"

"Molly—"

"No, Alex. I don't know how to do that." I thought I had a hold on this whole game plan of hers, but I'm absolutely spiraling, here in the middle of campus. *Spiraling!*

"Molly, I—"

"I've literally never asked a single person out in my life. Nor have I ever been asked out! I don't think I've ever even asked someone to hang out as friends. How do you expect me to—"

"*Molly! Shut up for a second!*" She raises her voice, holding her hands out in front of her. "*Jesus Christ.* You are so *fucking* dramatic." She laughs. "Three weeks ago I watched you spill a drink on a girl while trying to get her number. I *know* you don't know how to ask someone out. That's why it's *in the plan.* That's why you're going to ask . . ." She puts her hands over her chest. "Me."

"What?" I ask, plummeting back down to earth. She wants me to ask *her* out?

She sits up straight as a pole and tucks her long blond hair behind her ears and into her shirt to make it look shorter. "I'm a lit major, but Shakespeare sucks. I punctured a lung at rugby practice this week." She plasters the biggest smile she can manage to go with her breathy, high-pitched voice. "Are you going to ask me out or what?"

Oh. Ask her out *for practice.*

"Okay." I suppress a laugh. "First of all, she does *not* sound like that. Second of all, forget even asking her out, because I don't know what to do if she says yes. Or . . ." I bury my face in my hands. "*Oh my God*, what if she says no?"

"Look," Alex says, dropping back to her regular voice and

letting herself slouch again. She's quiet for a long moment as I watch the wheels turn in her brain, like she's deciding something. "We'll go on a mock date. Okay?" she finally says. "Step four is to actually go on the date. So, we'll practice both at once. You'll ask me out and then we'll go on a fake date, and then you'll be ready for the real thing. Cool?" she asks. "Now do it. Ask me. Er . . . wait!" She sets her sandwich down quickly on the curb, pulling out her phone. "Ask me over text. That's probably how you'll ask *her*. So you might as well get some practice."

She's right. Besides, seeing Cora be flirty with her teammate yesterday really lit a fire under me. I need to get this right so I can successfully ask Cora before it's too late. *Plus*, Natalie's concert is in six days. Alex has done so much for me. I'd really like to be able to follow through with what she needs from me.

My thumbs hover over my keyboard as I take in a deep breath and look down the street at the crowd of students starting to disperse back to their dorms. Where would I even ask her to go?

The movies, but that's so overdone. And we wouldn't be able to talk at all.

Dinner. *No. Too much* talking. And chewing.

Then it hits me. I can't believe I completely forgot for a second. It's been my dream date for as long as I can remember. I just never thought I'd *actually* get the chance to see it through. I think back to my childhood, all the weekends spent at the roller rink with Noah when we were kids, having to get off the floor during the couples' skate. It's perfect for a first date with Cora. We'd sort of have to stay close to each other, *and* if we're any good, we maybe could actually do the couples' skate.

Alex, do you want to go roller-skating with me tomorrow night? I type, adding and then deleting a smiley face emoji. I know Alex would tell me not to come on *too* strong.

"For real? You really want to go roller-skating?" she asks, audibly suppressing a laugh.

I look over at her, sending her my best glare. If *Cora* ever reacted like that, I would *die*. But she would never, because I'm sure she'd love roller-skating. And it's something I know I'm actually good at.

"You know, I used to win, like . . . *all* the girls' races when I was a kid!" I say, defending the one somewhat sporty thing I can do, aside from Ping-Pong.

"Wow, impressive. No wonder you're beating the ladies off with a stick," she says, every syllable dripping with sarcasm.

"Hey! Skating is getting cool again. Maybe you're the one who has to catch up with the trend for once." I shove her lightly in the arm.

"I know, I know. I'm just picturing you kicking a bunch of little kids' asses at the roller rink in front of Cora," she says, giggling.

"Isn't that exactly what you would tell me to do? Pick somewhere that I can impress her?" I ask, ignoring her comment.

"Huh. She learns," Alex replies.

I lift my head, surprised. "You sound impressed."

"I just hope you're as good as you think you are," she says.

"I guess you'll just have to wait and see," I reply.

"I guess I will." She looks down, and her thumbs glide across her screen.

A few seconds later a text comes in on my phone.

I would love to go roller-skating with you, Molly Parker. 🛼 ☺

My cheeks feel warm at just her words. I can't even imagine what it'll feel like seeing something like that from Cora. But it actually feels . . . not impossible now.

And skating circles around Alex Blackwood won't be such a bad feeling either.

CHAPTER 27

ALEX

I toss my eyeliner back in my makeup bag and lean back to inspect my face in the bathroom mirror one last time, exhaling slowly as I wrap my fingers around the cool porcelain sink. I bounce my leg up and down as I stare at my reflection, turning my head left and right and left again, my fingers running through my hair, trying to get it to fall *just right*.

Am I . . . *nervous*?

"It's *roller-skating*, Alex. How hard could it be?" I snort and pluck my phone off the counter. The screen lights up with a text from Molly, letting me know she's waiting outside.

I grab my wallet and keys from my bedroom and head down the stairs, slipping my arms into my faded-blue denim jacket along the way. I stop short when I push open the door to see Molly leaning against her car. She's wearing the high-waisted Levi's jeans and formfitting white T-shirt we bought together, along with a black-and-yellow checkered flannel that's tied tastefully around her waist. Her long hair lightly catches the breeze like we're smack in the middle of a movie instead of standing on one of the grossest streets in Pittsburgh.

I open my mouth to say something, but her eyes catch me off guard, a thin layer of mascara and eyeliner making the light brown stand out in a way I've never noticed before.

I don't think I've ever seen her wearing makeup.

"Shit," she says, pushing off the car and looking down at her outfit, her brow furrowing. "Did I screw it up?" She tugs at the shirt tied around her waist. "It's the flannel, isn't it? I *knew* I should've just worn a button-down instead. . . ."

"No. You just . . . look . . . you look . . . really pretty," I manage to get out, looking at the way the jeans accentuate the curve of her hips.

Molly's hips, I remind myself, and pull my eyes quickly away.

Her head swings up in surprise. I clear my throat, hurriedly course-correcting. "You know, like, *objectively*, of course. That's what Cora will say anyway."

"Oh," she says. The both of us just stare at each other.

Say something, Alex. Why am I so tongue-tied? *Who am I?*

I scratch my neck and point at the car door. "We should . . ."

"Right! Yeah." She fumbles with her keys and unlocks the car door with a beep before she pulls it open and motions for me to get inside.

"So chivalrous," I tease as I slide past her.

She rolls her eyes, but the tension breaks like I hoped. "Honestly, Alex, get in before I slam the door on you."

We both laugh as she jogs around the front and gets into the driver's seat. The radio hums to life as we pull off down the road. The drive to the roller-skating rink takes us on a scenic view of Pittsburgh, the city skyline illuminated in the golden light of the setting sun.

It's no Philly, but . . . it's actually kind of nice. Beautiful, even, this city I've escaped to. I crane my neck to gaze out the car window at it until it fades from view, the highway taking its place.

"Conversation topics," I say as we drive. "What are you thinking?"

Molly shrugs, her hands tightening on the steering wheel. "Right. I've got a bunch. I was thinking I'd start by asking her about bio class. Follow it up with some rugby talk. Maybe just . . . see how her day is going?"

"*Yes*," I say, nodding. "But especially that last one. People *love* to talk about themselves."

Molly shoots me a look, one of her eyebrows rising. "Tell me about it."

I grin. "Whatever she starts talking about, ask follow-up questions. Build a conversation off that. It'll show you're listening to what she's saying, and there's nothing better than feeling like you're being heard."

Molly nods, taking it all in.

When we arrive twenty minutes later, the rink is surprisingly packed. The smell of old carpet, feet, and whatever greasy food the concession stand is churning out fills my nose, and I'm relieved the lights are dim except for the glittering silver disco ball in the center of the rink, because I'm pretty sure this place should *never* see the light of day.

"The car door move was a nice touch," I say as we buy tickets, leaning closer to her so she can hear me over the enormous speakers blasting out "September" by Earth, Wind & Fire. "*Next*, I'd say you should at least offer to pay for Cora. Especially if you ask her on the date." Molly freezes, her hand still in her wallet.

"Should I . . . pay . . . for you now?"

I pull a ten out of my pocket, shaking my head. "We don't have to practice that part. I mean, this isn't a real date."

She nods, and we both fall silent as the cashier counts our change and begins the hunt for our skate sizes. When she returns with them, we both reach at the same time, and our arms brush lightly together.

Hmm . . . maybe roller-skating *isn't* a terrible date idea after all. Definitely not in my usual wheelhouse, but I can admittedly see how it has all the makings of a solid first date. Some flirting, a little hand-holding, maybe something from the snack shack? It could work.

I can't help but laugh as Molly tests out the wheels on

276

both our pairs, spinning each one individually, before nodding her approval, like she's sampling a fancy wine at a Michelin-starred restaurant.

This is going to be quite a night.

Getting the skates *on* is no trouble at all.

Actually trying to use them is hell itself.

After I stutter-stepped across the black speckled carpet, saying as much of the Hail Mary as I know, I ventured onto the glossy wooden floor.

Which was . . . a huge mistake.

Immediately I clutched at the wall for support as skaters whizzed past. And every time I've tried to move since then, I can feel my legs flailing in two different directions.

So, naturally, I have decided to just stop trying altogether and cling to the wall for dear life.

"You've just got to go for it!" Molly says as she skates in small circles, *backward*, right in front of me.

I glare up at her, my fingernails digging into the wall as I clomp my way forward. "If I just *go for it*, I'll—"

The words aren't even out of my mouth before they come to fruition. I wipe out *hard*, the skates sliding out from under me as I ass-plant on the wooden floor. The base of my spine practically splinters into a million pieces. I lie there, flat as a pancake, staring up at the white ceiling as the disco ball sends out glittering rays of light.

I turn my head to see Molly whiz past, doing a very quick spin stop just in front of me.

"*Very* graceful," she says, obviously enjoying this.

"Don't talk to me," I say, my eyes moving from her face back to the ceiling. "Just leave me to die."

"Well, you never listen to me," she says, smiling as she leans forward. "So, I'm not listening now."

She holds out her hand, raising her eyebrows at me, and I let out a long sigh and grab on. She pulls me up, but to my surprise, she doesn't let go once I'm upright.

"We'll take it slow, okay?" she says, her fingers warm and soft as she slowly begins to skate backward, pulling me gently with her. I can feel my stomach actually flip over.

"Now, *this*," I say, as I quickly slip my hands out of hers, "is an excellent move to pull with Cora."

The words are barely out of my mouth before I begin to flail wildly, but Molly grabs my shoulders, keeping me balanced.

I grin sheepishly at her, and she shakes her head at me.

Her fingertips slide down my arms, taking my hands again, her grip firm as we glide across the floor. We go around and around in circles, getting faster with each lap that passes. I practically glue my eyes to our skates and the steady rhythm they're keeping, so I barely notice the silence between us.

Right, left, right, left.

"See?" she whispers, her voice barely louder than the music. "This isn't so bad."

I look up to meet her gaze, ready to tell her I think I *literally* broke my ass when I fell, but the words get caught in my throat.

Her face is inches from mine, the light from the disco ball glittering in her dark eyes and dancing across the gloss on her lips. She leans closer on the turn, until our chests are almost touching, and the sweet smell of her floral perfume overpowers the dirty-sock aroma, familiar and safe and almost dizzying.

It's so unexpected, my heart begins to hammer noisily in my chest.

I honestly can't tell if it's because of the impending doom of a fall, or . . . Molly.

And I'm not sure I want to try to figure out the answer.

Natalie's face flashes in front of my eyes, and I quickly pull my hands out of Molly's, wobbling slightly as I skate past her. "I got this."

My fingers curl into fists as I concentrate on not dying and ignoring whatever *that* was. *One foot in front of the other, Alex. One foot in front of . . .*

I look to the side as an actual kindergartener flies past me, fast enough for the breeze to nearly topple me over.

"Just think," Molly says as I sway backward into her. Her hands reach out to steady me before I can drag us both down to the floor. "Maybe one day you'll be as good as a five-year-old."

I snort, the tension breaking in an instant. "Doubtful."

"So how do you think it would go?" Molly asks, skating backward as I begin to wobble my way forward again. "If I came here with Cora?"

"Probably pretty well!" I give her a sideways look as she loops gracefully around to skate next to me. "I mean, I'd *definitely* start off with that hand-holding shit *before* she shatters her spine, but that's what practice runs are for, I guess." I nod, completely back to business.

She wants to be here with Cora. Not me. Everything is fine. If anything, this just shows I'm a good teacher.

She nods in agreement, giving me a small smile, but I can practically feel the confidence radiating off her.

I spend the next hour chasing Molly around the rink, although "chasing" is a bit too strong of a word to use.

I probably resemble a literal toddler running after Usain Bolt.

Every time I begin to flail, her hands reach out to keep me upright, and the both of us dissolve into laughter.

"God, you are *so* bad at this," Molly says, shaking her head after I nearly nosedive into the wall.

"It's a gift," I say just as a voice crackles over the ancient loudspeaker, "Rock with You" by Michael Jackson cutting out in the middle of a verse. "It's the time you've all been waiting for! A prize-packed game of limbo is about to begin in the center of the rink."

Yeah, that is literally the *last* thing I'm waiting for. When I try to make a break for nonslippery land, Molly grabs my arm and pulls me into line.

"Molly, I suck at limbo *on land*," I say as the music starts up again, "Limbo Rock" pumping through the speakers. "Do you see how tall I am? I mean, by all means, do this with Cora, but Cora is a *lot* shorter than me."

"It's the first round. All you need to do is lean your head back," she says as we move slowly forward, kids, teenagers, and adults alike dipping under the wooden bar like it's nothing.

I eye the chest-level bar warily, stutter-stepping carefully forward when it's my turn.

Just as I am about to dip my head back, though, my right skate gets caught on my left one and I go tumbling forward, conking my head on the wooden bar on my way down. Hard. The music cuts off abruptly as a collective "OOOH" rings out from everyone in the limbo line.

Everything is dead silent. Quiet enough to hear a pin drop.

I sit up, rubbing my forehead, my eyes meeting Molly's, and . . . we absolutely lose it. I don't think I've ever laughed so hard. She doubles over, *howling*, while I roll around on the ground, trying to catch my breath. Soon everyone joins in, and Molly is wiping tears from her eyes when she finally glides over to me.

She holds out her hand, nodding toward the exit. "You wanna get out of here?"

"Yeah, that's probably a good idea," I say as she pulls me up and safely off that hellish glossy wooden floor. Our fingers pull apart as soon as we hit the speckled carpet, but the both of us are still giggling.

When we sit down on the wooden bench by the skate return, Molly angles her body toward me, her face growing serious. There's a glimmer of concern in her brown eyes as she reaches up to lightly touch the bump forming on my forehead. Her fingers are cool and gentle and more dizzying than the limbo-bar-induced concussion I just experienced.

I have absolutely underestimated how good she would be at this.

"You need any ice?" she asks, nodding toward the concession stand. "I can go get you some."

"Uh, no." I shake my head, and she pulls away, turning her attention to untying her skates, while I try to silence the unexpected, unsteady beating of my heart.

Molly might not need any practice at all.

She kicks off her skates and stands. "Well, I'm going to get you some anyway," she says, her eyes studying my face. "Couldn't forgive myself if your moneymaker had a bruise on it!" she calls over her shoulder.

"Ha ha, yeah," I awkwardly blurt out because my brain has apparently decided to stop functioning completely. I watch her go, letting out a long groan as I bend back over to finish untying my skates.

My phone buzzes in my pocket, and I quickly pull it out, a text from Tonya lighting up the screen.

Just saw Tommy leaving your mom's place. Thought I'd let you know.

Shit.

CHAPTER 28

MOLLY

Even though it's well after dark by the time we get back to Pitt.

Even though I'm completely exhausted.

Even though my ankles are aching from two straight hours of roller-skating.

I'm not quite ready to say good night yet.

So instead of dropping Alex off at the red door of her apartment building, I park across campus, right outside the Cathedral, where it's usually fairly quiet, away from the bars and nightlife.

"Good call. Make the date last longer," Alex says, looking over at me as she unbuckles her seat belt.

"Yeah. Totally," I reply, trying to act like that's definitely what I was doing.

We step out and start walking down the quiet sidewalk, bumping shoulders every once in a while. Alex has been unusually quiet since I returned with the bag of ice at the roller rink.

"You good?" I ask, checking in.

"Yeah. I'm good," she responds, followed by a big sigh. It doesn't seem like she's good, but after a couple of minutes of silence, I hear her laugh and look over to find her shaking her head at herself.

"You thinking about limbo?" I ask with a smile.

"All of it," she replies, and soon we're both just cracking up over all the things that happened tonight.

"I think this is the first time that I actually feel a little at home here," Alex says, catching her breath from our last bout of laughter.

"I know what you mean," I reply.

There's something about this night . . .

It's everything I hoped college could be but never actually believed it *would be* after I walked into that single on move-in day.

It's everything I've been waiting for but somehow so much more.

This is definitely a night I'll remember. Alex, too, if that bump on her head scars.

"I'm not sure I've ever actually felt at home . . . anywhere. It's nice," she says, a lump in my throat forming over the fact that she's never even felt at home *at home*.

"I'm glad," I reply, bumping into her lightly.

The cool fall air makes goose bumps rise to the surface of

my skin, so I untie the flannel from around my waist and slip it on, leaving the front open.

Alex makes a left, taking us farther away from her apartment and toward Schenley Park, the Pitt arts building glowing in the light from a large stone fountain out front.

"Come here," she says, her voice slightly fried from all the hours we've spent yelling and cracking up today. She takes my hand in hers and pulls me onto the concrete steps of the Carnegie Library. I don't even ask why we're going to the library so close to closing time on a Sunday. I just let her tug me the rest of the way up, because I'm learning that good things happen when I let go a little.

She releases her grip on me when we make it through the glass doors and into the vestibule. It actually feels odd *not* to have her hand in mine after pulling her around the rink for so long. I chase her through the main floor, past the coffee stand where she cut me in line, and toward the stairs, huffing and puffing behind her as we jog up two flights and come out on the top floor, where I've never been. She walks slowly through the dusty stacks, autobiographical works giving way to historical fiction. There isn't a single other person up here with us, and I'm about to ask her what we're doing, when she finally stops in the middle of an aisle and turns to face me.

"Do you hear that?" she asks, her chest heaving under the buzzing fluorescent lights.

But the only thing I can hear is the sound of both of us trying to catch our breath.

"I don't hear anything." I shake my head.

"Exactly. Just dead silence," she says, letting her eyes close as she sits down on the floor, leaning up against the bottom shelves.

I step forward and slide down onto the floor beside her, wrapping my hands around my knees and picking at the stitching on my jeans. As we sit here in the quiet, I have this urge to tell her something that I've been thinking about for a while now.

I'm not sure I want to. I don't want her to be weirded out, but as I sit here in the silence with her, it's the only thing on my heart right now. As excited as I am to do all this with Cora, this practice run . . . means something different to me.

And I want her to know.

"Alex?" I say, staring at the lines of books across from us.

"Yeah?" she replies softly.

"I want to tell you something, but don't laugh. Okay?"

"Okay," she whispers. I take a deep breath, my mouth feeling dry.

"You drive me absolutely crazy, but . . . you're the best friend I've ever had," I tell her, my voice shaking a little.

She doesn't say anything back, but out of my peripheral, the way she looks at me says it all as she slides her right foot across the floor until it rests up against my left. We're both quiet for a long time, until she clears her throat.

"I've never, uh . . . brought anyone here before. . . ."

"To the library?" I ask, looking over at her with a squint.

"No, Molly." She huffs out a laugh. "Just let me . . ." She motions like she has more to say, but she just doesn't know how to get the words out.

"Oh, *sorry*," I whisper, waiting for her to continue.

"When I was younger and my parents used to fight, I would bike to the library, and I would sit down on the floor, hidden behind the rows and rows of books, and I would just read. There was no screaming or breaking shit. It was just quiet." She closes her eyes, and I readjust my position, hoping not to interrupt, afraid she'll stop talking. She continues. "By the time I got to high school, my mom's drinking was . . . I can't even . . ." She shakes her head, deciding to move on. "She would never listen to us, never go and get help. And then just when I thought things couldn't get any worse, when my mom was spending entire weekends passed out on the couch and we didn't even have money for food, my dad just . . ."

I watch her eyes glaze over with tears, her mouth trying to form something more than a stutter.

"He left me. He just left me there to scrape up whatever was left." She shrugs, a sharp intake of air catching her off guard as she finally opens up to me. "And I did, but it just got so much worse, and *oh my God*, I just feel like my whole life has been me trying to scrape by. With everything. My mom.

Money. My relationships." She pauses, looking over to meet my eyes for the first time since she started talking, her breathing ragged. "I don't want to live my whole life like this. Where the library is the only place that feels safe because I'm alone."

I've never wanted to make someone feel better so badly in my life.

"Alex, you don't have to," I tell her with as much confidence as I can.

"You sound so *sure*. Like I can just change my major to English, and we spend the next four years reading and eating frozen yogurt and walking around at night asking each other stupid questions, and somehow everything won't fall apart."

"It won't," I say, my chest hurting for her. "If there's one thing I've learned from you, it's that you have to go after what you want or nothing will ever change. Alex, your life doesn't have to be the same as your parents'. And you don't have to major in something you don't even like just because you're afraid of that. Some things have to fall apart because they don't belong together, but some things belong so much they could never break."

"That stuff only seems possible when I'm hanging out with you," she says, her eyes focused on the carpet. "I've never met someone like you."

"What, awkward? Anxious? Socially inept?" I ask, helping to fill in the blank.

"Good. You're just . . . good, Molly," she replies, looking down at me beside her. "Cora's going to be lucky to have you."

And suddenly I feel a need to ask the same question I asked her when we first agreed to the plan. I know the original reason, but things feel so different now. Different in a way that I can't exactly put into words, because I can't quite figure it out myself. "Why are you doing this?"

Alex snorts a laugh, but then she goes quiet like she really wants to figure out the real reason before she tells me. "I . . ." She takes in a big breath and lets it out slowly, her eyes tracing the books across from us. "I want to prove to *myself* that I can be good too. I want to be someone who can be trusted and relied on. I want to be someone who can actually open up."

She looks back at me, our eyes level for once as she slouches against the shelf behind us. "You've been pretty open with *me*," I tell her, noticing for the first time the subtle lines of yellow braided through her green eyes.

"It feels different with you," she says softly, letting her head fall toward me just a smidge, barely enough to even notice.

But I notice.

The air between us is almost intoxicating.

There's something electric about it.

"If this were a real date," Alex whispers, "this would be the part where we kiss."

My breath catches in my throat, the pain in my ankles

long forgotten, now replaced with an aching in my chest.

I can't tell if it's happening or it just feels that way, but it's almost like the space between us is closing, closing, until . . .

A text rings in on my phone, the sound jolting both of us out of the magnetic pull. Alex looks away quickly, shuffling a few inches in the other direction as I pull out my phone.

"It's Cora," I say, and for some reason I feel almost guilty. But then what I read stops me in my tracks. "Oh my God. She wants to get dinner with me on Friday. Study together and then get dinner." I turn my phone to Alex, who quickly grabs it out of my hands. "*She's* asking *me* out, right? That's what's happening here?" I ask.

"Uh." She holds the phone closer, emojis galore. "Yeah. Definitely a date," she says. "Guess you can officially skip step three."

Holy shit, I'm *finally* going to go on a date with *Cora Myers*.

But . . . I don't feel as excited as I thought I would. I convince myself it's probably just that studying and dinner don't quite have the same fun factor as the roller-skating night we could've had. It has nothing to do with—

"Wait, Friday?" Alex hands my phone back. "That's September thirtieth. That's Natalie's concert. It's *perfect*. She can see all of it firsthand—you with Cora, because of *my* help. You should ask her to come! And then I'll be there if you need me. We can, like . . . double," she says.

I look up at her for a second, trying to decide if that's what

I *want*. I'm not sure what exactly just happened between us here, but I'm feeling things for Alex Blackwood that I never thought I would *ever* feel for her. I don't want it to be weird. But . . . I can't deny I also really need her there to help me on my first date, so I don't totally screw it up with Cora on my own now that we're not skating. Plus, she's right. It's the perfect opportunity to tell Natalie how much she's helped me, and after everything she's done, I owe Alex this.

"Go on. Text her back. This is everything you've been waiting for, right?" She tosses the ball back into my court, but she doesn't quite meet my eye.

"Uh, right. Yeah totally." So I reply, typing up a flirty text to Cora.

Dinner sounds great! 😍 But I've maybe got something better. Do you want to go to a concert with me? I can promise sweaty people and overpriced sodas 😉 😄

I show it to Alex, and after a pause she taps the send button for me.

Cora answers quickly, YES!!

Alex is right. This is everything I've always wanted, everything I never thought I could have. It's *Cora*. I'm not going to screw it up over one night, one moment lost in the library with a girl I absolutely couldn't stand a month ago. A girl who is obviously very much interested in someone else.

So, it's settled.

Friday is step four. I've got a real date. My first date. With Cora Myers.

Just the two of us.

And Alex.

And Natalie.

Perfect.

CHAPTER 29

ALEX

I can't get up the apartment stairs fast enough.

I whirl around the banister, my head spinning as I push through our door and almost run smack into Heather.

"You good?" she asks, a steaming Styrofoam cup of noodles in her hand. "You look a little . . ." Her voice trails off as she gives me a once-over. "Frazzled."

Frazzled?

Alex Blackwood does not get frazzled.

Definitely not over *Molly Parker*.

"Yeah, I'm totally cool," I say, letting out a weird laugh as I head down the hall to my room. "Totally fine!" I add, closing and locking the door behind me. I rest my back against it, sliding down to the floor.

What the fuck was that?

I squeeze my eyes shut, pressing the palms of my hands against them, but I still see Molly's face painted against my eyelids, steadily leaning forward, her lips close enough to . . .

I pull my hands away and shake my head, the image fading.

"Come on, Alex. Don't make it more than it is," I mutter as I slide my legs straight out in front of me, my shoes knocking together.

I mean, I haven't kissed *anyone* in a *whole month.* That's practically a record! It's no wonder this fake date had me all flustered.

But my brain keeps circling back. To the skating rink, the smell of her floral perfume, the feeling of her hands in mine. To the library, her brown eyes in the soft light, her gaze filling my stomach with butterflies. It didn't feel fake.

"Shit."

I slide farther down, lying completely flat on the carpeted floor. I watch the headlights of a car driving past outside dance across my tile ceiling, my heart thumping through the fabric of my T-shirt.

I like Molly.

The thought comes to me out of the blue, shocking at first, but then . . .

I repeat it over and over again, finding a scary truth in the words.

I like Molly.

Roller-skating-for-a-first-date Molly.

Can't-even-ask-a-girl-out Molly.

Dresses-like-a-sixty-year-old-woman Molly.

I groan and roll over onto my side, tucking my legs up as the thought of her clothes brings with it the thought of Mrs. Parker, her smiling face and her salt-and-pepper bob of hair. The adoring way she looks at Molly. The conspiratorial way she winked at me when we met.

. . . How much she'd hate me when I would inevitably break Molly's heart because *apparently* Natalie's right.

Natalie.

The girl I have history with. Who said she loves me, despite all the reasons she shouldn't. The girl I just spent the last *month* working my ass off for, to prove that I *can* be a good person. That I can be real and honest and open up to people.

Only . . . all I did was open up to the wrong one.

It was just . . . for the first time it didn't feel claustrophobic or awful. It was . . . so easy. Tonight, at the library. Two weeks ago, in her dorm room.

My stomach sinks through the floor, and I reach out to pick at an unruly carpet strand.

I guess I'm exactly the person Natalie said I was.

Someone who can't be trusted all the way in Pittsburgh.

Although, this . . . *this* is worse. I've never had this happen to me before. Flirting and dating and hookups, sure. But not . . . *whatever this is.*

I mean, it's not like it even matters anyway.

Molly likes Cora. Perfect, sunshine-and-rainbows, everything-Molly-could-possibly-dream-of Cora. They make sense in all the ways we never would. Cora defended her that night at the party when I said something really shitty. She's from her *hometown*. She's not . . . well . . .

Like me.

Broken. And bound to hurt her no matter how hard I try not to.

I lie on the floor, curled up into a ball, until I can completely tuck away all my wrong feelings into a neat little box. A box labeled DO NOT OPEN. A box that takes me until the sky turns pitch-black to completely construct.

I'm going to fix this.

I'm not going to derail now just because I did my job a little too well.

Molly belongs with Cora, I belong with Natalie. Natalie who loves me despite all my glaring flaws.

This Friday we're both going to get our girls. And it will be like this never happened at all.

The next afternoon I find myself chopping a mountain of onions so big it could probably bring the entire city of Pittsburgh to tears.

I swipe my elbow across my eyes, squinting through the pain as I slice through the pile with a knife duller than a biology class lecture.

"Got ourselves a nice day today," Jim says, playing weatherman from the front of the storage unit, a cigarette dangling from his mouth as he cranes his neck back to look at the sky. "We need it. Haven't had a good day in a shit long time."

We sold out twice last week, but I've learned Jim loves to be dramatic.

Today, though, I'm not in the mood. I finish cutting the onions and hop down off the truck, pulling my blue latex gloves off and tossing them in the trash can.

Leaning against the truck, I pull my phone out of my pocket to see a text from Natalie. She let me out of jail after I had one of her bandmates get her a caramel Frappuccino from Starbucks before their show in Chicago.

It's honestly starting to get a little old, and increasingly difficult, to find ways to get out of it. Especially when I feel like it happens . . . kind of a lot.

Already in Ohio! See u Friday 😌

I hesitate over the keypad, my thumbs frozen in midair as a whisper of uncertainty swims into my stomach. But I push it away and send back a Can't wait! peppered with more emojis than a middle-aged mom's Facebook post.

I pocket my phone and head to the back to help Jim cut fries. He eyes me as I take over the fry cutter, slamming my way through two boxes of potatoes in record time, my brow lined with sweat despite the cooler weather.

"You good?" he asks, an amused smile on his face.

"It's nothing." I roll my eyes and shove another potato into the cutter, then pull the lever down with a loud bang. "Just . . . girl troubles."

I don't even expect him to respond, but Jim chuckles and squishes a lid on one of the overflowing fry bins, grunting as he picks it up. "I've been there. Couldn't keep 'em off me back in the day."

"Really?" I ask, and he smiles, sliding the bin onto the truck before pulling his phone out of his pocket.

"Don't sound so surprised," he mutters as he squints down at it. After a couple of taps, he holds up a blurry picture of high school Jim, clean-cut and wearing a varsity letterman jacket, two cheerleaders tucked under his muscular arms.

It looks like an entirely different guy.

"No fucking way," I say, my head swiveling between the photo and present-day Jim.

He pockets the phone. "Crazy what ten years of drugs and alcohol can do." He grabs another box of potatoes off the storage shelf and drops them at my feet. "I'm sober now, thanks to a rehab up in Erie and my weekly AA meetings, but I lost it all. My friends. My family. My fiancée."

With a long sigh, he sits down on the edge of the truck and pops a cigarette in his mouth, lighting it. "She was my high school sweetheart, but she up and left me after a week-long bender. Can't say I blame her."

He stares off into the distance, a puff of smoke billowing slowly out from between his lips. "Alcohol was my way of running away from things, y'know?"

I nod, feeling angry as I think of my mom. How alcohol is her escape, everything in her life following right behind her the second she puts a bottle to her lips. Her responsibilities, her relationships, her ability to even be a functioning human, let alone a parent.

But then . . . I think of myself. I might not drink, but . . . I certainly run away from things in a different way. Just like my mom.

"I get that," I say, letting out a long sigh as I look down at the potatoes, the cardboard bending at the sides, trying to hold all the weight.

He grunts as he stands, pointing a thick finger at me. "Whatever the trouble is, don't run from it. Don't end up old and alone like me, kid."

"Jim. What the hell are you talking about? You're, like . . . forty."

"Eh. Whatever." He waves his hand at me, popping his cigarette back into his mouth and heading out of the storage unit.

I watch him go, but something about what he said stays with me. *Running away.*

I think about Natalie, how she said "I love you" that night in Philly. How she opened my eyes to something I never even realized about myself. How much certainty there is in that, in *us*.

And now here I am, sabotaging it. Just like I always do.

Why would I want to run away from that and pine after a girl who likes someone else?

I can't be the one who runs anymore, not like Mom. I have to stay. And if I can't make it with Natalie, I can't make it with anyone. I have to try.

I stoop to grab a potato, then slam it through the potato cutter, my mind completely and totally made up.

CHAPTER 30

MOLLY

The venue is small. There's maybe enough room for a hun-
dred people to stand between the raised stage and a big rectangular bar at the back of the building. Antique pendant lights
hang on long chains from the vaulted ceiling, and arched
opaque windows run the length of the two long walls. It looks
like a converted church.

"They're really good!" Cora yells into my ear over the
blasting speakers, her foot lightly knocking into mine on the
black glossy floor. I smile and nod my head enthusiastically,
but I've been so distracted that I haven't really listened to a
single song.

Distracted by Alex on the other side of me.

Distracted by the way she's been ignoring me all night
apart from making sure I'm going to tell Natalie about what
she's done for me.

Distracted by the way her attention has been glued to

Natalie onstage for the past thirty minutes and the way Natalie has been staring back at her. Like every line she sings is *only* for Alex's ears. Like they are the only two people in the room.

I take a sip of my Sprite and glance over at Cora.

She's got on an adorable blue dress with yellow flowers that bounces up to her thighs as she dances along with the music. Her lips are outlined perfectly in red lipstick, and the tiny diamond stud in her nose is sparkling under the spotlights overhead.

She catches me watching her but doesn't stop bopping along to the music.

She just smiles, that big bright smile that I have loved since ninth grade.

It's a smile that shakes me awake and reminds me that *I'm here with Cora Myers*, my absolute dream girl.

"I'm really glad you came, Cora," I tell her, my heart pounding in my chest.

"Well, it took you long enough to ask me," she prods. "Although, technically, I guess I asked you."

"Well, *technically*, we'd be studying for a biology exam right now if I hadn't brought up the concert, so . . ." I shrug a shoulder at her playfully. I can feel my nerves bubbling up, but it feels different from that night at the party when I could barely even look at her. I'm not nervous that I'm going to screw it up. I think I'm nervous that . . . this might actually work.

That I might *actually* get the girl of my dreams.

"True," she surrenders. "Then, I guess I'm glad you asked me. Really glad." She knocks her soda into mine, and we both take a sip as a roaring applause makes its way through the audience. Alex glances in my direction for a split second before focusing her attention back on the stage. Natalie blows kisses to the crowd, and Alex whistles loudly over two fingers as the band makes its way offstage.

A couple of minutes later, Alex is waving someone down, but I can't see over the heads in the crowd. Soon Natalie breaks through and makes her way over to us, a few people around her pointing and whispering to their friends.

As I watch her get closer and closer to Alex, I wonder if they'll kiss. It's been almost a month since they've seen each other, after all. But they don't, and I exhale, relieved. Instead, Alex wraps her arms around Natalie and pulls her into a close hug, whispering something into her ear. I turn away, looking back at the bar, which is teeming with people trying to get drinks before the headliners start their set.

"What'd you guys think?" Alex asks, opening up the circle to include Cora and me.

"You were incredible!" Cora says to Natalie. "I had no idea Alex was dating a rock star."

I can see Alex physically tense up at that. I wonder if it's because she's worried that Natalie might think Alex hasn't talked about her much, her *girlfriend*.

"Yeah, well"—Natalie flips her long black hair over her shoulder, batting her mascara-caked lashes—"she's a lucky lady." Alex relaxes a little, and it's so weird to see her nervous. It's all just so . . . not her.

But I guess they worked out all their issues or they wouldn't be here.

"Hey, baby, go get me a water," she says to Alex. Like it's not even a question.

"Of course," Alex says. "I'll be right back."

"I'll come with you." Cora raises her empty cup. "Molly, you want a refill?" she asks.

"No, I'm good. Thanks." I shake my head, and Alex gives me a look as the two of them disappear into the crowd, leaving me here with Natalie. Being here alone with her, I feel my anxiety kick up again, a tightening around my chest. But I think about Alex, and even though she's been weird to me all night, I owe her this.

"Hi, I'm Molly." I reach my hand out, and Natalie takes it after a two-second hesitation, which she spends looking me over. I feel that familiar sweat come over me. *Push through it, Molly.* "Alex really is great. She has been helping me out a lot," I say, readying myself to tell her all about how she helped me get this date with Cora, about how she's a different person from the girl she left in Philly. "For the past month, we've been—"

Natalie interrupts me with a snort and rolls her eyes.

I stop and look at her, confused.

"Don't go thinking you're anything special," she says. "It's clear you're just a lost little puppy looking for attention. And Alex will give it to anyone . . . for a while. That's just Alex."

I step back as she stares me down, making me feel small, making me feel like the person I was before I came here, before I met Alex. And as much as I want to defend my friend, as much as I want to tell Natalie that she doesn't even deserve to be in Alex's life . . .

I just . . . can't.

And soon Alex and Cora return with drinks.

"You guys talk about me while I was gone?" Alex asks, looking directly at me. I take a step back, uncurling my fingers.

"Only the good stuff." Natalie wraps her hand all the way around Alex's waist and pulls her close, and this time she does bury a kiss in her neck. "Right, Molly?" she asks, shooting daggers across our small circle at me.

I stare back at her for a moment, trying to come up with something to say, but instead, I just nod.

"I'll be right back," I say, avoiding Cora's gaze as I head off to find the bathroom, pulling my phone out as I squeeze through openings in the crowd, my blood practically boiling.

Meet me by the bathroom, I text Alex, and then I wait.

CHAPTER 31

I try not to spill my fresh drink on about a million people, until I finally spot Molly leaning up against the black-painted wall outside the bathrooms.

"Dude, what are you doing?" I ask, pointing my thumb back toward the corner of the bar we left Cora and Natalie at. "You can't just leave your date. Have I taught you noth—"

"I don't like her," Molly says, cutting me off midsentence. Her face is about as serious as it gets, dark eyebrows pulled together in a frown.

"Cora? What do you mean you don't like her?" I ask, wondering where the hell this conversation is going. They just flirted their way through the Cereal Killers' entire set.

"No. Natalie."

I give her an incredulous look. "What? You don't even *know* her."

Molly leans closer, no trace of timidity. "I know enough

to know you deserve better than *that*. A lot better."

"What are you even *talking* about?"

"I don't like how she treats you," Molly says, crossing her arms over her chest.

I shake my head, letting out a laugh, even though this doesn't feel funny at all. A flicker of the past few weeks of her icing me out and hanging up on me flashes through my mind, but I push it away. I have to stand my ground. I'm not running away now.

"Well, if the last month has taught me anything, it's that you don't know shit about relationships, Molly." I take a step closer, glowering down at her. "I mean, you can't even ask a girl out without a detailed tutorial."

Molly flinches but doesn't back down. "I know what a healthy relationship looks like, Alex, even if I haven't been in one. And that is not it."

"Well, *sorry*, but we weren't all raised in the perfect little family, with a white picket fence, and two-point-five kids, and *Beth* for a mom." I size her up, from the determined look on her face to the white-knuckled fists her hands have balled themselves into. "Why do you even care? You've got your dream girl."

The fists tighten, her jaw locking in frustration.

"Because I'm trying to *help* you, Alex, even though you've been ignoring me *all night*. You're my—"

I don't let her finish. I don't want to hear her say the word "friend" . . . for too many reasons. "Well, we're done helping each other, aren't we? You got Cora. Natalie's back. The plan is done, if there really ever was one. You know, I just *made up* all the steps, because you needed them so much. Who gives a shit about step five anyway?" I gesture between us, me and her, *us*. "We don't have to do this anymore."

And then the words tumble out of my mouth before I can stop them. The ones I can never take back. "We don't have to pretend we give a shit about each other."

Instantly I see them hit their mark.

And it is . . . even more awful than I could have possibly imagined, watching the small piece of Molly's heart I managed to find a home in over the past month absolutely shatter.

Her eyes widen, and she takes a step back, accidentally knocking into the wall behind her, tears forming at their corners.

I look quickly down at my scuffed Converse, squeezing my eyes shut as she brushes past me into the crowded room of people.

"Nice going, Alex," I mutter, kicking at the wall.

I turn my head, watching as she grabs Cora's hand, and the two of them disappear out the door and into the night. Into their happily ever after.

In one gulp I down my drink, then my eyes lock with Natalie's across the room, my own happily ever after that I *won't* sabotage laid out right in front of me. I slam the empty glass on the counter and push through the crowd to Natalie, reaching out for her, ready to take it.

"I can't open it." Natalie giggles, stumbling into me, the room key tumbling out of her hand and onto the carpeted hotel floor.

I scoop it up, swaying, before sliding it through the lock, the door clicking open.

"Got it!" I call to the empty hallway, making her laugh even harder.

I'm well past my two-drink limit, and we both know it.

The door is still swinging shut when her lips find mine, our bodies press together, her fingers lace in my hair. All of it with a desperation that makes me feel, well . . .

Wanted.

Like things are how they should be.

Like no time has passed at all. No fighting. No distance. No Molly.

Her face pops into my head and I push it away, focusing instead on the feeling of Natalie's shirt beneath my fingertips. I pull it off, and our eyes lock as she reaches up to push me lightly backward, her arms wrapping around my neck as we go stumbling back into the oversize bed, kicking our shoes off as we go.

She smells like the menthol cigarette she smoked on the way over here. The Victoria's Secret spray she keeps tucked into her guitar case. And . . . despite myself, I can't help but think of the soft floral perfume Molly wears, how this one is musky and rich in all the ways hers isn't. Natalie's hands move down my body, her fingers quickly undoing the button of my jeans, slowly pulling down the zipper. . . .

"*Stop,*" I say before I even realize I'm saying it, wrenching my mouth off hers.

We both freeze in surprise.

She pulls away to give me a quizzical look, her eyes narrowing as we stare at each other.

I push away from her, sitting up as I run my fingers through my hair. "I don't know. I just feel like maybe we should . . . talk."

Natalie laughs, her eyebrows rising in surprise. "*Alex Blackwood* wants to talk?"

"Yeah, I mean, this past month has been kind of . . ."

She kisses my neck, not even listening to me. I want to tell her about the plan. About my mom. About working the food truck with Jim.

I want this to be different this time.

"Natalie. Come on. I'm serious."

She stops, groaning as she rolls off me and stands up from the bed, crossing her arms over her chest. "*What,* Alex?"

"What do you mean *what*?" I say. "This is what *you* wanted. You wanted me to be real with you. To be honest. And open. And here I am *trying* to, and you won't even listen to me."

"Well, I don't mean *right now*." She leans forward, tugging

311

at my T-shirt. "I mean, I haven't seen you in a *month*."

I bite my lip. "But what about what *I* want? What if I want to talk right now?"

Natalie rolls her eyes. "What? Do you want to talk about all the ways that Molly girl took my place? Or do you want to bitch about your mom's alcoholism? Like, come *on*, Alex. Opening up is never going to be your thing."

I wince. Her words are like a slap to the face.

Like my worst fears realized.

But . . . I *was* able to open up to someone. At the library. And on a printed comforter in a small dorm room not too far from here.

And . . . all at once I see the truth. She never wanted to listen to me. Never was *really* there for me. She just wanted to control me.

This isn't love.

The fighting. The lack of trust. Feeling like I'm walking on eggshells or always trying to get out of trouble. Being manipulated over and over again, never really knowing what she wants from me.

If anything, it reminds me of, well . . . my parents. What I thought was normal.

I guess I thought if I just put my head down and scraped by, it would be fine. We could make it work.

But love isn't something you scrape by for.

When I think of love, what I really, truly want, I know deep in my bones that it isn't this.

"I . . ." I take a long, deep breath, squeezing my eyes shut as I collect my thoughts. "Natalie, whether or not you want it now, you always wanted me to be honest with you. To tell you how I feel," I say, knowing what I have to do. "And . . . I finally feel like I can."

I meet her gaze and shake my head. "I don't want this."

Natalie lets out a long, frustrated sigh, pulling her hair up into a bun as she talks. "Let me guess. I was right. This is about Molly?"

I think about her hand in mine as we ran through the library. Walking around and around the streets of Pittsburgh after getting frozen yogurt. When she wrapped her Pitt scarf around my neck. Her smile as she pulled me safely around the roller rink, catching me whenever I was about to fall. That *moment* as we sat on the floor in between the stacks, our legs touching, the air filled with an undeniable electricity.

"I'm crazy about her," I admit. To her. To myself. To the both of us.

If looks could kill, I'd be dead on the floor right now.

"But that's not what this is about. This is about how you treated me. Telling me to go left and then being mad I didn't go right. Making me feel like I'm never good enough. Like you're doing me a *favor* by caring about me." I shake my head.

313

"I ghosted you *once* because I was scared and hurt and afraid, and yeah, it was shitty of me, but you do it *all* the time, Natalie. I'm always doing something wrong in your eyes."

Natalie snorts, and a twisted smile creeps onto her face. "And what? You think it'll be better with someone else?"

I shrug. "I don't know. I just know I want to be with someone that I feel comfortable sharing myself with. I want to know I have someone to talk to about my life, and my problems, and . . . I don't know! Changing my major to English. And I don't have that. *We* don't have that."

"This is so typical. Running away and closing off because you can't handle something real."

I shake my head. Before tonight I would have believed her. But not anymore. "I'm . . . not running away, though. I'm running *to* something. *That's* what's real. *None* of what you've told me has been real."

"Alex," she says, putting her hands on my shoulders. "Come on. That's bullshit and you know it. No one knows you like *I* know you. I know the good *and* the bad. The *real* you. I know your history. I know, at the end of the day, you're just a fucked-up girl, and I've been with you the past six months despite all that, through flirting and lying and *everything*. Even the stuff with your mom. Why would you just throw that out now?"

I look around the room. At my shoes kicked off by the door. At Natalie's shirt lying on the ground. At *Natalie*, staring at me like . . . I'm worth absolutely nothing.

And it's like the answer I didn't even know I was looking for. Why I couldn't say "I love you" to her that night in Philly. Why I could never really be certain.

She just . . . wasn't the one.

I stand, pushing her hands off my shoulders. "Maybe I couldn't open up to you because *you* weren't worth it."

Her eyes widen as I take a step forward, the two of us face-to-face. "I might not deserve a girl like Molly," I say, my voice low. "But I know I can sure as hell do better than this."

And with that I jam my feet into my Converse and head out the door, making sure to slam it behind me like I did on that night a month ago.

Only this time it actually feels good. This time it feels right.

CHAPTER 32

MOLLY

When I wake up the next morning with puffy eyes, there's a small part of me that actually believes I'm going to pick up my phone to find an apology text waiting to be opened.

Pretty stupid of me.

I drop my phone back onto my bed, and for the first time in a long time, I fully take in the horror that used to be my room. My clothes are *everywhere*, shirts thrown onto the floor, pants strewn over every bedpost. My books and binders are lying across the floor, mixed together with dirty socks. I've been so caught up with Alex and Cora and the plan that I haven't really noticed how bad it's gotten.

High school Molly would've had a *stroke* if she'd seen this.

I spend the next couple of hours putting everything back in its place, the way it used to be. The way it should be. An extra pang of sadness hits me as I refold the pile of sweatpants that Alex destroyed before we went to the mall.

This usually helps. Cleaning tends to have a healing effect on me, but by the time I finish, I actually feel worse, because I spend the whole time thinking about how things ended with me and Alex last night.

I pull out my phone, my thumb hovering over my mom's contact, but I stop myself. I've basically been ghosting her for two weeks. What kind of message does it send if I give in and call her now, when everything has gone to shit? She's just going to think I *need* her in the way that I used to need her, and that's not what I want, but I need to get out of my head. I need to get out of this dorm.

So I decide to take a ride over to Noah's house.

When I arrive, he puts a pause on whatever Netflix documentary he's watching, and I plop down next to him on the couch. "What's up?" he asks.

"Not much. Needed to get out of my dorm. Just got done cleaning, because it kinda . . . exploded. There was crap everywhere," I reply.

"Really? You're always so . . . neat," he says. I think of my makeup, which was scattered all over my desk from the two hours it took me to apply it before roller-skating and then again before the concert.

"Yeah, well . . . for once I actually had something to do besides clean." I laugh pathetically at myself.

"How was that concert?" he asks.

"Fine."

"How's Cora?"

"Fine."

"And Alex?"

"Fine," I say again.

"So everything's fine, huh?" he asks, clearly picking up on my tone.

"Not really," I reply, letting the sadness seep into my voice as I slouch against the couch.

"What happened? What's wrong?" he asks.

"Alex turned out to be kind of a jerk after all." I tell him what happened last night, what she said to me at the end of the concert.

"Well, maybe you should talk to *her* about it. It sounds like things were pretty tense with her girlfriend. Maybe she didn't mean—"

"I'm not going to talk to her, Noah. I was just some stupid project for her. We aren't friends. We aren't anything. I'm done," I reply, tears pressing against my eyes as I try to swallow my frustration. "I never should've taken your advice. I never should've gone to that stupid party."

"Molly, come on. You don't mean that. Don't be so dramatic," he says with a familiar tough-love honesty that reminds me of someone else. It's something I don't think he would've said to me a month ago. "I can see how much happier you've been since then. I mean, you're like . . . with Cora. Isn't that what you've always wanted?"

"I don't know. I guess so," I reply, but unbelievably it still feels like I have to convince myself that I can be happy without Alex in my life. "Can we just watch . . . whatever this is?" I ask, pressing play on the remote, and Noah seems to accept that I don't want to talk about it anymore.

About an hour in, a text buzzes in from Cora that makes me feel lighter.

Want to come hang out? Watch a movie?

Alex *was* right about one thing. I've got someone better. Someone who I *really* like. Someone who actually *wants* to hang out with me, even after the catastrophe that was our first date.

I can still fix this.

That afternoon when I arrive at Cora's dorm, she already has a movie cued up on her computer, which is plugged into the HDMI port on her TV. There's popcorn on her desk and several varieties of boxed candy for my choosing. It's *really* cute. *She's* really cute.

"Ready?" she asks, her hand hovering over the space bar. *Oh.* I didn't expect to just start watching the movie right away. I thought maybe we'd hang out. Ask questions and get to know each other a little better. Or perhaps talk about the ending of our date last night.

We didn't really speak at all about what happened after. When I pulled her out in the middle of the headliners' set, she noticed I was crying and stopped me on the sidewalk to ask me what was wrong. I didn't want to talk about it at the time. I *couldn't*. So I just shook my head, and she just put her arms around me and held me close.

But in that particular moment, no one could really make me feel safe, not even Cora.

We took the city bus back to campus, my head pressed against the glass as Cora scrolled through her phone next to me, both of us stealing glances at each other every few minutes. When we stepped off the bus, I tried to talk to her, but I still couldn't get the words out.

"Molly, it's okay. Maybe we can talk about it tomorrow?" she said. She was *so* understanding. I think if I'd just had some more time, if we could've walked the block a couple of times or sat on a bench, I could've talked to her. But after that, she gave me a hug goodbye and crossed the intersection away from the quad.

It all felt so . . . unresolved.

"Um, Cora, before we start it, I wanted to apologize about last night. I kind of ruined everything and I couldn't explain then, but Alex and I, we kinda got into a . . . fight, I guess." I sit down on her bed as she sits back against the wall by her computer.

"I didn't want to pry, but . . . what happened?" she asks. I can't exactly tell her the truth, that Alex has been helping me get her to fall for me for the past month and I stupidly believed that made her my best friend.

"Uh . . . she was basically using me. I don't think we're friends anymore. I'm not sure we ever were." My chest aches as the words leave my lips.

"Is that a bad thing? She always seemed a little superficial to me," she replies, surprising me with such a judgmental statement. I think of how much Alex hates when people treat her like that. Despite everything, I find myself still wanting to defend her, until I remember all the things she said to me. I shouldn't even be wasting more breath on her now. I'm here to watch a movie with Cora, not talk about Alex. So I push the subject from my mind.

"Let's just watch the movie. I'm exactly where I want to be . . . with you. Thanks for giving me another chance," I say.

She presses play and steps across the carpet, plopping down on her bed beside me. I thought we'd be watching a cute rom-com or something, but no. Turns out Cora is *way* into horror, which is something even *I* didn't know. Her pick for our movie date is *The Grudge*, and to be honest, I watch most of the movie through the cracks in my fingers. Even so, it's totally worth it. Every time there's a jump scare that elicits a shriek out of me, Cora scoots a little closer.

About halfway through, she puts her hand between us on the bed, palm up. I lay mine down there next to me, my heart pounding in my ears so loudly that I can't even hear the movie anymore.

She tosses a Skittle into her mouth, and when she sets her

hand back down on the bed, it's another inch closer to mine. A minute later she reaches for another one, and this time I feel her hand sliding into mine, until our palms are flush, our fingers intertwined.

Instead of my heartbeat picking up, I think it actually slows down. And weirdly . . . I feel like I'm missing that flutter in my stomach that I always had anytime I even thought about Cora.

Now I'm here, holding her *actual* hand, and . . . it just doesn't feel like I thought it would. But then I remind myself that I am Molly Parker. I am an overthinker, and I tend to create problems out of nothing. I take a deep breath and let it out, forcing myself back into the present, into this moment that I never thought would come. I'm not going to mess this up.

On Monday morning I take my usual chair beside Cora and Abby and set my backpack up on Alex's chair. I keep my head down, staying in conversation with the two of them so I don't have to see when Alex comes in.

The professor begins the lecture, and I glance back at our old seats, but they're both taken by other students. I scan the room, searching for any sign of her: a shock of blond hair, a notebook filled with doodles, the smell of a 7-Eleven turkey sandwich with extra mayo. But she isn't here.

She's probably still locked away with her cool girlfriend.

I'm brought back to the present moment when Cora slides her hand onto my leg under the table.

It doesn't matter.

Alex is not my problem anymore.

I try my best to focus on the PowerPoint slides in front of me, but when I open my binder, tucked into the sleeve is the sloppily written note Alex wrote out to invite Cora to breakfast.

I run my fingers over it, tracing the indentations in the paper and replaying the chaos from rugby tryouts and the frozen yogurt shop, all the ridiculous questions we asked each other on the walk back to my dorm, and the roller rink.

It hurts to think about, but I also can't help letting out a quiet snort of a laugh as I picture Alex taking herself *out* with the limbo bar.

"What's up?" Cora whispers, leaning toward me.

"Oh, uh." I open my mouth to tell her, but there's just too much to tell, and how could it ever translate? "Nothing, just thinking," I say, slipping the note back into the sleeve and turning the page.

Tuesday, Cora and I meet up for a study session at the library. Our books lie open, notes scattered across the small wood table between my cup of tea and her coffee with six sugars.

"Molly," she whispers.

I lift my head to find her holding out one of her AirPods across the table. I smile, taking it from her and slipping it into my ear, cringing just the tiniest bit when Broadway music blasts through the tiny speaker.

After a few songs it becomes clear the *entire* playlist is Broadway. I know I'm probably the only gay on earth who feels this way, but . . . I can't stand show tunes. I don't dare tell her that, though, because it's obviously her jam. Maybe if it's her favorite, one day it'll be mine, too. I push through for as long as I can.

"Oh my God." Cora laughs from across the table, looking at her phone. "My teammate Hallie is *literally* the funniest person I've ever met. God, I love her."

My stomach sinks, and suddenly it feels like I'm blowing it, like I'm letting her slip through my fingers. I need to make a move. I need to solidify this before it's too late.

"Hey, Cora, um . . . what are you doing this weekend?" I ask, trying to sound confident as I attempt to casually slide the earbud back to her, but of course it goes *flying* off the table.

Too much, Molly.

She shrugs as she bends to pick it up. "Not sure. What about you?"

Even though I'm trying not to think about her, I *need* to do this, to not chicken out, so I try to channel that day at Bigelow Bash when I asked Alex to go roller-skating.

But everything from that night comes with it. Including

what happened after, when she led me to the top floor of the library, letting me into the part of her life that she had always kept to herself.

And the way she looked at me . . .

I force myself back here with Cora. I want to be the one to ask her on a date this time, but suddenly roller-skating doesn't sound as appealing.

"Same," I reply lamely. "Nothing planned."

She sets her highlighter down on the table. "I think there's some sort of student art gala happening across the street at the Carnegie art museum on Friday. Abby was telling me about it."

"Do you like art?" I ask, thinking about how every time I'm in an art museum, I just end up looking for a bench to sit on until I can leave.

"I love it." She gives me a knowing look from across the table, clearly waiting.

"Cora." I laugh.

"Yes, Molly?" She raises her eyebrows at me expectantly.

"Do you want to go to the art gala with me?" I ask.

"I would love to," she replies. "I think it's, like, a big deal, actually. Fancy formal dress. So, bust out your *finest* attire, Molly Parker. I can't *wait* to see you in a dress!" she adds.

"Oh, cool! Totally. Me too. I mean . . . seeing you . . . in a dress." I duck my head like I'm reading my notes to hide my panic. I don't think I've owned a formal dress in my entire life. I never even went to prom. If Alex were here, maybe she could . . .

Drop it, Molly. Alex is gone.

I'll have to bring in the big guns.

I'll have to swallow my pride and finally call my mom.

I just hope she isn't pissed that I've ignored all her calls this past week.

CHAPTER 33

ALEX

"Thank you, have a nice day!" I call out to our last customer, sliding the window shut with a long sigh while Jim clatters around behind me, closing up shop.

My phone buzzes in my back pocket with an incoming call. I can't deny the tiny swell in my chest as I look down at the screen, a small part of me hoping to see Molly's name staring back at me after almost a week of silence, even though I know it's on me to reach out and apologize.

I just . . . don't know what to say. When I left Natalie's hotel room, I thought I could just go right up to her and tell her how I feel. How sorry I am. But . . . I knew she was with Cora, and it felt wrong to interrupt, like I didn't deserve to. Especially after what I said.

I skipped bio and English class this whole week because I couldn't face her. Couldn't stand watching her and Cora flirt while she ignored me completely. Even though I deserve it.

There's no denying the fact Pittsburgh feels empty now. No Molly to hang out with. No plan to focus on. Just plugging away in classes I don't really like.

Aside from work, I just sit around the apartment or wander around the library, texting my ever-elusive mom, reading books, trying to find a way to say how sorry I am.

I let out a long sigh as I look down at the phone screen. Of course it's not her.

It's an unknown number, the first three digits a familiar area code from back where I grew up.

I have no doubt that it's a call concerning my nonexistent car's extended warranty, and I almost let it go straight to voicemail, but my finger accidentally hits the accept button.

Shit.

I hold the phone up to my ear. "Hello?"

"Is this Alex Blackwood?" an unfamiliar voice asks, its tone serious.

Oh no.

"Uh, yeah. This is Alex."

"Alex, this is Officer McHugh from down at the county jail."

My eyes widen and I reach out, grabbing on to the soda fridge for support. *The county jail.*

"We have your mother, Donna Blackwood, in custody here. She was in an accident around five thirty this morning. Ran a . . ." His voice trails off as he rustles through some paperwork. "Tommy O'Neil's car right into a telephone pole. Took her until an hour ago to sober up enough to give us a phone number."

The call I always dreaded getting is finally here.

Why the fuck did he let her drive?

"Is she okay?" I ask as my insides turn to ice. Jim swings his head over to look at me, his eyebrows raised.

"Miraculously, there isn't a scratch on her. No one else was involved in the crash, but she was heavily intoxicated at the time of the accident and clocked in . . . well above the legal limit."

Just what I was hoping not to hear.

"She's looking at a DUI with a license suspension." He clears his throat. All those years of hiding her keys, of driving her around, of policing everything she did, for nothing. Having Tonya check in on her. Practically forcing her to text me once a day. *Selling her car.* And now *this*? "Are you able to . . . ?"

My ears are ringing too loudly to fully make out what he's saying. I meet Jim's gaze, and I think he can tell because he takes the phone and puts it on speaker. Words jump out at me as he talks to the police officer on my behalf.

"Pick up."

"Help."

"Drive?"

I nod, and he relays the information to the police officer.

When he hangs up, he puts the phone down on the

counter and reaches out to take both of my shoulders in his thick hands.

"We have to go pick up your mom, okay?" He nods out the window of the truck. "I'll drive you."

"I . . ." My voice trails off, and I shake my head. "Thank you."

He gives me a gruff, reassuring smile. "Don't worry about it, kid."

We quickly pack up the truck and fly back to the storage unit, because there's no way this death trap is making it across the state to Philly. We hop into Jim's rusty forest-green Ford Explorer, and he cleans off the passenger seat so I can slide in, chucking snack wrappers and empty water bottles into the back seat.

We stop off at my apartment on the way to the turnpike so I can grab bail money. My hands freeze over the two jars I've spent all semester saving up. I thought my money was destined for rent payments, and textbooks, and maybe, just maybe, meals out and frozen yogurt and roller-skating with . . . But now . . .

I shake my head and quickly swipe both of them into my backpack before sprinting out the door and back into the car.

Jim whips through the streets of Oakland to the highway while my phone GPS guides the way.

Pennsylvania flies by as Jim's headlights shine through the darkness. I press my forehead up against the cool glass of the window, watching the painted white line whiz past as dusk turns to night.

"You okay?" he asks. For Jim to be initiating a conversation, things have to be pretty serious.

I pull my head away from the window and look over at him. "I don't know yet."

"Is this . . . a normal occurrence? How long has she been an alcoholic?"

"I . . . she . . ." I stammer, struggling to string words together, struggling to admit it. "A while," I finally say. "I've *always* been afraid something like this would happen. *Especially* when I left to come to Pittsburgh. It just feels like . . . this day has been coming for a while." I let out a long sigh and look down at my hands. "I should never have left."

"No way," Jim says, shaking his head. "Listen to me, okay? From someone who knows from experience, you can't be responsible for her anymore. She has to be responsible for herself. You're going to be honest with her and lay out the facts, and we're going to get her some help, Alex. Tonight. Some professional, honest-to-goodness help. And *you.*" He looks over at me. "You're going to go back to Pittsburgh, and get your degree, and stop carrying the weight of another person around."

His words hit me hard.

I didn't even realize how *exhausted* I am. How heavy this weight has been. How scared I've been for *years.*

"We've also got a double next weekend at this big music festival, so I can't have you quitting now," he says with a wry smile, and a laugh escapes my lips.

As we get closer, the familiar Philly skyline comes swinging into view, and I watch as Jim takes the familiar exit to a completely unfamiliar place.

My leg starts to bounce up and down as I peer out the window, and as the thought of *picking up my mother from jail* and making her accept the fact she *actually needs help* circles my brain, my teeth start to chatter too.

He pulls into the parking lot but waits in the car as I head inside. The sterile fluorescent lights shine painfully bright after our drive in the dark.

"Hi," I say to the woman at the front desk, sitting behind a glass window. My eyes flick around the room, pausing on the huge door behind her, the patch on her shirt, the blue waiting chairs to the right of us.

What do I even do?

"I'm, uh, here to pick up Donna Blackwood. I'm her daughter. Alex."

She makes a note, then calls down to holding to bring my mom out.

I hold my breath, listening as a door opens in the distance. The sound of footsteps echoes loudly down the hall, until finally, the gray door behind the front desk swings open, and an officer escorts my disheveled mom out.

She looks . . . *extremely* worse for wear. Her black T-shirt is stained, her brown hair unkempt. I do some math. *Nineteen hours.*

This is probably the longest she's gone without a drink in close to a decade.

She refuses to meet my gaze, her eyes locked on the tile floor beneath us.

"Here's what she came in with," the front desk lady says, sliding a plastic bag with my mom's phone and wallet across the desk to me. It's a haze as she goes over paperwork, the fine my mom is required to pay, what this means for her driver's license.

I grab a pen and take notes, my anger mounting with each line I write, my mom sure as hell not listening even though *she* should be the one keeping track of all this. She should be the one worried about hearings and appeals and what to do next.

When the woman is done, I grab the bag of my mom's stuff, nodding to the doors. "Let's go."

I turn on my heel and slam through to the outside, the cool fall air making my skin prickle as I try to keep it together. I pace around the parking lot, my mom a shadow just behind me. Jim is leaning against his SUV, discreetly not looking at the both of us.

I spin around to face her, and she looks up at me, her eyes teary.

"Alex . . . ," she starts.

"No." I shake my head. It's time for my mom to stop

running too. To finally hear me. "I just left *school* to drive five hours to pick you up *from jail* after you crashed Tommy's car *into a telephone pole*. Do you understand that? Do you understand how fucked up this is?"

She doesn't say anything. She just stares at me, her eyes wide and slowly welling up with tears.

"No. Don't pull that card. I am *tired* of this. I am tired of giving you money I need for school just so you can blow it on alcohol. I am tired of worrying about getting a call like I got tonight, telling me you crashed a car, or hurt yourself, or *worse*." Tears start to stream down my cheeks, and I wipe them away with the back of my hand. "You need to get help, Mom. You can't keep living like this. *We* can't keep living like this."

"Alex. No one was hurt," she says with a laugh. "You can't kill a telephone pole."

"No. But you can kill yourself," I say, my chest heaving. "You *are* killing yourself."

She doesn't have a response to that, so I keep going.

"I know . . ." My voice cracks, and I pause, trying to collect myself. "I know it's been hard since Dad left. Trust me. I do. But I can't keep taking care of you. You need to learn to take care of yourself. I can't be your husband, and your mom, and your daughter."

I've spent so much time *fixing* people, but . . . I never bothered to help myself. Until now.

"You are *going to get help*, or I . . ." My voice trails off as I glance over at Jim. He gives me a small, encouraging smile. "Can't have you in my life. Not if you refuse to even try. Not if you are on a one-way path to killing yourself. If you won't do this for you, *please* do it for me."

I watch as her face changes from shock to confusion to understanding.

And finally . . . she nods, agreeing.

"The second that car hit that pole, I thought of you," she says, a sob escaping her lips. "All I could think about was how much I'd let you down. How much I *keep* letting you down, Alex."

I reach out and pull her in, her body feeling so small and fragile despite the amount of pain it's caused.

I give in to the tears, all the ones I swallowed for the past few years, from this past week, all of it crashing down on me at once.

"I'm sorry, baby," my mom says, her hand reaching up to gently stroke my hair for the first time in years.

And even though things seem almost impossible to fix, at least holding tightly on to each other, I can't help but think maybe we can both climb out of rock bottom. That maybe it isn't too late to talk to Molly, if I can just find the courage to.

When we get in the car, Jim talks to my mom about his experience and the rehab he went to in Erie.

"I spent a night or two in jail myself," he says, giving her a wry smile. "Nothing makes you want to get clean more than being stuffed in a holding cell with a communal toilet in the corner."

My mom smiles weakly from the mess of his back seat.

"No bullshit, but I think this place could really help you out. It definitely got me on the right track."

When she agrees, we drive through the night to Erie, pulling over every now and then for my mom to dry heave on the side of the road, the withdrawal symptoms slowly setting in. About halfway there, I join her in the back seat, letting her lay her head down in my lap while I gently stroke her sweat-drenched hair, wincing as her body rattles away like a leaf in the wind.

When we get there, Jim knows just where to go and who to talk to, and we get my mom set up in a room. I help her into bed, and she curls up into a ball, looking so small beneath the white knit blanket as the doctor monitors her vitals.

I wait until she falls into a fitful sleep before sneaking off down the hallway to pay as much as I can in advance, the two jars of savings hopefully enough to make a dent.

When I get there, the blond woman behind the desk who helped check my mom in gives me a big smile. I'm surprised she has this much enthusiasm after working the night shift.

"I, uh, was wondering about the bill?" I slide my backpack

off my shoulder and unzip it to pull out the two jars. "I can pay some of it now. . . ."

She waves her hand. "It's totally covered."

I squint, my hand frozen over one of my jars. "What?"

"Yeah, Jim swung down here a couple of minutes ago and enrolled her in the same residential program he was in here at Erie Endeavors. It covers the cost in full. About a month or so here in the facility, followed by an intensive extended-care outpatient program to help her transition back to daily life."

It's not often that I'm knocked completely and totally speechless, but . . . this is definitely one of those moments. I look down at the two jars in my backpack, my eyes stinging with tears.

Mechanically, I turn and head back down the hall to her room, slowing outside of it when I hear Jim and my mom talking.

I peer around the corner to see him leaning up against the wall, two enormous coffees in his hands.

"She's a good kid," he says. "Pain in the ass, but she works hard. Doesn't complain. A hell of a lot better with people than I'll ever be."

My mom smiles at that. "You'll take care of her? While I'm in here?" she asks.

He shifts, looking down at the two cups of coffee. "I get the feeling she's been taking care of herself for a while," he says as he takes a small sip. "But yeah. I'll keep an eye on her."

My mom nods, her eyes closing sleepily. I lean against the wall as Jim comes out into the hallway, closing the door behind him. When he sees me, he holds out one of the coffees, and I take it gratefully, giving him a playful nudge.

"Guess this kicks me out of the running for employee of the month, huh?"

He snorts and takes a swig, leaning against the wall next to me. "Oh yeah. Your ass can kiss that goodbye."

I let out a long sigh, the adrenaline from the past twelve hours giving way to a bone-deep fatigue. "I owe you one, Jim." I look up at him. "Thank you. For everything."

"Least I could do," he says, and an awkward silence settles over us.

Clearly, neither of us is particularly good with showing our emotions.

"Sorry you're missing your shift at that farmers' market this morning."

"That place is the worst. They always park us by the porta-potties, so it's damn near impossible to sell out," he says, rolling his eyes. "Those fuckers."

"Those fuckers," I echo. And despite everything that's happened, I can't help but laugh.

CHAPTER 34

MOLLY

On the phone call with my mom, there was no mention of how distant I've been, no mention of all the calls I've missed or the texts that have gone unanswered. Honestly, I think she was just happy to be talking to me. But then, after I asked if I could borrow one of her formal dresses, she kept *insisting* that she come down again so we could take another trip to the mall . . . just the two of us. I was able to get her talked out of that, but then she wanted to come down and help me get ready.

We finally came to an agreement when she insisted on *at least* meeting Cora for lunch.

And honestly, I thought it might be a good idea. Meeting parents seems like a big step in a relationship. Maybe that's what step five in the plan was . . . meet the parents. Not that it matters now.

Honestly, the idea of two of my favorite people meeting

excited me. Things went so well when she met Alex that I wasn't worried about it.

At least not until now, sitting here with the two of them around a small table at Point Brugge, my and Mom's favorite lunch spot.

"So, Cora, what are you majoring in?" my mom asks as our waitress sets down a Reuben with a side of fries in front of her.

"I'm doubling in English lit and history, with a minor in French," Cora says, pausing to thank the waitress for her Pittsburgh Salad. Lettuce, cheddar, boiled egg, and bacon, topped off with the classic Pittsburgh pile of fries.

"Fries . . . on a salad," Cora says, looking down at her plate. "Do you like that, Molly?"

"Well—" I start, but am interrupted by my mom.

"It's our favorite part!" she says, answering for me. My skin prickles as she sinks her teeth into a handful of her own and winks at me.

"I could never get used to it," Cora replies, rolling them onto a napkin with her fork before pouring out her dressing. "Anyway! I'm really into Greek mythology right now. I've been reading this book on the origins of Apollo. . . ." Her entire body lights up with that excitement that first caught my eye in class. I smile, watching her go on as she starts digging into the nitty-gritty of the book, about Apollo traversing the known world and finding a place to build his temple and . . .

My cheeks start to hurt, so I let my smile drop down into a straight line.

I look over at my mom, and I can practically see her eyes glazing over as Cora speaks.

"We're—" I try to switch topics and tell my mom that we're in biology together, but Cora sort of plows over me with more details of her book.

I never realized how much she likes to talk. I was so glad for it at the party. She would fill the silence when I was too nervous to say anything. So I just never really noticed, but . . . now that I want to, I can't get a word in.

I feel a layer of sweat coat the back of my neck as I watch the scene drag on in front of me. My mom has clearly checked out of the conversation even though she's still trying to be polite by offering an "oh" and "uh-huh" every now and again.

She hates her. My mom hates her.

God, this was such a terrible idea. I just thought . . . I thought she'd like her as much as I did.

As much as I *do*.

Maybe Cora's just nervous to meet my mom. *That* I can relate to.

By the time we make it through lunch, I've barely eaten any of my sandwich, because I'm a little puddle of stress and anxiety. So I pack it into a to-go box for later, then follow my mom back out to her car, Cora walking beside me.

"Thank God she liked me. I was so nervous," she whispers,

looking not nervous at all. I smile and nod, surprised but also relieved she couldn't tell what my mom really thought.

When we get to the car, my mom pulls four long dresses out of the trunk for me to choose from.

"Which one do you want?" she asks, fanning them out for me. There's a blue one with white flowers, a sage-green one with a deep V cut, and a sleek black one that looks the most promising if I *have* to choose, which I do . . . because I can't just wear my new jeans to this student art thingy. There's another one, but it's so far from what I like that I don't even—

"Oh my God! *This one!*" Cora yells, clutching on to a bright red, floor-length dress . . . the fourth one.

"That's what I was thinking!" I reply, plastering a smile onto my face.

"Really? I would've guessed the black one," my mom says, looking at me suspiciously.

"No, I like the red one," I reply, taking it from Cora and heading for the passenger seat. Why can't she just let me handle this for myself?

The ride back to campus is dead silent as I look at the red dress on my lap. The *bright* red dress.

Cora and my mom exchange pleasantries before Cora hops out at her dorm. I tell her how much I'm looking forward to tomorrow, and then I watch her head through the door of her building.

I don't say anything as we sit there, parked on the side of

the road, and neither does my mom. Which never happens.

Her voice finally cuts through the deafening silence. "Cora seems nice. Do you like her a lot? Is it everything you thought it would be?"

"Don't do that," I tell her, chewing on my knuckle as I stare out the window.

"Do what? What'd I do?" she asks.

"I know you don't like her."

"Molly." She sighs. "I'm really, really happy for you."

"But you don't like her," I repeat, frustrated with how much her opinion still means to me after all this time.

"I just need to get to know her better. You know how I am. It takes me a while to warm up to people."

"Really?" I ask, looking over at her. "Because it didn't take you any time at all to warm up to Alex."

"What do you want me to say?" she asks, shrugging her shoulders. "Yeah, I liked Alex. But because you were so happy at the mall that day. You're different with her around. In a good way, I mean. You were more . . . *you* than I've ever seen you with other people."

"You didn't even give Cora a chance, and you clearly don't know *anything* about Alex. I don't think you really even know *me*," I say in a harsher tone.

"What is *that* supposed to mean?"

"Nothing. Forget it," I reply, struggling to hold everything inside.

"You don't answer my calls or texts for a couple of weeks and you think I don't know you anymore? I know you better than anyone. I know for a fact that you don't like that dress."

"This *isn't* about the dress!" I snap at her like I never have before. "It's about *me*. I'm *trying* to move on from high school, but you just keep dragging me back! I'm practically a different person than the one you dropped off here a month ago, and that scares you. Of *course* you don't want me to date Cora, because that would mean I would actually have someone in my life who's more important than *you*." My mom flinches, her eyes looking glassy, but I've needed to tell her this for a long time. I just never seemed to be able to find my voice until right now. "When I'm around you now, I feel like I just revert back to the person I don't want to be anymore. You know that thing that happened at the food court, when you were rude to that Korean guy?"

"I wasn't rude, Molly. I—"

"Yes, you were. Do you know how that makes me feel? It makes me feel even more uncomfortable in my own skin than I already am. I love you, Mom, but I don't want you to be my only friend. I don't want to hate being Korean like you do. I don't want to hate who I am anymore, and I don't want to be strangled by anxiety for my entire life. I'm tired of shutting everyone out because I think I'm not good enough. I'm tired of stuffing myself into a mold because I'm terrified to let people see *me*."

I catch my breath, turning toward the passenger window again, because I can't stand her looking at me the way I just *know* she is. Like I'm a stranger sitting in her car. I've never talked to her like that before.

I wait for her to argue with me, to try to convince me that I need her or that she needs me, but she doesn't do any of those things.

"I'm sorry," she says, her voice as quiet as a mouse. I look over at her to see that she's not looking at me like I'm a stranger at all. She's looking at me like I'm the person she loves most in this world and I just broke her heart, which is so much worse.

"I'm sorry that I've held on. I'm sorry if my issues with being Asian have affected you. I *never* want to be the type of parent that makes you feel like you're not good enough or that holds you back in any way. That was never my intention, Molly. I promise you. I want you to make your own decisions and do what you want and date who you want and have a life that's your own and not just ours, but . . . I'm still your mom and I'm going to tell you when you're wrong, and you're wrong about one thing." She raises her eyebrows at me as if to ask permission.

I nod.

"I think you're *incredible*. And I don't think that's something new about you that has just come out over the past month. I think you've *always* been incredible. I think you can do anything you want to do in this life. I think you can have *anything.*" She turns more in her seat to face me, looking right into my eyes as I try to blink away a few tears. She continues. "And you should be with someone who agrees and sees that too and wants to be as selfish with you as I have. Just don't settle for anything less than *exactly* what you want. Not for me and not for someone else. That is the only thing I care about, because you deserve the very best, Molly Parker. You deserved it a month ago, and you deserve it now. You should be with someone you can always be yourself around. Someone you don't have to try so hard to impress." Her eyes flick down to the dress in my lap.

"It's just a dress," I reply.

"As long as that's all it is."

"That's all it is," I tell her, maybe trying to convince myself, too.

She takes a deep breath and looks out her window. "And I know my relationship with my heritage is a little screwed up, but I also can't just flip a switch and make it go away, not with how I grew up. I've tried."

"I know," I reply, acknowledging that I could never fully understand what she's been through.

"But I'll keep trying. Because I really don't want you to end up with the same issues as me. I don't want you to feel ashamed of a single part of who you are." She turns to look at me, and I give her a small smile, taking her hand in mine across the center console.

"I'm sorry I shut you out. You didn't deserve that . . . like, at all."

"How about I lay off the phone calls and you meet me for lunch in a couple of weeks to tell me all about the art gala, or . . . as much as you want to tell," she says. "And please invite Cora. I'd really, genuinely love to get to know her better."

"That sounds good," I say. As I start to gather my stuff up, she reaches across the car and puts her hand gently on my cheek.

"Hey." Her thumb rubs circles against my skin. The muscles in my body that have been tense since lunch finally loosen a little. "It doesn't matter what I think or what Noah thinks or what anyone else thinks. Just follow your heart, babe. You always have." Her hand drops back to her lap.

I nod, then open the door to step out onto the sidewalk. "Thanks for the dress and for lunch." I hold up the garment bag and the to-go box. "Love you."

"I love you, too. I'll see you both in a couple of weeks," she says, and I give her a small smile before jogging across the street to the quad when the light turns green.

I feel a little lighter, like something's finally resolved. But not everything.

It *should* be that simple.

If *I* like her, that's all that matters.

And I do like her.

I have everything I've been dreaming about for the past four years.

So why does it feel like I *am* settling?

CHAPTER 35

ALEX

I get back to Pittsburgh late on Friday, when the sun is already drifting close to the horizon.

Now that I don't have to spend every waking minute worrying about my mom, I spent the whole trip staring out the window, thinking about, well . . . Molly.

How she's the only one who would understand the enormity of what happened. What last night meant for me. How sharing that part of myself with her that night in the library made such a difference.

If I can finally stand up to my mom and tell her how I feel, I can do the same for Molly.

And even if she's with Cora and I've missed my chance—if I ever even had one—I owe her an apology for hurting her and for lying. Because she's the best friend I've ever had too.

And if I can't have more, at least maybe I can earn her trust back and have that.

When Jim drops me off, I tap on her Instagram story from two hours ago to see a boomerang of Noah holding up an enormous slice of pizza, in the kitchen we made palachinkas in.

She's at Noah's.

And so even though I want nothing more than to just collapse into bed, I find myself weaving through the streets on my bike, the wind stinging my eyes as I whip around corners, the green street signs a blur as I fly past.

Before I know it, I turn onto Mintwood Street, the soles of my Converse dragging along the pavement as I look up at the lopsided white house on the corner.

I didn't realize just how much I missed her until this very moment.

I pull out my phone to call her, but just as I hit the green phone icon, the screen turns black, the battery completely drained from my night of driving across Pennsylvania.

I let out a long, slow exhale.

I know this is an out. I know I could just run away.

But I don't want to.

I lean my bike against the steps, then jog slowly up to the front door. My fingers curl into a fist, and I reach out, hesitating, before lightly knocking.

I don't think I breathe until the door swings open, my heart jumping in my chest as . . .

Noah appears.

"Alex! Hey," he says as he leans against the doorway. He nods behind him to the inside of the house. "Molly's not here."

"Oh." I swallow, nodding. "Do you . . . maybe know where I can find her?"

"She just left to go to this thing at the art museum." He hesitates and pulls his eyes away from mine, rubbing the back of his head, like he knows how much this next part is going to sting. "With Cora."

Even though I should've expected this, the wind still gets knocked right out of me.

"Right! Totally. Yeah," I manage to get out, my hand finding the cool metal of the railing as I stumble down the top step. "Uh, thanks, Noah. I actually gotta . . ." I point behind me, my voice trailing off.

I turn, almost mechanically, and head down to my bike, trying pretty damn hard to keep it together.

"Alex!" he calls after me. I look back, and he jogs across the porch and down the steps and stops right in front of me. "I . . . I love my sister." He looks down at me, a small smile on his lips. "I was a little scared when I saw she got stuck with a single. Scared she would struggle to make friends. Scared it would be like high school all over again."

He reaches out and puts a hand on my shoulder. "But I'm not scared anymore. She's finally figuring out who she is, and I think that has something to do with you. So . . . thank you for that."

I look down, kicking lightly at the bottom step. "Well, she's got Cora now."

He shrugs. "Yeah, maybe. But that doesn't mean she doesn't miss you."

Yeah, right. Tears sting my eyes, and I scoop up my bike, hop quickly onto it, and pedal off down the street without another word.

My legs burn as I head back up the hill and across the bridge to Oakland, my chest heaving as I pedal as hard as I can, flying through side streets and around turns.

We don't have to pretend we give a shit about each other.

But we weren't pretending. You can't pretend to feel the things I felt with her. I've tried.

I slam on my brakes as the stoplight in front of me flicks to red, the one part of the route home I was hoping I could just sail past.

The Carnegie Museum of Art towers just next to me, completely consuming my peripheral vision.

I should've just run the red.

I turn my head to see a thin trail of students milling about just inside, visible through a wall of enormous glass windows. Black suits and long, colorful dresses, drinks clutched in their hands, smiles plastered on their faces.

I want to go in. To find her. But that would be selfish. I want to talk to her, but I don't want to ruin her night. I know that an event like this can only end with the two of them together.

Still, a part of me is searching for her. Wanting to see her pass by in a long black dress, her head thrown back in laughter, Cora just beside her. Wanting nothing more than to have her just feel happy and like she's completely herself.

And loving her just enough to have Cora be the person to give her that instead of me.

Loving her.

The realization startles me more than the car behind me honking. I nearly topple off my bike as I'm brought back to reality. The light in front of me has *clearly* changed to green without me noticing.

I wave my apology and coast down the street and onto the sidewalk, then park my bike in the bike rack outside the library.

I can't go back to my apartment. Not yet.

I head up the steps and take a deep breath as I push inside, winding up the stairs and through the stacks to the spot I came to with Molly, the smell of old paper and bindings filling my nose as I slide slowly down to the floor.

I close my eyes and lean my head back against the shelves, letting the silence wrap itself around me.

I think about my mom, up in Erie, finally getting the help she needs after all this time. Of Molly, only a few doors away, probably holding Cora's hand like she held mine that night at the roller rink.

The library used to be a place to quiet the pain and the heartache, to escape from it, but now . . . it feels like a place to let myself feel it. To let the dam break.

I pull my knees up to my chest, the tears I've been holding in since I got back to Pittsburgh finally beginning to fall.

CHAPTER 36

MOLLY

My heels are completely frozen to the marble floor under me as I take in the girl standing in front of me.

A green, floor-length dress that's just tight enough to show off every single one of her curves, the neckline plunging down well past her sternum, a ruby-red necklace hanging over the bare skin of her chest, matching her earrings and, not coincidentally, my dress.

"Oh my God, Cora. You look . . ." I smile, meeting her bright eyes. "Beautiful."

She lets out a giggle that echoes through the foyer, her heels clicking over to me.

"Back at you. The dress looks *so good*. We made the right choice," she tells me. I look down at my mom's sparkly red dress and the pair of two-inch heels that hopefully won't be my cause of death tonight.

"Thanks," I say, trying not to be too obvious as I pull the fabric down so it sits a little flatter.

"Shall we?" she asks, offering me her arm, a thin gold bracelet dangling from her wrist.

I blush and wrap my hand around her upper arm, letting her lead me into the gallery.

Whatever step five was in the plan, I think it's safe to say we're well past it.

We walk up to one of the many bars floating around the gigantic room.

"Hey, could I get two glasses of chardonnay?" Cora asks, surprising me, but unfortunately, she can't quite manage to pull it off like . . . well, like some other people can. The bartender, dressed in a white shirt and a black bow tie, sees right through it. He pours two ginger ales into champagne flutes without a word and slides them across the bar to us.

"It was worth a shot," I whisper.

As we begin to walk around the show together, I spend most of the time looking at all the students dressed up in their fancy clothes, wondering if they're *actually* having a good time. I'm not sure how anyone could *like* all of this. I've never been much of an art connoisseur, but the idea of looking at the art right in front of the artist makes me *real* nervous.

"Oh, hey. This girl's in my lit class," Cora says, tugging me into an exhibit.

I follow her into an area with paintings hanging on makeshift walls in the middle of the room. Each painting looks a lot like the one before it, amorphous blobs of various sizes and skin colors on canvases ten feet tall.

"Lindsay?" Cora asks, approaching a girl a couple of inches shorter than me, dressed in a velvet blazer and oxford shoes. She lifts her chin, squinting at Cora for a second before recognition floods her face.

"Cora." She smiles approvingly, obviously as entranced by Cora as everyone else. "Hey. It's great to see you."

"You too." Cora peeks back at me. "This is Molly," she introduces me, and I reach out to shake Lindsay's hand. "I didn't know you'd be here. This is your exhibit?"

"Yes, it's called *Race Place.* I've been working on it for almost two years now," Lindsay says, proudly looking up at her masterpieces, her blue eyes shining against her milky-white skin.

"Tell me what it's all about," Cora says. Lindsay starts telling us about how each piece represents the erasure of race in American culture and the journey she's been on while trying to figure out how to translate what she's learned into this particular medium.

I try to listen at first, but it all sounds so rehearsed, so dry, that I just can't rein my attention span in for long enough. Maybe I should've just asked Cora to go roller-skating after all. It would've been ten times the fun. Crappy chicken tenders, root beer, and maybe even a little limbo.

"It was nice to meet you, Molly," Lindsay says, snapping me out of my thoughts. She moves on to speak to another student who has wandered into her exhibit. I look back up at the largest painting with Cora next to me. I'm trying to understand how each painting represents something different when all ten of them look *exactly* the same.

Also, I think I could've painted them myself, but I'm pretty sure that's a crappy thing to say at an art showing.

A funny thought hits me as I look up at the oversize painting, the brown, black, and tan shapes all pressed together. And once it hits, I just cannot unsee it.

"Hey." I lean over, already laughing as I try to whisper in Cora's ear. "Doesn't it kinda look like . . . gigantic butt cheeks?" I laugh a little louder. It *really* does.

But Cora doesn't laugh with me. She just squints and shakes her head.

"Uh, not really. Not to me," she says.

"Oh, yeah. No, they really don't. Sorry." I point my thumb over my shoulder. "You want to keep walking around?"

She smiles and nods, letting my unfunny joke thankfully fall into the past.

As we move around the room, Cora comments on a ton of paintings and drawings and sculptures, but just like she didn't see the butt cheeks, I don't see half of what she sees in them. Nonetheless, I stick by her as she talks to a million people about a million different pieces, my face feeling tired from having to smile every time she looks my way. I wish it were just the two of us, but Cora seems to thrive off social interaction, so maybe this is how it will always be. . . .

As we move on through the exhibits, a text buzzes into my phone.

It's from Noah.

Alex was just here looking for you. She left, but thought you should know.

I suck in a sharp breath as a ringing in my ears blocks out all the sound in the room.

Alex was looking for me.

Why was Alex looking for me?

I wonder if she came to apologize.

I wonder what she wanted.

I wonder if she would've thought that painting looked like . . .

Yeah. I smile to myself. *I know she would have.*

And we would've laughed about it together, just the two of us, because no one else would think it was funny, but it wouldn't matter. And then we would go get frozen yogurt and walk around campus as late as we wanted, talking about all the things that we've never talked about with anyone else.

The good. The bad. It wouldn't matter. We'd talk about *everything.*

God, I miss—

No. I don't. Because it's like she said. None of that was real, so what is there to even miss?

What is real is that she's selfish, cocky, a *horrible* skater, brutally honest . . . though that's funny at times, independent, loyal, easygoing, and—

"Hey, Molly." Cora's voice pulls me out of my head, back to the art gala that I just can't seem to stay present at this evening.

"Yeah?" I ask, blinking away the past and realizing that we've made our way into a secluded corner all by ourselves.

Cora stands in front of me, wringing her hands together nervously, which is a look I haven't seen on her before. She reaches out and scoops up my hand in hers, taking me by surprise.

My breath feels caught in my throat, the room spinning like the marble under my feet has turned to jelly, and Cora is right here in front of me, looking into my eyes.

Her hand feels so . . . noticeable in mine, foreign, like it maybe shouldn't be there. When Alex took my hand to pull me up the stairs and into the library, it seemed to belong there so much that it almost didn't feel like anything at all.

"I'm really glad you came with me tonight. I want to tell you something," she huffs out.

My chest is so tight that it hurts.

"I . . . uh. I'm having some feelings for you," she says, and I feel my lips lift into a smile at the words I never *ever* thought I would hear from her.

This is it. I did it! *We* did it.

Again Alex's face pops into my head, her curious green

eyes with the strands of yellow in the center, her small nose, her pale lips.

Cora takes a step closer to me, the toes of her heels touching mine, and just like in the library, it's almost imperceptible, but I can feel the space closing between us.

I picture Alex slouched against the books, her foot up against mine. Telling me about her life, about the future she so desperately wants for herself. The future she could finally see.

Cora slides her hands up my wrists, up my forearms, holding my elbows in her palms. She starts leaning into me, her eyes closing slowly.

I try to close mine too, but . . . None of this feels right. None of it feels like it was supposed to.

And then I remember . . .

I remember how electrifying the air felt between Alex and me as we looked at each other that night in the library. Like there was this uncontrollable force pulling me toward her.

I remember the way I could feel my heart beating in every single part of me.

How I would've given everything to be close to her.

As I watch Cora lean in, just a few inches away, I realize that no matter how beautiful she is, no matter how perfect I thought she was for me, *this* is not *that*.

It never could be. Because the Cora I thought I could love existed only in my head. She wasn't real. And while she's still gorgeous, and funny, and magnetic . . .

For the first time, I get it.

I understand.

There's a difference between a fantasy and, well . . .

Love.

"Cora." She freezes, her face so close to mine that it's blurry. "Cora," I repeat, and she straightens up. My eyes coat with tears at the thought of knowing what I have to do. "I am . . . so, *so* sorry, but I can't do this," I whisper, wiping away a tear.

"What?" she asks, leaning away from me.

I take a deep breath in. "Cora, I have liked you for *so* long. You really have no idea. And when I came to college, I wanted things to be different. *I* wanted to be different . . . for you. I'm not really the person you've gotten to know this past month. I don't like rugby or show tunes or art. I hate this dress. I think I look like a Christmas ornament, and I can't even feel my feet in these heels. Alex has been helping me become the person I thought you would like, but . . . I guess I ended up becoming, well . . . *me.*" I step backward out of her grasp, catching her hands in mine.

"Cora, I . . . I just want to be friends."

She looks hurt, and stunned, but she nods, falling back a couple of steps.

"I'm sorry. I actually have to go, okay?" I ask, giving her hands a squeeze.

. . .

Stumbling out into the cool night air and down the sidewalk in front of the Carnegie art museum, I find my phone in my purse and dial Alex's number as quickly as possible. It doesn't even ring once before I hear her automated voicemail.

I hang up and dial again, my chest feeling like it's going to rip open.

Straight to voicemail.

Shit!

I stop at the corner, putting my hands on my hips as I realize how much my feet are killing me from these death traps.

I remember all the stuff she said to me at the concert, and that little voice in my head tells me that this is a bad idea, that she really doesn't care about me and she's just going to say the same thing again and it's never going to work.

But I shut it right up, because all that stuff she said to me that night was such bullshit. I should've seen right through it at the time, but at least I can see it now.

She wasn't pretending. Moments like the one we shared in the library could only come from something real.

I *have* to talk to her.

I *have* to tell her how I feel.

I hold up my phone and redial her number one more time as I cross the street in the direction of her apartment.

As I listen to her voicemail again, I catch a glimpse of something out of my peripheral that makes me stop dead on the sidewalk, my phone still up to my ear.

A fluorescent-orange bicycle locked up right outside the library.

Of course.

I run up the concrete steps, taking them two at a time, which ends up being a big mistake. On the top step, my ankle gives out beneath me, and I grab on to the railing before the heels do too much damage.

Oh, fuck these.

I peel the shoes off, clutching them both in one hand, and then practically rip the door off the hinges with the other.

I sprint through the main floor in my long gown, and even though that turns pretty much everyone's head, for once I don't give a shit.

I just have to get to her.

I strain my muscles to make it to the top floor, then swing around the railing, struggling to catch my breath as I fly through the stacks, each one blurring into the next, until . . .

There.

I stop, looking down at her on the floor with a book in her lap, and even though I just sprinted to get here as fast as I could, now I pause, the events of the last month washing back over me just from seeing her again. . . .

The party and biology.

Our bet at the coffee shop.

Rugby tryouts and frozen yogurt.

Shopping with my mom and trying Korean food.

Ping-Pong.

Limbo.

The concert.

Our fight.

Cora.

All of it.

Leading me here.

Leading me . . . to her.

CHAPTER 37

ALEX

I turn the page of the book I'm holding, but the words all blur together. Every sentence I've tried to read for the past hour is impossible to retain.

Letting out a sigh, I close it, surprised to see a flash of red when I turn my head, sparkling sequins shimmering faintly under the dim library lights.

It takes me a minute to register what I'm seeing.

Molly. Here. In a sparkling red dress, her hair pulled away from her face, her lips a matching ruby.

She looks . . . beautiful.

And happy. Her smile practically outshines her dress.

She's probably made things official with Cora at their little art museum gala. Maybe they even kissed, tucked away in the corner of an exhibit on pastels or watercolors.

I clear my throat and stand, sliding the book back into its place on the shelf. "I didn't pin you for a sparkly-red-dress kind of girl," I say, my eyes fixed instead on the book's gold lettering along the edge, the peeling tape sitting over the faded label.

When she doesn't say anything, I know it's my time to talk. To apologize.

I take a deep breath, slowly pulling my fingertips off the spine of the book.

"I, uh. I took my mom to rehab last night," I say. "And the whole ride back to Pittsburgh, all I could think about was how you were the only person I wanted to tell and how I'd screwed it all up. How sorry I am for what I said the night of the concert. Because you were right. About Natalie. About everything. But I didn't want to hear it, so instead, I just tore it all down and hurt you." I let out a long sigh and turn to face her. "Molly, I didn't mean what I said—"

"Is she okay? Are you okay?" she asks, and I can't deny the tears that swim into my eyes.

"Yeah. She ran a car into a telephone pole, but . . . she'll be okay. *We'll* be okay," I clarify. "But I want *us* to be okay too."

There's a moment of silence, and then she takes a tiny step closer.

"Did you ever think we'd date?" she asks over a ragged breath.

I freeze, her words catching me off guard. "What?"

She raises her eyebrows at me, and I notice her chest is heaving, a pair of heels hanging in her right hand. Was she *running*?

"Me and you," she says, pointing between us. "Did you ever think we'd date?"

I open my mouth, struggling to find the right thing to say. All that comes out, though, is a single word. The truth. "Yes."

"Do you still?" she asks, rubbing salt in the wound.

I shake my head, pulling my eyes away from hers. "You like Cora."

She's silent for a long, heart-pumping moment. All I can do is look at the hem of her dress, the tiny rays of light reflecting off the sequins onto the floor.

"Every second I've spent with Cora this past week, I was thinking about you. About how I wanted to be with *you*." I hear her let out a long breath of air. "It was like you talked about. Real versus fantasy. It took me a long time to realize, too long, but being with you made me feel better than any fantasy I'd ever played over in my head. Like the person I never knew I could be. The person I *am*."

I lift my head to see her taking a step closer.

"That's how I knew you were lying that night. I know the real you. Just like you know the real me," she adds.

Her face is inches from mine, her eyes warm and earnest, the air between us buzzing with electricity. She parts her lips, hesitating before she speaks around her smile.

"It was always you, Alex."

And with those words, the barriers I've put up to shield

myself from the world are finally knocked down. The boxes where I've locked my feelings away completely disintegrate. Until it's just Molly and me and that force that's been pulling me toward her since the very beginning. But neither of us is fighting it anymore.

I close my eyes, frozen in place as Molly stands up on her tippy-toes, and I almost entirely forget how to breathe. Her lips barely graze mine, but somehow they manage to set my whole body on fire.

I reach for her, but before I can even pull her closer, she lunges forward, knocking me back into the shelves. A few books fall onto the floor with scattered thumps, but she doesn't stop kissing me. I wrap my arms around her, my hands grabbing on to her hips as I pull her body up against mine. I hear her heels hit the floor, and then her hands are sliding up my neck, into my hair. There isn't a single inch of space between us, but somehow she still doesn't feel close enough.

I've kissed . . . plenty of people, but it has never been like *this*. The floor and the ceiling and the stacks of books all melt away, everything fading except for the two of us, the feel of her sequined dress beneath my hands, my heart hammering so hard in my chest that I'm *sure* she can feel it.

When we eventually pull apart, she rests her forehead up against mine, and a small smile dances onto her lips as she sways back and forth in my arms. "You know, you never told me what step five is," she says.

I laugh and give her a small shrug. "That's because I've never gotten to it."

She pulls away, raising her eyebrows at me. "What is it?"

"It's pretty simple," I say as I reach up to tuck a loose strand of hair behind her ear. "Step five: tell her how you feel."

My hand slides down to rest against her cheek, my thumb gently tracing her skin.

"And how do you feel?" she whispers, like she doesn't know she stole my heart, piece by piece, that first day in biology class, and that night we got frozen yogurt, and at our roller-skating date, bruised forehead and all.

"Like I'm so in love with you, Molly Parker."

And . . . it feels right. The words I've been so scared of for years suddenly come easier than I ever thought possible.

"I love you too, Alex Blackwood," she says, and it's all the things I never knew an "I love you" could be, meeting me exactly as I am, without a single condition.

It's coming home instead of running away.

Her hands unlock behind my neck, sliding down in between us. "Well, I guess I got the girl after all," she says.

"See? I told you my plan would work."

"Shut up." She laughs and reaches out to grab the collar of my T-shirt, tugging me into another kiss.

And for once I actually do.

ACKNOWLEDGMENTS

This entire book, being able to cowrite something with my best friend and wife, has been an absolute dream come true. I have so many people to thank for making this possible.

First and always foremost, an enormous thank-you to our incredible editor, Alexa Pastor. This book, from start to finish, through the many rounds of revisions, went so smoothly, and it is ALL thanks to you. Your notes always blow me away, and it is just the COOLEST to watch the stories we have worked on together take shape and get drastically better thanks to your guiding hand. Cheers to book four, Alexa!

I am filled with SO much gratitude for my amazing, amazing agent, Emily van Beek at Folio Literary, for seeing the potential in this story, and for the time and care you show not only me and my writing, but also Alyson's. You are the absolute best!

Also, a HUGE thanks to Elissa Alves for genuinely crafting the most lovely submission packages known to man. They are truly a thing of beauty!

To Justin Chanda, Kristie Choi, Julia McCarthy, Audrey Gibbons, Shivani Annirood, and the rest of the wonderful team at Simon & Schuster: THANK YOU, THANK YOU, THANK YOU. I am so grateful to all of you, and I feel so fortunate my stories are in your hands.

To Siobhan Vivian, for teaching the class at Pitt that got

me a wife, my career, and the best mentor a girl could ask for. Writing Youth Literature 1 & 2 truly changed my life, and it's all thanks to you.

Thank you to my mom, Ed, Judy, Mike, Luke, Lianna, and Aimee, for being the team I can fall back on for support, games of Moonrakers, and family dinners. I love you all!

And last, but certainly not least, thank you to my wife, my coauthor, and my best friend, Alyson Derrick. It is an absolute honor to have gotten to be a part of your first book, and I can't wait to be your biggest cheerleader for all the books to come. I am so proud of you, Ace. I love you.

—Rachael

This is insane. I can't believe I'm actually writing acknowledgements right now. There are so many people who have helped me get here.

First, thank you to Siobhan Vivian for reading our "shitty" first draft, and for tearing it to absolute shreds. You've made this story so much bigger and so much better than it ever would've been. Thanks for always taking the time to help me and Rachael. Whether it's giving us a job, getting us a job, or just meeting us for breakfast, I have never had a teacher who has cared so much. I'm really glad to call you my friend.

To Emily van Beek, the agent of all agents (IMO), thank you for taking me on. Thank you for believing in me as a coauthor and a solo author. It has been an absolute pleasure getting to know you this past year.

Thank you to my editor, Alexa Pastor, for putting so much time and care into every single round of edits. I was truly amazed at how much better this book got from draft one to draft two, and that is all thanks to you. And thanks to Kristie Choi, Justin Chanda, and the rest of the crew at Simon & Schuster for all your hard work, and for making my dreams come true.

Thank you to my mom, the Beth to my Molly. Thank you for being the best friend I needed so badly during the last couple of years of high school and my transition into college. Thank you for all the nights spent watching crappy SyFy movies while eating chips on your bed. Thanks for all the doubles you worked so we could have a bomb-ass Christmas. Thank you for the trips and the laughs and the hugs and for always, *always* being there for me, even now.

To Dad, thanks for showing me that the best things in life come from family. Thank you for raising me to "rub some dirt in it," but also teaching me that it's okay to cry. And . . . where would I be without your unfailing support of my very first fictional protagonist ever, Lolytosh Dinkus? Perhaps working a food truck. Thanks for always believing in me. I love you, Daddy (in a southern drawl).

Thank you to my two older brothers and some of the very best friends I could've asked for. Mike, thanks for always getting me hype about *everything* in life. I think you are one of the most special people to ever walk the earth. And to Luke, thank you for your friendship and your advice and for always listening. Getting to reconnect with you two as adults has been so wonderful. I really love you guys.

To my grandma. I just want to tell you that you're the strongest, toughest human being I have ever met. I look up to you even more now than I did when I wrote that poem in elementary school. You were and always will be my hero. I love you.

And finally, to my wife. Thank you for those weird and wonderful two weeks at the start of our senior year. Thank you for being my friend first and for being patient and for letting me get there on my own. I don't know why it took me so long to figure out that it was always going to be you. You are everything I needed but never knew I could have. I'm not sure how I ever lived my life without you. I love you, Rachael Jane. I will always love you.

—Alyson